By the same author

The Treasure of the Unicorn Zephyr, Book Guild Publishing, 2015

The Devil Returns Twice as Deadly, Book Guild Publishing, 2015

NO TURNING BACK

FRED SMITH

The Book Guild Ltd

First published in Great Britain in 2017 by
The Book Guild Ltd
9 Priory Business Park
Wistow Road, Kibworth
Leicestershire, LE8 0RX
Freephone: 0800 999 2982
www.bookguild.co.uk
Email: info@bookguild.co.uk
Twitter: @bookguild

Typeset in Garamond

Printed and bound in Great Britain by CPI Group (UK) Ltd, Croydon, CR0 4YY

ISBN 978 1911320 784

British Library Cataloguing in Publication Data.
A catalogue record for this book is available from the British Library.

To Martyn Green, for his expertise and invaluable help

Contents

1

Sins of the Father

Backed by the towering cliffs, and formed relentlessly by waves of the Atlantic Ocean, an apparently endless beach becomes lost in the distant haze. The overhead threatening grey skies promised rain, heavy rain. In its brooding shadow, sea birds prepared to shelter from the onslaught to come. Many mysterious legends were formed in this enigmatic part of Ireland, where sunshine and rain could change in the twinkle of an Irish eye. Nature was about to unleash her dark, harsh, and unrelenting fury. Soon the skies above the cliffs, rising six hundred and fifty feet above sea level became devoid of all bird life. Instead they occupied every nook and cranny of the cliff face, even birds from the salt marshes blown off course clung for survival here.

The sharp crack of lightning and its accompanying booming rumble of thunder startled the two horsemen, who concentrated on calming their skittish horses. James Williams was a guest of his college friend, Noel O'Brien, or Nobby as he was affectionately known. The pair were spending the last two weeks of a break from their studies from Cambridge University in England. Shortly after negotiating a rocky outcrop, Noel's horse began to limp rather badly.

After he had examined the horse's leg, Noel informed James with great concern, 'I'm afraid she cannot go on, you must make all haste to get off the beach, James. I know of a cave where I can shelter with my horse till the storm blows itself out.'

James replied, 'Are you sure, will you be all right?'

Noel smiled. 'I have been familiar with these surroundings, since my early childhood. The tide is coming in, but I will be quite safe; the back of the cave is well above the high tide mark. Now hurry, tell my relatives I am safe, you are in more danger from the incoming tide than I am.'

In the cave Noel spoke reassuringly to his horse, which seemed to calm the panic-stricken and bewildered beast. Unwittingly they had become refugees from nature's aggressive invasion, and shared the shelter of the cave with many species of sea birds. As he removed the cumbersome saddle, the incessant noisy hiss of torrential rain made it impossible for Noel to think clearly. He blamed himself for making the silly mistake of leaving it so late and being caught in a storm, he should have got off the beach much earlier. Instead the majestic towering cliffs, which he proudly showed his friend, had lured him into this stupid predicament. His feathered friends shifted uneasily, and tried to shrink even further into the comfort of their feathers. After a while the severe intensity of the deluge abated, changing to a more serene steady patter of rain. Daylight was fading fast; Noel would be resident here for the night, it seemed. This would be no big deal for him, as he had been schooled by his father from a very young age in the art of taking care of himself. It was always his friends and loved ones who did the worrying on such escapades as this.

Meanwhile James had safely made it off the beach and was alarmed at the ferocity of the fast incoming ocean. The storm had turned the sea from its former tranquillity into a wild, fearsome beast. As the night wore on Noel wrapped himself snugly into his riding cape, and reflected on the many issues blighting his friend's life.

The latest issue was a rumour circulating round the college, blackening his father's name, and it weighed heavily on his mind, he would have to deal with it immediately on his return to England. James was grateful that his friend had invited him along to his home in Ireland to talk things over. He found it most beneficial as their talks had narrowed the suspects down to one person by the name of Atkinson. They knew he came from somewhere in the south west of England.

Without managing to achieve much sleep, Noel was eventually brought back to reality by the noisy flapping of the wings of departing birds, flying off into the new dawn. His horse snorted, but he noticed she was keeping her weight off the affected leg. The angry sea was now more docile, but it would be another hour or so before it retreated and allowed its prisoners free access to the outside world once more. Noel sat gazing out to sea; after the storm everything felt renewed and invigorated, and he too felt elated. Gentle waves lapped lazily onto the shore, bringing with it sea beans. He knew their journey started on eastbound currents, after falling from tropical trees on the banks of the Amazon – they were not beans at all, but tree pods.

He broke from his idle thoughts when he became aware of the three horsemen in the distance riding through shallow water towards him. It was James accompanied by two stable boys.

James shouted, 'Good morning, Nobby, are you well?'

Noel smiled. 'Yes, of course. I'm ready for some breakfast; I'm starving.'

James looked bemused and informed Noel, 'The two lads will attend to your lame horse. Come, take the spare horse, we will have breakfast together.'

Sea gulls squawked noisily, as they wheeled high above the cliffs. James looked up at them as they made their way along the beach, and noticed a white tower. It was Brad's Tower, named after a rich landowner long ago in the past. They would soon be back to the inviting comfort of Noel's home.

After breakfast, they had lots to do, as the following day they planned to return to England. James had arranged for Noel to stay with him in London after their return to Cambridge. He was also keen to confront the perpetrator who was blackening his father's good name. Little did he know it wouldn't be as simple as he had first thought.

***

Mary Williams tended to the floral display of hanging baskets and window boxes, which her husband had provided for her enjoyment, around their house. Robert Williams, in his retirement, had bought this house in Ludgate Hill within sight of St Paul's Cathedral because he had strong ties to the area. He had lived here for several years before he met his beloved Mary. She paused in her task, taking in the everyday sounds of London's busy life. She looked up; the sun was high in the cloudless sky and cheeky house sparrows squawked back down at her. It was then she noticed the two horsemen approaching and her heart leapt with joy. As the riders dismounted, she recognised her son.

'James,' she shouted. 'My dear boy.' She was gripped in a strong hug. She was aware her son was so much bigger than she remembered, when she lovingly bounced him on her knee as a child all those years ago. She was overcome with emotion as she heard his gruff voice.

'Mother, how are you? Is father at home?'

Mary gazed back through moist eyes. 'Not at the moment, he's having lunch with friends, but what are you doing here, is everything all right at university?'

James grinned. 'Slow down, Mother. First let me introduce you to Noel, a colleague from university.'

Mary chuckled, 'Sorry, darling, I'm so glad to see you.' Then, turning to Noel, 'I'm pleased to meet you. Come, let's get your horses stabled.'

On his return home, Robert Williams was overjoyed to see his son; they both enjoyed catching up on what was happening in their lives. Then Robert asked, 'How are you doing at university?'

James shifted uneasily on his chair. 'Bit of bother there, I'm afraid.'

Concern on his face, Robert asked, 'What's happened?'

James was quick to respond. 'There are some ugly rumours circulating, Father, besmirching your good name.' James continued, 'There is no easy way to say it, Father, I want to know if there is any substance behind these accusations.'

Robert's mind was in turmoil, he had committed indiscretions in the past. Then he blurted out, 'Let's go to the Wild Boar Inn in Holborn, where we can talk.' It was more a command than a suggestion.

There was a general air of busy banter when the three of them found a quiet comer. This suited them well, had it been evening it would have been much rowdier. Robert looked questioningly at James, who launched straight into the issue. 'I returned to Cambridge in the hope of getting to the root of these rumours, however, the main perpetrator didn't show up for this term.' They fell silent as a serving wench placed three foaming tankards of ale on their table. Robert thanked her as he paid for the drinks.

James took up where he had left off. 'I can't deal with my studies while these ugly rumours are freely doing the rounds.' Robert was keeping a cool head, as he sipped his ale.

'What do you know of this chap?' he asked. Noel responded, 'All we know is his name is Atkinson, and he is from Wiltshire, but he didn't show up this term.'

Robert was gripped once more with dread. It was in Wiltshire where he committed his most damning indiscretion, but the name of Atkinson was like a knife driven through his heart. He was aware of James's voice, dragging him back to reality. 'Does the name mean anything to you?'

Robert paused, as he looked around the room, then answered, 'I once crossed a man by that name from Wiltshire; it's possible he may have a son your age going to the same university. It looks like I may have to repay him a visit.'

James reached out, and gripped his father's wrist, 'In that case, I'm coming with you.'

Robert looked incredulously at his son. 'I will take care of my own mess, I don't need you to look after me; besides what about your law studies?'

James toyed with the tankard in front of him, 'I've been wanting to talk to you about my studies; the truth is I'm doing everything from your point of view. Have you ever thought what I want to do?'

Robert frowned. 'Well, isn't it?'

James looked his father straight in the eyes, 'No, it isn't. I've long had a passion for engineering, and with the inheritance you have provided, I thought this is the profession I would like to undertake as from now I'm going to assist you to clear your name, then I can pursue my dream career.' Robert leaned back in his chair, exhaled, and uttered, 'Phew, one cannot accuse you of being indecisive.'

After a moment's silence, they both smiled and Robert raised his tankard and said, 'Here's to us.' As the tankards clanked, they were joined by a third. 'Don't forget me,' said Noel. They heartily quaffed, then Noel bought another round.

Robert said, 'Do you know this is the very ale house where I met your dear mother.'

James replied, 'Really? There is so much I don't know about you two.'

The pleasant tranquillity of the Wiltshire countryside was effectively transformed at the passing of the two horsemen. As they moved beneath the trees of roosting crows, the whole flock noisily took to the air. Robert remarked, 'That's called a murder of crows.'

James smiled as he answered, 'You would think we were murdering them, from the racket they're making.'

Memories flooded Robert's brain as they crossed the elegantly arched stone bridge. 'I remember years ago, I had to attend to some business here. This bridge replaced a wooden bridge, which at that time had been swept away during heavy flooding.'

James surveyed the bridge. 'It's a very fine bridge, much more substantial than wood. How did you overcome the disaster?' he asked.

Robert cast his mind back all those years ago, 'Oh there is a ford, and also at that time a ferryman.' He then realised if this line of questioning continued, he would find it difficult to explain a phantom ferryman, so quickly changed the topic.

'You will remember my good friend, Sir Stewart Pelham; he has been the squire and magistrate here at South Downesmere for many years, he will be pleased to see you.' James noticed how quickly his father had changed the subject, and instinct told him his father was hiding something. His father was right, however; the squire was indeed overwhelmingly pleased to see them. Although normally busy, he swept aside his previous engagements to accommodate them.

'Robert, how nice to see you, and you too, James. My, how you've grown – you were just a wee whippersnapper, not knee-high, when last I saw you.'

With the pleasantries over, the squire was curious to know the reason why his two visitors were here to see him. 'What can I do for you?'

Then James explained, 'I'm having a spot of bother at Cambridge, sir.'

The squire looked at Robert. 'Really?' he was genuinely interested, mainly because it got him away from his normally drab daily business, and secondly, he was intrigued as to why he could possibly help.

They had just been served with tea, and Robert had just put his cup down to say, 'Do you have a man in your employ by the name of Seth Atkinson?' The squire narrowed his eyes. 'I used to employ him, but had to let him go.'

Robert sat forward. 'Why was that?' The two looked at each other.

'The fellow was getting ideas above his station, one day the fellow took my horse, which made me late for an appointment.'

Robert nodded his head, 'I remember the occasion well, that was down to me, I'm afraid. The fellow took a disliking to me, and orchestrated a vendetta against me. He hates me to this very day. In retaliation I told him you had given him permission to take your horse, knowing he would have a hard time to explain himself.'

The squire raised his eyebrows, 'Good heavens. I had no idea; he was a surly chap, anyway. It was only a matter of time, I suppose, when he would have crossed the line.' He turned to James, 'However, what's this got to do with you, James?' The squire couldn't help but notice how alike the two of them were.

James explained, 'One of the students is blackening the name of my father. All I know about him is that he is from this area, and his name is Atkinson.'

The squire's face lit up. 'Ha,' he exclaimed. 'Now I understand, Seth has sons. His youngest, by the name of Jacob, is studying engineering at Cambridge.' He glanced at Robert, and in a hushed voice, mused, 'Sins of the Fathers.' Then continued, 'When I dispensed with Seth, he set up a timber business, and has done quite well for himself. I'm not a vindictive man, and helped him as much as I could. I understand he has the most up-to-date sawmill anywhere here in the South West. He employs a large workforce which includes all his close relatives, here on the estate.'

Robert was quick on his feet, and faced the squire. 'I do not wish to interfere with anything to do with your estate, but it is important I pay him a visit.' The squire beamed his approval, spreading his hands outwards. 'It's not a problem, my dear friend. When you meet him you could remind him of my generosity, should he become truculent.'

With the squire's support he allowed David one of his stable hands to be a guide for Robert and James and show them the way to the sawmill. Robert knew David from those early days, long ago when the stable lad helped him battle through huge snow drifts to retrieve his horse.

David told Robert the sawmill was very much up to date, with fine modern machinery. He often visited, as he had helped Harry, an old school friend, find work there. Harry tried to find work as an estate worker, but the squire was having none of it. Harry was a bit wayward, and had gained the reputation as a poacher. The squire was strict; there wasn't a hope he would employ him.

On arriving at the sawmill they found it a hive of activity. Harry was in charge of a huge Shire horse, which was dragging a large tree trunk to an open shed that housed a steam engine, working various individual machines. At the far end of the shed, horses pulled fully-laden wagons of finished beams on their way to customers. Seth met them open-mouthed.

'Hello Seth,' smiled Robert, 'it's been a long time. You've done well for yourself.' Seth's face turned black as thunder. He grimaced, and snarled, 'No thanks to you.'

Robert continued light-heartedly, 'Now then Seth, sour grapes will get you nowhere.'

Seth scanned around, as if expecting more surprises, 'What are you doing here, what do you want?'

Robert tapped him on the shoulder with his riding crop,

'Some place more private, for an amiable chat.' Seth glared back in defiance. 'Must I remind you the squire is a very close friend of mine,' informed Robert.

Seth scowled. 'Come into the office, follow me.'

On the way James spotted Jacob, who looked away in an effort to ignore them. James called out, 'Hi, it's Jacob, isn't it?' Jacob was clearly embarrassed, and stopped to confront James, and suspiciously asked, 'What are you doing here?'

James held out his hand. 'I'm James Williams, I believe you're at Cambridge with me.'

Jacob warily took his hand. 'I know who you are, what are you doing here?'

James firmly shook his hand. 'My father and I are here to find out why you are spreading rumours besmirching our good name.' Jacob was clearly not prepared for such a confrontation. 'My father is very upset at how your father treated him in the past; he has had a hard life, not made any the easier by your father's interference.' James began putting Jacob at ease by his easy-going preamble. 'Yes they're in the office now, hopefully sorting things out.'

In the office Seth's raised voice could be heard outside, 'I had to start from scratch with this business; I lost my job because of you.' Robert remained calm throughout, 'Don't you see what a blessing that was in disguise, Seth? You have worked wonders here. Might I remind you that you started this feud when we first met by sending me on a fool's errand to find the ferryman, when you knew all along that he was dead.'

Seth smiled at the thought. 'I did, didn't I?' It still amused him after all this time.

Meanwhile, outside, James and Jacob were getting along reasonably amiably. Jacob told James he was finished with Cambridge, he wanted to work alongside his father at the mill. He had some engineering plans of his own he wanted to put into the business.

James then told Jacob that he too wanted to devote his time to engineering. He would like to establish a workshop of his own, but in the meantime he had a favourable inheritance which he could use for investment. He looked up. 'Oh, oh,' he said, which alerted James to the fact their fathers had concluded their business and were coming towards them. Much to the surprise of the two young men, their elders seemed to be on the best of terms; they did not expect such a dramatic change of heart.

Robert broke the ice, saying, 'What's this new contraption?'

Seth indicated to his son and explained. 'This steam engine is the brainchild of Jacob here. We are having a few problems with it, which I hope Jacob will soon put right. When he does I can see it doubling our output in no time.'

James turned to Jacob. 'I'm impressed, how did you get onto this?'

Jacob was keen to discuss his involvement. 'When my father started this business, tree trunks were sawn manually over a pit. With one man on top of the trunk, and a second in a pit below, each on the end of a huge rip saw, it was back-breaking and time-consuming. I made enquiries and found a firm by the name of James Watt in Manchester who could supply an engine. The only problem was that most of the components had to be sourced locally. Also, our machine shop wasn't up to it. However, I heard of a chap up north who could supply us with a steam engine, plus set it up so that it was up and running. I travelled up north to meet him and discussed the merits of using steam power in a sawmill. He helped me with drawings and plans on how to make it work, and, *hey presto*, here we are. We are experiencing problems every step of the way, but I'm confident it's only a matter of fine tuning to sort it out.'

James was intrigued, 'Who is this chap, and where is he from?'

Jacob's face shone with enthusiasm. 'His name is George Stephenson from Northumberland. I have arranged to meet him for further talks. I'm travelling up there next week.'

James couldn't hold back his excitement. 'Do you think I

could accompany you; this is just the sort of thing I want to get involved in. I'd love to meet him.'

Jacob said, 'I don't see why not, I'm sure he would like to meet you also, I happen to know he is looking for investors. Some of his work is on hold because of lack of finance.' Jacob continued, 'One of his engines was installed in a colliery, which was so efficient it replaced horses used to transport wagons of coal from the mine. It's given me the idea to install a similar arrangement here at the sawmill, just think a fully automated system, without the need of horses. Apparently, the race is on to produce a steam-driven wagon, a horse less wagon, and George Stephenson is at the forefront with his designs.'

James was impressed. 'I can see you're fully caught up in streamlining your father's business by your enthusiasm.' Jacob gave an affirmative chuckle, and James caught the black brooding scowl of one of Jacob's brothers in the background, so he mentioned to Jacob, 'That chap there doesn't seem too happy about the changes you propose.'

Jacob turned and explained, 'That's Matthew, one of my elder brothers. He thinks the world owes him a living; he is jealous and needs to grow up.'

Robert and Seth both looked at one other in wonderment, both happy at how well their son's friendship was developing. Seth informed them, 'I would like to put together a team of engineers to travel with my son to meet this engineering genius.'

Robert asked, 'What's stopping you?'

Seth's shoulders drooped, as he answered, 'Finance.'

'The answer is staring you in the face,' replied a jubilant Robert, as he slapped his son on the back. 'Behold your sponsor.'

'What do you say, James?' Events were happening at a fast rate, at least too fast for James. He was formulating a response, as he gathered his wits. 'Well, getting involved in engineering is certainly my aim; however, some form of structure needs to be set up. I would need to enter into some form of legal contract.'

Robert was impressed at his son's forward-thinking, 'Yes, of course. How about we find lodgings for the night, then we all meet up in the morning and thrash out a plan of action?' James tentatively agreed, he was naturally cautious but went along with his father's wishes. He was aware there could be trouble from Seth's family; he had seen it in other industries, where not everyone embraced modernisation.

Before going to the local tavern, Robert decided to call on the squire, to put him in the picture. The squire was genuinely interested, and said, 'How strange after all these years of animosity, you two, of all people, entering into life-changing decisions together.'

To which Robert replied, 'I'm not part of this venture, I'm simply doing what I think is right for my son.'

Then the squire mused, 'Strange how life takes us on a mysterious journey of twists and turns. Nonetheless, there is no need for you to use the local hostelry; I'd be honoured for you to accept my offer for you to be my guests, and stay the night here.'

The following morning a short meeting was held at the sawmill, where nothing was fully decided until James arranged to put some legal documents together. It was time he paid a visit to the Financial Adviser, Sir Richard Hutchinson. On their journey homeward, James questioned his father. 'One thing bothers me, Father, I get the feeling you are not telling the full story of your first visit to South Downesmere.'

Robert looked enquiringly at James. 'What do you mean?' he asked.

James followed through with, 'On that particular night, the river was so violent that the wooden bridge was swept away. I understand that there was a ford crossing but obviously unusable owing to the dangerous state of the river. Apparently your feud started with Seth when he sent you on a fool's errand to find the ferryman. It was a fool's errand, because the ferryman was no longer with us, he was dead.'

Robert was dreading telling his son the truth, he knew where this line of questioning was going.

'When you got to the ferryman's cottage, how did you cross the river? I know you were at the cottage, because David took you back the next morning to collect your horse. Someone must have helped you, as all three boats were all drawn up into the boat shed?'

Robert squirmed in his saddle. 'It's such an unbelievable story, I have only told a chosen few the true events of that night. Angus the ferryman appeared and took me across the dangerous turbulent waters of the river, for the exorbitant sum of three pieces of silver – the exact amount he owed in taxes. I have found most people disbelieve this is what happened. It's the only story I have; it's up to you to believe or not.'

2

Rainhill's Tragedy Revisited

Ruth Swales saw to the daily running of the law firm, as she did every morning. She prepared herself a well-earned cup of tea, after seeing to the needs of the solicitors in their various offices. She also busied herself preparing a tray of tea and biscuits for her boss, Richard Hutchinson, who would arrive mid-morning regular as clockwork. They had worked together ever since Richard had started his law firm as a young man, many years ago. Now in his middle age the successful business afforded him the luxury of starting later in the day.

'Good morning, Ruth,' he greeted her, as she poured hot water into the teapot. 'What have we got this morning?' She gave him a cheery smile, and said, 'If you would like to go through to your office, I have something rather special for you th_____ 'There's no hurry – it's scheduled for 11 am.'

As he entered the office, he called over his 'Something rather special – sounds interesting.'

She followed, carrying the tray, and pointed out the le his desk. 'It's from James Williams. I knew you wouldn't war of the junior solicitors dealing with it.'

Richard beamed, he trusted her completely. 'Quite right, Ruth. What's he been getting up to now I wonder?' James was the son of his best friend Robert, and he was his godparent.

As boys, Robert once saved Richard's life when they were high up in a tree looking for birds' nests. Richard slipped and prevented himself from falling by grabbing a branch of the tree.

However, his fingers were slipping; if it hadn't been for Robert scrambling down to him and grabbing his wrists, he would surely have fallen. They were so high up it would certainly have been a fatality. They had a strong special lifelong brotherly bond ever since. Ruth said, 'I've got some of your favourite biscuits,' as she left quietly, closing the door behind her.

Richard was intrigued; he picked up the letter requesting this appointment. As his godparent he followed the progress of James's education closely, all the way to university. He would do all in his power to assist him in any way possible. He whiled away the time, lost in thought, till a knock on the door brought him back to reality. Miss Swales popped her head round the door to announce the arrival of James.

'Oh good. Ruth, show him in please,' he rose and extended his arm across the desk, they shook hands. 'Good morning, James, what can we do for you?'

After James told him the extraordinary encounter his father and he had at South Downesmere, Richard sat back in his chair and uttered, 'Phew, I remember Seth Atkinson, all too well, I had him down as a no-good ruffian. I am most surprised he has done so well for himself. However, your father did the right thing in admonishing him as he did. As for this scheme of yours, to leave your studies for an engineering career, are you absolutely sure this is what you want to do?'

James had complete trust in Richard, and had often listened to his wise words, as he was growing up, and had always called him uncle. Now as an adult, he afforded him the title of sir. He was instantly at ease, 'I've given it serious thought, sir. I'm not going into this venture with my eyes closed, and I realise that I must protect any financial investment I make with a legally-binding document. That's why I'm here, seeking your advice.'

Richard leaned forward, putting his elbows on the desk, and after interlocking his fingers, said, 'So this newfound friend of yours, Jacob, you have told me he is trustworthy, but what is he bringing to the table? Firstly, you've only just met him; secondly, all I can see is that he can help you get a foothold into the engineering world. If I were you I would proceed with caution; you have the assets, so therefore protect them. Form your own company, and ensure that you alone control it.'

James pursed his lips, in thought, 'That's just what I expected you to say, sir.'

Richard rested his chin on his knuckles, and with a smile said, 'Excellent, I'll draw up some papers, naming you head of your own company. I would ask that you would keep in close contact with my office, and any transactions or decisions will be run by me first.'

James beamed, 'Thank you, sir.'

Then Richard said, 'By the way, how is your father? Well, I hope?' James clicked his tongue.

'He is quite well, sir. He is still trying to live my life for me, that's if I let him.'

Richard laughed, 'Oh, your father always was a dominant force, but I can see he may have met his match in you. I have an enormous high regard for him, did you know he once saved my life? If it wasn't for him, I shouldn't be here right now.'

James returned Richard's wide-eyed look, 'I didn't know that, I'm finding out all sorts of things about my dear papa.' Richard relished telling the story. James said, 'I had no idea, he often told me stories when I was a child, but there was no hint of that.'

Richard was in a talkative mood. 'We had many escapades in our younger days, he was like an elder brother, always there looking out for me. Many events happened that neither one of us will care to admit to. If our past were to catch up with us, we would both be in dire straits.' He tapped the side of his nose, and looked round as if he were checking no one was listening, 'Confidentiality, eh?' This amused James; he could see how his father and this, his best friend, had a special relationship between them.

When next they met, Jacob and James had much to discuss, with James making his position quite clear. 'Your father's idea, Jacob, of getting a team of engineers together is a bit premature; it's too early to be thinking that far ahead, at this moment in time.' Jacob nodded his head, 'It would appear both our fathers want to live our lives for us, don't you think?'

James agreed, 'Yes, let's get ourselves up north and meet your genius engineer.'

There was a general air of excitement, which buzzed round the small village hall, on the outskirts of Newcastle. The majority of the audience were from working class stock, mainly made up from the local workforce of coal miners from the immediate area. The odd few like Jacob and James stood out in stark contrast because of the way they were dressed, but in particular because of their southern accents; however, what they all had in common was their collective interest in engineering. The highlight of the evening was to be a talk by the renowned engineer, George Stephenson.

However, after the preliminary announcements, the guest speaker was introduced. A thunderous applause erupted which announced the arrival of the guest speaker, who entered via a door at the back of the hall, and he had to negotiate a pathway through the throng of back-slapping well-wishers.

George Stephenson gave a brief outline of his life. He had followed his father down a coal mine and worked as an assistant fireman; he was ambitious but not educated. Eventually he got a job at Killingworth mine, as a wagon-wright, where he tested the safety lamp. After half an hour, he invited the audience to a question and answer session, whereupon a multitude of hands went up amid raucous demands from the questioners. One chap at the front asked, 'How much testing was done before the safety lamp was accepted?'

Stephenson waited for the noisy throng to settle down before saying, 'It was given its most rigorous test by taking it into an area contaminated by fire damp; it was a most volatile and hazardous situation. The biggest problem was getting someone to go with me.' The hall burst into an explosive eruption of laughter.

When order was restored, the next questioner asked, 'Is it true you were thinking of going to America?'

Stephenson answered, 'Yes, that's quite true. I had planned a trip, which I had arranged with two sponsors, but they both pulled out at the last minute.'

One man shouted, 'Why was that, then?'

His reply caused another ripple of laughter, 'They both fell for the fatal charms of the fairer sex, and got married.'

Shortly after foregoing the chance of a trip to America, he went on to relate how a large colliery became inundated with water. Advice was sought from one of the leading civil engineers of the time, John Smeaton, from Leeds. He was responsible for the design of bridges, canals, harbours, and lighthouses. After meticulous calculations he designed a beam engine, to solve the mine's flooding faults. Unfortunately, after its installation, it failed to do what was expected. Stephenson worked out the pressure on the piston would have to be eight pounds per square inch. This being an atmospheric engine they had never been known to work so high. News soon reached the ears of the colliery manager, that Stephenson was boasting he could solve the problem.

He was summoned to appear at the manager's office to explain himself. Thinking he was in trouble, and could lose his job, because of what he had been saying, Stephenson was reluctant to attend. However a friend, who was an overlooker at the colliery, advised him. 'It's in your best interests to go, I am willing to go with you for support.'

However, full of dread and trepidation, he confronted the manager. He was questioned about what he thought was wrong with the engine, and if given the chance, how long would it take to make the necessary alterations. 'Three days,' he replied. This meeting took place one Sunday afternoon, and Stephenson informed the manager he would start first thing the next day. The manager, being a forceful man, told him in no uncertain terms that he wanted him to start immediately. So it was that Stephenson started alterations, that very afternoon. After alterations the engine was ready by Wednesday; Stephenson never left the engine, working on it day and night, till the moment it started up. At first nothing happened as there was very little load on the engine, then it gradually got up to speed, soon in a short time the water was dispersed.

Shortly after that event, the great engineer John Smeaton died. One man asked, 'What alterations did you make, that varied from that of such a renowned civil engineer?'

Stephenson replied, 'Mr Smeaton laid down the ground rules, which I didn't agree with. The size of the jet pipe needed to be considerably larger for condensation, and elevated the cistern to a higher position. However, we should not berate the man; he has done marvels in the engineering world. Were it not for his sudden demise I'm sure he would have come to the same conclusion as I did.'

When the meeting came to an end, Jacob pushed his way to the front, and held out his hand saying, 'Jacob Atkinson, sir.'

Stephenson smiled. 'Oh yes, from Wiltshire, if I remember correctly.'

Jacob carried on, 'That is correct, sir, and this is a colleague, James Williams. He's an investor, looking to sponsor engineering projects.'

Stephenson was immediately interested. 'You are a rare breed, Mr Williams. Pleasure to meet you, I wish you had been around five years ago. How is your sawmill going, Jacob?'

Jacob shifted uneasily, 'Not as well as expected, sir.' Soon they were in deep discussion, with Stephenson making hurried sketches, as he explained how to overcome the various problems.

Eventually he turned back to James, and engaged him in his latest project to build a working locomotive engine, which was inspired by a Cornishman, called Richard Trevithick. His engine was built for a Tyneside colliery owner, which was a huge success, and encouraged several engineers, including Stephenson, to build their own engines.

Stephenson had just finished an engine for Killingworth Colliery, capable of pulling a thirty ton load up a hill at four miles an hour. He named his engine Blucher, after a Prussian General, and was currently working on a much-improved design, which he hoped to enter in the Rainhill trials. He named his new engine Rocket.

It was a most fruitful and rewarding journey, both for Jacob and James. Jacob had answers to problems which persisted with their engine, and James had the necessary contacts, required as an investor. Stephenson had just successfully assisted in the running of the Stockton Darlington railway line, and was currently working on the Liverpool and Manchester railway. James had been invited to invest in major railway projects, at the same time lending a hand at the sawmill.

Seth was pleased that the rate of production was increasing, and James pointed out that if anything were to happen to their steam engine, production would grind to a complete standstill.

'What do you suggest?' Seth wanted to know.

'I would seriously contemplate on having a stand by engine, also I believe Jacob is working on a hydro turbine. He thinks it's feasible to harness the power of the river.'

Seth scratched his head, 'It's beyond me. You young fellows, what will you come up with next?'

While Jacob was experimenting on his latest venture, he found he was very much limited with his choice of materials, and lack of a suitable place to work. He put his problems to James. 'What I need is a proper workshop.'

James agreed, 'Yes, of course, I agree. I have been giving it a lot of thought, draw up some plans, and I will help you, I have been organising a workshop of my own. We can run the two projects in tandem.'

Six months later saw the completion of Jacob's workshop. James was steadily forging ahead with his. The difference being his premises were much bigger, as he was incorporating a foundry; he had realised the importance of being able to produce his own castings. Within the year, he carried out a recruitment campaign, to employ a skilled workforce, which included an apprenticeship scheme. The following year his fledgling business started to slowly teeter on to success, then gain momentum. His business started to expand, and his order book looked healthy, all under Richard's watchful eye.

Vast changes were being made in steam engine design, with James trying to keep abreast with modern technology. He kept a close eye on Stephenson's progress, who announced he had a revolutionary engine in *Rocket*; his engine was ready and waiting to be entered in the Rainhill trials. It was these trials that would decide the system to be used in further railway lines of the future.

At the Rainhill steam trials, in 1829, there were ten hopeful candidates, competing for a prize of five hundred pounds. Only five locomotives were entered for the trials, with *Rocket* being one of them. Out of the five, two were dogged by bad luck, the two engines were, *Cycloped*, and *Perseverance*. *Cycloped* wasn't a steam engine at all: it was powered by a horse on a treadmill-like arrangement. Unfortunately, the horse fell through the floor rendering the contraption incapable of competing. *Perseverance*, while being transported to the trials, fell from a wagon carrying it; the damage was extensive.

Of the remaining three entrants, judges questioned the legality of *Sans Pereil*, as it was over the weight limit specified. In spite of this it was allowed to compete, then after reaching a speed of sixteen miles per hour, had to retire owing to a cracked cylinder. That wasn't the last to be heard of her, as later in her career she was purchased by the Leeds Liverpool line.

Novelty was the smallest locomotive, weighing only two tons, and it reached a speed of twenty-eight miles per hour; however she was forced to retire after joints started to blow, bringing her debut to an end, much to the disappointment of her many admirers. George Stephenson had commissioned the building of *Rocket* to the Bridgewater Trust in Manchester. When *Rocket* was completed, Stephenson requested that one of their men be the driver for the duration of the trials. The manager of the works said, 'I'm sorry, sir, we do not have anyone available to undertake such a role.'

Stephenson was in deep thought as he muttered, 'Umm,' then his face lit up in a smile as he caught sight of a young apprentice. He had noticed this young trainee during the building of *Rocket* to the now transformed magnificent finished machine. The young lad was most noticeable because of his interest and dedication throughout the many stages of *Rocket's* build. 'How about that young fellow there, he seems to show a genuine overall interest in engineering?' Not stopping, Stephenson carried on, fearing the manager might dismiss the suggestion out of hand. 'Could you spare him? An apprentice can easily be replaced.'

The manager thought long and hard. 'Mmmm,' he expelled slowly, 'I suppose we could arrange something. Young Entwhistle would have to agree of course. Have a word with him, see how he feels.'

The apprentice was surprised, as the renowned and much revered master engineer confronted him.

He could hardly believe he was being offered a position to work alongside such a great man. 'I understand the working of a steam locomotive, sir, but to actually operate one and be the driver is quite beyond my capabilities.'

Stephenson admired the young lad's honest reply, and asked, 'How old are you, Edward?'

The lad was overwhelmed, and answered, 'I'm fifteen, sir.'

After a long pause Stephenson explained, 'Steam locomotives are in their infancy and you will be one of the very first of many drivers – this will be a prestigious occupation. I will teach you everything you will need to know.' And so, Edward's new and exciting career diversion began at the Rainhill Steam Trials.

The following days saw young Edward Entwhistle become one of the youngest drivers of a steam-driven locomotive engine. As his confidence grew, so did his skill at the controls.

Stephenson never left the young lad's side, until he was quite certain he fully understood the intricate workings of his machine. At the trials *Rocket* performed well, managing a running time of twelve miles in fifty-three minutes.

People thronged the railway tracks at Crown Street Station, Liverpool – a district of Edgehill. The Prime Minister, the Duke of Wellington, was travelling with other VIP guests in his own carriage. The train carrying the distinguished guests stopped to take on water halfway along the route at the Parkfield watering station, some seventeen miles outside Liverpool. At this point the VIPs got out to socialise and stretch their legs, despite being warned against this by railway staff. Amongst the important people was the local MP William Huskisson, who had fallen out with Wellington over the issue of parliamentary reform.

Huskisson thought that because of the general mood of good will, this would be a perfect opportunity to heal their long-standing rift. He made his way between the two lines towards the duke, who remained in his carriage. Huskisson opened the carriage door and the duke, on seeing his political adversary's warm welcome, held out his hand.

At this point *Rocket* was leading the cavalcade on the opposite track, and was bearing down on the spectators at an alarming rate. The crowd, alerted to the danger by warning shouts from the horrified railway staff, scrambled back onto the safety of their carriages. Not so nimble was Huskisson, who was half in the carriage and hanging on to the door. Stephenson noticed the open door, which was in line with their speeding loco, too late. Edward had his hand on full throttle as it smashed into the door, splintering wood, and dragging the unfortunate victim under *Rocket's* wheels. The poor man's left leg, up to his hip, was severely smashed.

Stephenson was quick to react, and immediately organised the transportation of the badly injured politician to Eccles. There he was attended to by Doctor Whatton. Huskisson asked him, 'Tell me candidly, what do you think of my case?'

The doctor replied, 'It is very bad. I fear, sir, you cannot survive.'

He went on to ask, 'How long do I have?'

The doctor told him, 'It's impossible to say exactly, not more than four to five hours, at most six hours.' Then precisely at nine twenty, in severe pain, he died.

Further down the line, mingling with the crowds, was James who was accompanied by his father, Robert. News of the disaster came filtering through the crowd, it sent a shiver down Robert's spine. He was no stranger to these parts; it held bitter memories of his wife Mary's relatives, who were murdered at Rainhill.

When he first met his wife Mary, Robert was in trouble with the law. Mary's aunt and uncle were implicated, in that they had helped a known felon. Robert had planned to flee to the colonies with Mary and her relatives. It was here, while waiting at a safe house, that disaster struck and they met their demise.

James noticed the sudden change in his father's mood; the news of the accident seemed to have radically changed him from being carefree one minute to morosely despondent the next. 'Are you all right, Father?' Robert looked visibly shaken, saying, 'I do hope the poor fellow isn't hurt too badly. This place has unhappy memories for me.' He then went silent once more, not wanting to dwell too long on past events.

Public subscription was rapidly taken up. Sufficient funds covered the cost to erect a magnificent tomb and mausoleum in memory of William Huskisson MP, which still stands in the centre of St James Cemetery.

3

Mob Rule

The silence in Richard Hutchinson's office was most palpable, and it accentuated the muted sounds of the busy London life outside. James looked across the desk to the frown on the face of his mentor, who was first to break the silence. 'I'm all in favour of investing in the railroad, but do urge you to err on the side of caution. This northern chap, George Hudson, has gained a reputation of being' – there was a pause while Richard thought about how best to articulate his true meaning; he then continued – 'not altogether wise in his judgement, he may be heading for a fall in my opinion.'

James retorted, 'He is just one of many investors, they can't all be wrong. The way I see it the railways are the way forward; there will be no stopping it.'

Richard was impressed by his protégé. 'I agree wholeheartedly, James, my boy, I am merely advocating the need for caution. In your line of business there is a great deal of risk, and uncertainty. The very people you are attempting to help are your biggest threat – I refer to the Luddites.'

James did not want to come across as being indifferent, but continued to press home his side of the argument, 'Yes, sir, we are already aware of possible trouble from that quarter, but I'm certain common sense will prevail.'

Richard nodded. 'I just want you to be aware of the dangers; a mere three years ago a terrible uprising by the workers in Lancashire resulted in many deaths.'

What Richard was referring to was the riots in Lancashire in 1826, which spiralled out of control over several days. In a well co-ordinated attack, it started in Summerseat on Monday 24th April near Bury. Following a mob rule of 'break nothing but the power looms', the jubilant loom breakers went about their work with impunity. The wanton spree of destruction continued on Tuesday, then through into Wednesday. They attacked all mills that embraced the new technology, culminating in a black tragedy in Lancashire history.

Bury magistrates ordered special constables to keep watch on the advancing mob. They occupied rooftop vantage points to monitor the crowd. Men from the Rifle Corps, commanded by Captain Goldtrap, stood guard in the town's market square. More soldiers were ordered to protect the town. The mob marched through the hamlet of Brandlesholme, to a factory in Woodhill, belonging to James Hutchinson. Before the troops knew what was happening, the factory was besieged by hundreds of rioters. Captain Goldtrap was ordered to get his men to the factory in double quick time. The men inside were busy destroying the machinery as the militia arrived. The troops were greeted by shouting and jeering, amidst a hail of stone-throwing by the crowd. Captain Goldtrap on his horse managed to force the crowd away from the main gates. Skirmishes broke out as the troops forced the rioters off the premises. A large stone was thrown with force at Captain Goldtrap, which hit him on the head and knocked him to the ground.

A sergeant went to his aid, through a hail of stones, and seeing his captain bleeding profusely ordered two men to take him to the safety of the factory. A sixteen-year-old James Buskey was identified to be amongst the stone throwers, and was immediately arrested. He was later seen to be running off after managing to escape. Two others, Harry Melling and Edward Yates, were also among the stone throwers, with Melling being identified as the perpetrator responsible for bringing the captain down. After a chase both were caught, and arrested.

Melling's behaviour was the final act which altered the militia's stance. The prisoners were taken to Bury and placed in a dungeon to await sentencing. The crowds were dispersed, routed by the militia, and they scattered, miles from home. There were many accounts of the military firing on the rioters, resulting in multiple fatalities. The wounded managed to escape or were taken in and given shelter. The exact number of fatalities may never be known, but it remains a dark day in the history of the weaver's trade.

The following days saw an alliance between special constables and the military, as they went about their business arresting suspected rioters. Their tactics were to strike in the early hours, when people would least expect them. More often doors were smashed down, before occupants could reasonably be expected to answer. The suspects were then dragged out, to be hauled off to the nearest police station. There they would wait in solitude to answer for their crimes in front of a magistrate.

It would take many weeks for the suspects to be apprehended, some left their homes to settle elsewhere, never to return. Conditions for the convicted, in Lancaster Castle, were far from ideal, the dampness and lack of heating led to epidemics of dysentery and cholera; however after examination by the castle surgeon Doctor John Smith, they would be pronounced fit to travel.

It was not uncommon for there to be deaths in the castle. From there they would be transported to Newgate prison, then on to the south coast to board prison hulks. Their final destination would be Australia.

James had made it a priority to find out all he could of the true facts leading up to the Lancashire riots. He could not, however, excuse some of the decisions made by those in charge. He came to the conclusion that there was a serious lack of sensible judgement here, and if handled differently, the whole unfortunate episode might well have been avoided. He put his thoughts to Richard, who confirmed he thought along the same lines. 'Yes, James, I totally agree; the whole affair was allowed to escalate out of control. Make sure you don't make the same mistakes.' James understood what was expected of him as he ventured forth, creating his engineering firm and foundry.

James was friendly with an old weaver. When he passed by, he often stopped to have a chat. His name was John Marsden, and he lived alone with his daughter. His tale as a young man was most strange indeed. He appeared one day in the small hamlet of Mitigate, in the Rossendale Valley. He was a skilled weaver who produced fine linen, and soon won orders for his work. Owing to his odd behaviour of shunning everyone, he gained a dubious reputation of being rather odd. He set up his loom in a hut on the moor near an old stone pit that had filled up with foul smelling water. He hid himself away from everyone.

There was much gossip in Mitigate, about why the young man appeared so gaunt and pallid. His furtive behaviour did nothing to endear him to the outside world. Rumour had it John Marsden had been a devout religious man. When funds went missing from his Methodist church, suspicion fell onto him. He was unable to prove his innocence, and so he fled and was soured by life.

He worked at the loom long into the evenings, finishing his day by straining to see by candlelight. Soon he earned more than enough to keep himself, and took great joy in amassing a great fortune. Gold and silver were kept in leather bags, and his hoard was kept beneath the floorboards under his loom. As the years passed he would delight in his middle age to take out his treasure. The glint of coins by candlelight thrilled him. However, his cosy way of life came crashing down one evening. He had just returned from a visit into Mitigate, to find his treasure gone. He was struck with dread, and dashed into the nearest tavern and screamed that he had been robbed. Many from the village were not interested; it only confirmed that the strange fellow was off his head.

But John's loss did win him the friendship of some of the locals, and one in particular – Mrs Stewart – who visited him. She left him a delicious apple pie, for which he was most grateful. He thanked her kindly for her Christian charity. As he was left with no money, he began to leave his cottage unlocked. One evening he struggled home through a snowstorm. As he stooped to attend to the fire, he noticed a pile of clothing on the floor. Being short sighted he at first thought it was his treasure. But when he touched it he did not feel coins, beneath the folds, he felt a baby. He picked up the child; it brought memories flooding back of his younger days, when he used to nurse his baby sister.

The child's mother was later found dead in a snowdrift. At first Polly volunteered to care for the child, but John wouldn't hear of it. It was as though the child had replaced his treasure, he was not going to part with her. He started going to church, and had the baby named Elizabeth after his sister.

Polly supplied John with cast-off clothes her own children had outgrown. John delighted in the child's company, and would never leave her on her own. When he had to work at the loom, he would tie her waist with linen, and then attach the other end to his loom. He would never let her wander off to get into trouble. He called her Liz, and she called him Dad, they lived as father and daughter. As the years went by Elizabeth transformed the cottage into a lovely comfortable home.

Then, one year during a drought, the stone pit dried out and revealed John's lost treasure, alongside the skeleton of the thief who had stolen it. He had stumbled into the pit one dark and stormy night. The identity of the thief was never revealed.

Whenever James visited Yorkshire or Lancashire, he made a point of seeing John Marsden and his delightful daughter and was heartened to think how fortunate Marsden was to find lost treasure twice.

Because new jobs were being created in the railways, the new technology was being heartily embraced. But because the weavers were well established, new technology meant less manpower, and was regarded as a clear case of robbing the workers of their jobs. It was just a matter of educating the masses, because there would be no turning back.

4

The Night Watchman

In a clearing of the forest, Harry urged on the powerful Shire horse. The massive trunk of the oak tree was dragged like a child would disrespectfully trail a rag doll. Harry clicked his tongue twice. 'Come on, Samson, good boy,' he spoke softly, and the beast responded instantly. He steered Samson along the deep rutted track, gouged out by the previous tree trunks that had passed this way. Up ahead Seth came running towards them, and Harry commanded Samson to halt. Seth was breathing heavily, and could hardly speak owing to his mad dash to get to Harry as quickly as possible. He rested one hand on Samson's flank, and doubled up while he recovered his breath enough to speak. While Seth proceeded to breathe noisily, Harry said, 'What's the rush, boss?'

Seth straightened up and in between gulps wheezed, 'Unchain Samson, get up to the mill; there is a delivery of steel that needs shifting quickly.' Seeing the look of wonderment on Harry's face prompted him to explain in a high-pitched voice, 'The haulier is charging me waiting time, now move.'

Arriving at the mill, Harry was surprised at the intensity of work going on, he likened it to a hive of dedicated ants, everyone intent on fulfilling their particular task. He was ordered to transport long lengths of steel rails, which had just arrived, on specially designed wagons. He was told to deposit them along the track which led into the forest. A stationary steam engine was most noticeable, having just been unloaded under the directorship of civil engineers. These engineers were most conspicuous by their clipboards and commanded unquestionable respect.

It was obvious to all that the object of this exercise was to mechanise the hauling of timber to be drawn from the forest. At lunchtime Harry joined the rest of the team of men handling the horses, where speculation for the security of their jobs was being vociferously debated. One character in particular, Karl Kramm, had a lot to say: 'You mark my words, we will all be out of work soon, the way things are shaping up. The Atkinsons' main object is to increase production, and damn the rest of us.' A wave of noisy debate followed, interrupted by a friend of Harry's, Paul Simpson, who shouted, 'What can we do about it? The Atkinsons are in charge.'

This enraged Karl Kramm. 'We can withdraw our labour, that's what we can do,' he snarled.

At that point Seth appeared, and came striding into the group. 'What's all this then? Do I hear strike action being mentioned? Anyone not satisfied can go, and good riddance – now, get back to work.'

The surly workforce sullenly dispersed, and Seth grabbed Karl Kramm by the arm. 'I've got my eye on you, Kramm. This is your last warning – any more talk like that and you're out.' The pair glared at each other, and Seth venomously spat out, 'Have you got that?'

James was in his office pouring over a set of plans, when a commotion out on the shop floor interrupted his train of thought. His shop foreman knocked on his office door and quickly entered, holding out an envelope which had just been delivered. As James tore open the envelope, he recognised the messenger standing in the background as one of Jacob's men. As he scanned the letter he could hardly believe what he had just read. He had just invested a large sum of money in the sawmill for modernisation and the letter informed him, after the equipment was delivered, someone had maliciously damaged the consignment.

He beckoned the messenger to come forward. 'How much damage is there?' he asked.

The man had just ridden his horse flat-out for two hours. 'It's bad, sir. The master says he would like you to come quickly.'

James was worried. 'See to your horse, and get some rest, I will arrange for a team to accompany me back to the sawmill.' He turned to his foreman, 'I want Jones the draughtsman, and the new man from the casting shop; we will leave as soon as possible.'

On arrival at the site, they found the damage to be extensive, although mainly to cast iron components, which were easily damaged beyond repair and were vital to the running of the new installation. Jacob asked, 'What do you think, James, can we ask the engine supplier to make good the items that are damaged?'

James was already thinking ahead. 'It's not their responsibility. They sent the consignment in good faith, to re-order would be too costly, and more importantly it would take too long. It will be faster for us to produce the new castings ourselves. We will share the machining of the new components between your workshop and mine.' Jacob looked utterly dejected and James placed his arm round Jacob's shoulder. 'I can assure you I am not going to let this incident get the better of me. Before I left the foundry I instructed my men to get the furnace fired up.'

Seth turned up as the engineers were sorting through the shattered machine parts. 'How long will it take, do you reckon?' he asked, as if enquiring how many sugars do you take in your tea. James didn't care much for Seth, because of his abrupt attitude. 'This isn't a five-minute job, Mr Atkinson. Surely you must realise the enormity of the damage. I'm sure Jacob is aware of the severity of the situation; I suggest you take advice from him. Have you any idea who might be responsible for this?'

Seth barked back, 'Oh aye, I've a good idea – must be the horse handlers; I caught them having a right good rant about losing their jobs once the new engine is installed.'

James was quick to reply, 'Well, it's inevitable some jobs will no longer be needed, but you must assure them they will be wanted to fill more technical aspects of the new methods you are creating.'

Seth continued his ranting, 'Trouble is, they don't appreciate what we are doing for them.'

James was disappointed at his attitude. 'We cannot have a repeat of this behaviour. I suggest you employ a night watchman to be sure the same thing doesn't happen again. Now, if you will excuse me, I've a lot to do.'

Seth stomped off thinking, *Jumped-up young pup, just like his old man.*

It was a cold, miserable morning in the forest, and, just as Harry had predicted, it started to rain. The loggers had informed him there were felled trees up ahead, dressed and ready for hauling. He and Samson were on their way to the pick up point. Further up the track he spotted Paul with his horse, Atlas, sheltering under a tree. 'May as well stop for lunch when it's like this,' he called out. Harry couldn't agree more. 'Good idea, Paul,' he answered as he unslung his pack from around Samson's neck. The sky became gradually darker, and heralded in the low rumble of thunder.

'This is not a good idea, being under a tree during a thunder and lightning storm,' observed Harry.

Paul chuckled. 'It will only strike once. Anyhow, notice how I have chosen the smaller tree for shelter? The tallest will be hit first, don't you know anything, thick head?'

The conversation turned to the sabotage at the sawmill. Paul fixed Harry with a meaningful stare. 'I reckon old Karl is pushing his luck, tangling with Seth as he does.'

Harry made himself more comfortable by lying down, he raised himself up on one elbow, and asked, 'Do you reckon it was him who smashed all that equipment?'

Paul nodded his head, and broke the silence by replying, 'Oh aye, can't think of anyone else having the nerve to go that far.' Then, he said with urgency, 'Speak of the devil,' as he noticed Karl coming along the track with his horse, Hercules.

As Karl drew nearer, he called out, 'Just as I thought, you two are skiving again.'

Harry grinned. 'We are having our lunch break while the weather is like this.'

Karl joined them under the welcoming shelter of the tree. 'I thought you would have an excuse, but I can't blame you, lads, just common sense, isn't it? Although I can't think that old slave driver Atkinson would see it that way.'

Then Paul said, 'We've been talking about the damage to the new equipment, who do you think did it, Karl?'

Karl shook his waterproof coat. 'Well, don't look at me, I don't know, but whoever done it, cheers, says I.' Paul gave Harry a sly look of disbelief, which didn't go unnoticed by Karl. 'Hey, don't go blaming me, I haven't got anything to do with it.' Karl firmly stated his innocence.

Paul chuckled, he was in a mischievous mood. 'Well, you would say that, wouldn't you?'

Karl was beginning to become irritated by Paul's banter. 'Listen you, I had nothing to do with it. Any more talk like that could cause serious trouble, so pack it in.' With that he fastened his coat and led Hercules away.

'Phew,' said Harry. 'You don't want to be upsetting him, he can be quite nasty when the mood takes him.'

Paul smiled. 'Yeah, I know. Funny how he keeps professing his innocence.'

Harry looked amazed. 'Well, wouldn't you?'

A puzzled Paul muttered, 'If it wasn't him then who else could it be?'

Harry said, 'Just leave it be; no sense in badgering him, he could turn very ugly.'

***

Sir Stewart Pelham walked into the office of his estate manager, as he would periodically do at least every other day. He liked to keep abreast of what was going on, in and around the estate, 'Morning, Wilson, everything alright?'

Wilson smiled as he exchanged pleasantries. 'Morning, sir, yes no problems, except for the trouble at Atkinson's sawmill, but that's for them to deal with.'

The squire frowned, 'Yes, nasty business. Have they found the culprit yet?'

Wilson waited while his master was seated. 'No, sir, not yet. It's partly because of that trouble, I wanted to talk to you.'

The squire exclaimed, 'Oh really, fire away.'

Wilson pulled out a ledger, and consulted it as the squire lit his pipe. 'You will no doubt be aware that Charles Lewis is way past his retirement age, and quite frankly he is not up to the tasks he should be performing.' Mystified the squire asked, 'What's that got to do with the troubles at the sawmill?' he was intrigued to know. 'Well, sir, the financial backers of the mill are insisting they employ a night watchman, so I thought this is the perfect way of placing Lewis in another occupation. I wondered what you thought?'

The squire beamed, 'Excellent, Wilson. If Lewis is in agreement, it solves the problem of telling him his time here is finished.'

When Seth received the news that the squire wanted Charles Lewis to take up the vacancy of night watchman, he didn't object.

His business was after all located on the squire's estate, it wouldn't do to get on the wrong side of him.

On the first night of Charlie's watch he spotted a mysterious figure lurking in the shadows, but when he went to investigate, the intruder made haste and vanished. After the watchman made his report, it was decided that all important stock was to be kept locked in a secure building.

Meanwhile, Seth became more agitated and was convinced Karl Kramm was the perpetrator. Karl maintained his innocence, and stuck to his story, saying he knew nothing about it.

Charlie's second night was more fraught with danger. As the early shift came on duty, they found the machine shop in a state of disarray, with no sign of the watchman. Gearing on the stationary steam engine had been smashed again, rendering it useless. It would be a considerable length of time before the parts could be mended or replaced. When the watchman was eventually found, he was lying unconscious behind the workshop. Seth was furious and immediately sacked Karl Kramm on the spot, despite his protestations.

The unfortunate Charles Lewis took some time to regain consciousness, and it would be several days before he would be able to tell anyone what happened that night. In the meantime it was decided to have a team of men working through the night. Seth didn't want the mill to be vacant, thus leaving it vulnerable and open to attack. Karl Kramm spent his nights in the local tavern, telling all and sundry he was innocent and bad mouthing his ex boss. The night shift system seemed to be working well, as no fresh incidents were reported, much to everyone's relief. Meanwhile, Karl Kramm carried on with his drunken nights at the tavern, never letting up on his outbursts of insults against Seth.

However, disaster struck one week later. The team on the night shift had devised a working practice of taking a main break at three o'clock in the morning. They all met together for half an hour in a small hut, and then resumed their respective tasks. They could hardly believe the scene that confronted them, unbelievably the saboteur had struck again. It was inconceivable that such devastation could be inflicted right beneath their noses. The damage wasn't as bad as was first thought, however, Seth was furious and arranged for a constable to apprehend Karl and lock him up immediately. Karl continued his tiresome pleas of innocence, which fell on deaf ears. As Karl was put in a cell he said, 'I'm innocent. I was in the Red Lion all night; I can prove it.'

The constable said, 'Were you there between three and half past in the morning? Because that's when it happened.'

Meanwhile James had received an invite from his father to have a meal, and catch up with the latest news on his business venture. Naturally the main topic was his engineering works, and his investment in the sawmill. The sabotage of the high technology machinery intrigued Robert. 'So they have this Karl Kramm character locked up, have they?' he asked.

James confirmed they had, 'Yes, he has been very persistent in carrying out a non-stop campaign of harassment and wilful damage to expensive equipment. There was no alternative but to lock him up.'

Robert screwed up his face in a grimace of uncertainty, 'What I don't understand is, if the fellow persists he is so innocent, why has he been so damned careless, and reckless?'

James shrugged his shoulders, 'He hasn't really thought things through properly, has he?'

Robert raised his eyebrows, 'Or could it be that he actually is innocent?'

James frowned, 'Oh come on, Father. If it wasn't him, who else could it be?'

As it dawned on Robert, his face clearly lit up. 'He isn't the sole unfortunate worker who stands to lose his job because of modernisation. There are dozens like him, and just as devious, I suspect. I don't know, James, I have a funny feeling on this. I think you should have a word with this Kramm fellow.'

James looked alarmed, 'No, Father, I don't want to be interfering, and causing trouble, you know how volatile Seth's temper is.'

Robert smiled 'Yes I do. I know once he gets his teeth into something, he will not let go. A most obnoxious man indeed.'

James nodded in agreement, 'I don't particularly like his attitude; he's a loathsome chap, and I fully understand the dispute you had with him all those years ago.'

***

Karl Kramm's first night in the cell was most uncomfortable, and because of the cold he didn't sleep too well. He was relieved when he heard the cell door being opened; a constable brought him a mug of tea, and a slice of bread for his breakfast. 'Here's your breakfast,' he was gruffly informed. 'The sergeant will be with you shortly to charge you.'

Karl was most indignant whenever it was implied he was guilty, 'I'm innocent, I tell you. I didn't do it.' The constable left the cell with a wry smile on his face; he had heard that line more times than he cared to remember. His silent smile conveyed his contempt and spoke a thousand words. When the sergeant arrived, he came straight to the point, 'Mr Atkinson is pressing charges against you for criminal damage. You will be up in front of the magistrate first thing in the morning.'

Karl wrung his hands in despair. 'I keep telling everyone I didn't do it. I have an alibi: I was at the Red Lion all night.'

The sergeant said, 'You had better be sure of your facts, I will be checking your story. If you are innocent, as you say you are, you will have nothing to fear.'

After the sergeant questioned staff and customers at the Red Lion, Karl's story did correspond favourably for him. It was established that Karl was in such a drunken state after closing time, that two burly customers hauled him out and threw him into the stables at the back. The time then was confirmed at approximately 2:30 am. The landlord stated that he arose at 5:30 am to feed his chickens and check on Karl, who was snoring like a pig. Karl was then aroused at 6 am when the landlord sent him on his way home. The landlord went on to say there was no way Karl could have done what he was being charged with.

On hearing of Karl's alibi, Seth was not a happy man, and told the sergeant to drop all charges. If he didn't the case would be thrown out of court, it would make Seth to look like a fool. The sergeant was not the type to be put off, and being zealous, was determined to carry out his investigations further. The trail led him to the cottage of the unfortunate night watchman, who was struggling to regain some form of normality in life.

The sergeant was shown in, and Charles Lewis was still confined to his bed, he was struggling to remember what had happened on that fateful night. He was experiencing flash backs, and just as he remembered certain things, and tried to concentrate on them, they tended to fade away into obscurity. However, what did stick in his mind was that it wasn't the portly figure of Karl Kramm who attacked him, but someone of a more powerful athletic build.

On hearing of the latest developments from the sergeant, Seth could not accept the fact that Karl was innocent, 'If that scoundrel didn't do it, then who did?'

The sergeant shrugged his shoulders. 'You must accept the facts. Karl has a water-tight alibi, you must stop these allegations.'

Seth scowled, 'He must be involved somehow. I'm convinced he is part of it.'

The sergeant inhaled sharply, 'He may be involved, but you

have no proof. We must wait till Charles Lewis fully regains his loss of memory, then perhaps we may be able to pin down your saboteur.'

The following evening, the sergeant was urgently summoned to attend the police station immediately to deal with an incident of civil unrest. A man was detained in a cell, while a constable struggled outside to appease an angry mob. Surprisingly the man being held was accused of attempting to burn down Charles Lewis's cottage. Under interrogation, it transpired the arsonist was Nathan Stockwell, a horseman employed to fill the vacancy left by Karl Kramm on his dismissal. He was caught red-handed by Charles Lewis's burly son, who with the aid of friends and family forcibly dragged the culprit to the police station.

Nathan Stockwell answered 'No comment' to all questions put to him, refusing to be drawn into any kind of dialogue. But under a steady stream of unrelenting questioning, the sergeant gradually gleaned first one little bit of information, then a full confession of guilt. The truth, when revealed, was as alarming as it was shocking. It was well known that Charles Lewis was making a satisfactory recovery; it would only be a matter of time before he would be able to name his attacker. Nathan Stockwell was reminded he was facing a serious charge of attempted murder; however, if he revealed the name, or names, of whoever put him up to it, he would be dealt with far more leniently.

Armed with the full facts, the sergeant found himself at the sawmill, seeking an audience with Seth. He had to wait a full twenty minutes before Seth decided to see him. An irritated Seth brusquely demanded, 'Now then, Sergeant, what have you found out?'

The sergeant replied, 'Some surprising, and interesting, facts, Mr Atkinson.' Seth offered the sergeant a drink, to which it was declined, 'No thank you, not while I'm on duty. We are carrying out our investigation, and it would be most helpful if you would accompany me back to the station – it would be most co-operative.'

Seth wasn't too happy at the new turn of events, and showed it. 'I'm a very busy man, Sergeant, does it have to be now?'

The sergeant gave Seth a reassuring smile, 'I'm afraid so, Mr Atkinson, I also have Charles Lewis in attendance. It would be most helpful.'

Back at the station Seth wasn't too happy as he was placed in a room waiting to be interviewed. When at last the sergeant appeared, Seth voiced his annoyance, 'How long is this going to take?' he demanded. The sergeant placed a file on the table, and with a dead-pan face slowly opened it. There was silence as he appeared to be studying the paperwork. Seth was having difficulty keeping his temper under control, but stared at the sergeant as he waited impatiently.

Eventually the silence was broken, 'Are you aware Nathan Stockwell accuses you of paying him to burn down the cottage of Charles Lewis?'

Seth went red in the face. 'That's a downright lie, why would I do that?' The sergeant stared back, grim-faced, as Seth continued his rant, 'He's one of the horse hauliers, they've all got it in for me.'

The sergeant leaned forward and pointedly made eye contact, 'I've just finished interviewing Charles Lewis.' Then, changing his icy stare, he broke into a smile, 'He's regained his memory, and he can recall every single detail after that blow to the head.' Seth frowned as he was enlightened; the latest developments were startling to him. 'That's good news, isn't it, Mr Atkinson?'

Seth looked puzzled, not knowing where this line of interrogation was going. 'Yes it is,' he agreed, looking down at his shoes.

Then the sergeant dropped his bombshell, 'He says it was you who attacked him on the night of the sabotage.'

Seth looked confused, and said in a limp voice, 'That's ridiculous, why on earth would I do that?'

The sergeant placed his elbows on the table, in a more relaxed pose. 'You tell me, but all the evidence points to you.'

Seth carried on, but his rant appeared to have lost momentum. He replied in a not so convincing voice, 'What's going on? Don't you see it's a conspiracy against me?'

The sergeant slowly stood up to gather his papers, and put them in the folder. Then, without another word, left Seth to the silence of the interview room.

Back at the sawmill, Jacob was in consultation with James, when he became concerned that his father was still at the police station, well after lunchtime. James said, 'If you're that concerned for your father, why don't you go down there to find out what is going on?'

Jacob looked dejected. 'To be honest, I'm afraid of what I may find, he is not the easiest of people to get on with.'

James looked warmly at his friend. 'Come on, old chap, I'll come with you for support.'

Seth had been informed that damaging his own property was not something the police could deal with, but there were more serious charges against him, like arson, and endangering life. He was also accused of grievous bodily harm; it was not looking at all too good for him. Jacob and James were allowed to see him. Jacob asked him outright, 'Is it true these accusations against you?'

The two friends were shocked when Seth with his head bowed replied in a barely audible voice, 'Yes.'

Wide-eyed, James enquired, 'Why?'

Still with his head bowed, Seth couldn't face them, 'I was having so much harassment from the men handling haulage that I thought by damaging the machinery, they would be blamed. Then public opinion would be on my side.'

Jacob was horrified at what he was hearing, 'But, Father, what about Charles Lewis, how could you?'

Seth buried his head in his hands, 'That was a mistake, it was not meant to happen. I could have bluffed my way out of all this, but what with Charlie regaining his memory, the game's up.'

James spelled out the obvious to Seth, 'The magistrates will no doubt come down on you very hard. The very best you can hope for is a custodial sentence, although I doubt this very much. You could be deported to the colonies, but you must realise there is a much more severe punishment. You have lost your rising empire, your family, everything.'

They left the pathetic Seth in his cell, and Jacob was visibly affected by his friend's summing up. Due to Jacob's silence, James was well aware of the turmoil his friend was going through. As they passed one of the interview rooms, they saw Charles Lewis drinking tea. James asked the sergeant if he could have a word with him. The sergeant agreed, 'Certainly, sir, if your friend Mr Jacob would like to sit down, he looks a bit shaken, I'll take you in to see him. We have finished with the old gentleman. I was just about to inform him that he is free to go.'

James said, 'Hello Charles, how are you? How are you feeling?'

The old man replied, 'Oh I'm feeling a lot better, things are getting clearer day by day,' At first the poor man was startled when the pair of them entered, and gazed at them confused. The sergeant said, 'You've had a busy day, Charles, I'll get one of my men to see you home.'

It was plain for everyone to see that Charles was in a disoriented state, James was mystified, he assumed he had made a full recovery, and ventured, 'I'm pleased you have got your memory back.'

Charles was struggling to keep up with what was going on around him, 'I'm feeling a lot better, but my memory is still foggy about what happened. The doctor says I may never remember what happened that night.' The cunning sergeant looked at James, with a smug smile on his face, and gently tapped the side of his nose.

5

Disaster at the Sawmill

Jacob, with the help of family members, took on the responsibility of running the sawmill. He had three elder brothers: Adam, Matthew and Mark. James got to know them well over the coming weeks, overseeing the company's newly appointed trustees; however, he soon found out that the true driving force behind the family lay with their mother. Mrs Atkinson was a strong-willed woman, and the engine behind their successful business venture. As regular church attendee, she was a devout Christian; it was she who guided Seth away from his natural desire to stray from the path of goodness. James now understood how a miscreant like Seth had flourished so well.

The newly formed company members excluded Seth, even though it was unlikely that he ever would return. The exclusion came on the advice of the investors; in fact they inserted a clause that stated there was to be a restraining order put in place, banning him from visiting the sawmill. Meanwhile, Seth faced an uncertain destiny, as he languished in jail waiting to answer serious charges. He had lost everything. At the very least, he was facing a long term of imprisonment, and his future was indeed bleak. Adam, being the eldest, was elected the new manager, and attempted to bring some form of normality back to everyday life. Unfortunately, the truth was he wasn't cut out for such a position. If it wasn't for his mother's guidance, he would not have lasted his first day.

James was spending more time at the sawmill, mainly to support his friend Jacob. Over the next few months, there were attempts made to develop a steam-driven vehicle that could be driven on the road without the need for steel rails to guide it.. People called it the horse less carriage, James had fired Jacob's enthusiasm to work on a new engine using an alternative fuel, namely gas and oil.

Technology was moving at an exciting rate, a German engineer, Nikolaus Otto, had perfected a means of using gas. But it had a mediocre reception; his fledgling engine was in its infancy and there was much work to be done to achieve perfection. The industrial revolution was in full swing, which was good news for James and his foundry, as work was going ahead non-stop.

To keep his furnaces up to suitable performance levels, James put his workforce on shifts, round the clock. This enabled him to keep up with demand providing castings for numerous engineering firms. James himself was working on a radical new engine, and spent whatever free time he had on design and development. However, he was rudely brought back to reality on the arrival of a specially delivered letter, the news it contained shook him to the core.

It informed him that one of Jacob's brothers, Mark, had been involved in an accident at the sawmill, and that he had sustained serious injuries. He lost no time in getting to the sawmill; Adam was the first person he saw. 'What happened, Adam?' he asked, holding the letter that informed him of the serious accident.

Adam was a tall man like his father, who indicated to James to follow him. 'We will talk in the office.' Adam was a man of few words, and in James's view, he would struggle to fill his father's boots. 'Mark was found buried beneath a fall of timber that was stacked waiting to be processed.'

James waited for more from Adam, but it became apparent that he would have to be satisfied with short answers. 'How did it happen?' he enquired.

Adam curtly replied, 'We don't know, one of the lads found him.'

Another pause, the incredulous James had to enquire, 'How is he?'

The short reply was, 'In a coma.'

James could hardly believe he was having this conversation; it was as if Adam was in a dream-like state. 'Where is Jacob?'

A pause from Adam, then, 'He is at the doctor's surgery with Mark.' James was glad to leave the office, he found Adam extremely frustrating, but unbelievably this was his natural self.

James hurried to the doctor's surgery, where he found Jacob and his mother. They were both distraught with worry over the young lad's present state. Mrs Atkinson managed a smile on seeing James, but her red-rimmed eyes belied the turmoil she was undergoing. 'Oh, James, it's good to see you.'

He hugged her, then shook Jacob's hand. 'How is he?' he wanted to know.

'It's not looking too good, the doctor's with him now,' replied Jacob.

Shock showed on James's face, 'How did it happen?' He was mystified over the whole incident. 'I've spoken to Adam but he's not forthcoming with news, I'm afraid.'

The old lady took James's hand, 'I'm sorry about Adam, it's his way, and he doesn't mean any harm, I'm sure.' She wiped her eyes, as she stifled a sob.

Jacob answered his question, 'One of the men found him, it looked as if someone had deliberately removed one of the pegs for the stack to collapse as it did.'

James was numbed with disbelief, 'What, that's preposterous who would do such a thing?'

The doctor's housekeeper made them all a cup of tea, while they waited patiently. They had not long to wait, but the sombre face of the doctor conveyed the distressing traumatic news he found so hard to put into words. Mrs Atkinson took in the silent message, and went rigid. 'Oh no, doctor,' she said quietly. Jacob put his arm around his mother, the grief-stricken old lady felt so helpless, as did the whole group.

The doctor spoke softly to her, 'His injuries were so severe, there's no telling what his quality of life would be like, had he survived.' News of Mark's death spread like wildfire through the sawmill, but more disturbing was that someone within the mill was a murderer.

The sawmill was closed immediately as a mark of respect until after the funeral. Then production continued at a slow pace, causing concern among the bankers, who in turn had to answer to the investors. Without Seth's input, Adam was happy to continue in tried and trusted old methods. The order book was healthy enough; however, production was not keeping up with demand. The demise of Mark weighed heavily on Jacob's mind, and he found it hard to accept and come to terms with the heartbreaking loss of his dear brother.

The suggestion that Mark's death was a deliberate act nagged at James. He spent a considerable time at the sawmill, and scrutinised the scene, where the alleged murder took place. He could visualise someone lying in wait at the top of the embankment, then, at a precise moment, releasing the heavy timbers. But who would do such a thing? There must be some very dangerous people here prepared to do anything to delay progress. James could feel the eyes of the mill workers on him. He could sense the atmosphere of hostility; it was most palpable. It crossed his mind any one of them could be the killer.

At a company shareholders' meeting, concern was shown at the lack of progress in modernising the works. Adam faced some embarrassing questions, which he failed to fully address. It was agreed that the team of engineers was to be allowed more say in the day-to-day running system that Adam had instigated. Some of the team were encouraged to work more closely with Adam and Jacob, to act as advisers. It was clear Adam needed guidance. James was aware also that Jacob was plainly affected by his brother's death; consequently his enthusiasm was seriously marred.

James made frequent visits to Mrs Atkinson's cottage; the pair shared their grief, and found a certain amount of comfort together. On these frequent visits long discussions took place, mainly on the affairs of the sawmill. Mrs Atkinson confided that Adam did at first hold a grievance against James, but had convinced her son that his intentions were for the good of all. Consequently, on one of James's visits Adam was present at the cottage, and James found a marked improvement in his manner towards him, it was also a lot easier to engage in conversation with him. Adam, like everyone else, found it difficult to believe that there was a murderer in their midst, and James was eager to follow up and find out as much as he possibly could.

James was puzzled, 'How could you see so clearly at night?'

Adam was finding this question frustrating. 'Because,' he stammered, 'it was a full moon, without a cloud in the sky.'

James then asked, 'I'd like to speak to Thomas Ellis, can you arrange that?' Adam called the office messenger boy, to find him.

When Thomas Ellis arrived Adam explained that James had some questions he needed to ask, but James cut in with, 'In private, if you don't mind. Leave us for moment, Adam.' Adam scowled and gave a questioning look as he reluctantly left the office. 'What were you doing that night?' James enquired, 'When you discovered Mark's body under the fallen timber stack?'

Thomas Ellis was wide-eyed, 'I was checking the timber to be processed for the day shift.'

James continued his hard stare. 'Is this normal practice?'

Thomas hastily replied, 'I have certain disabilities, which entitles me to perform light duties.' James swiftly summed this man up; he was too quick to justify his privileged occupation, when he hadn't been asked to comment on it. 'That will be all for the time being, Thomas. I may want to speak to you later.' When Adam returned, James asked, 'Is it safe to have one man with disabilities wandering around in the dark at night on his own?'

Adam answered, 'He shouldn't have been on his own. I understood Matthew would be going with him.' This left James confused, 'Then why did he go straight home on leaving here?'

Adam was also confused at that point. 'Now that you mention it, it never occurred to me to ask him.'

James was aware he was interrupting the running of the mill, but had many questions, 'What exactly are Ellis's disabilities?'

Adam took a sharp intake of breath. 'The truth is, Matthew asked me to put him on light duties because he owed him a favour. His disability is just a cover up.'

James took his leave from Adam. 'I won't disrupt you and your work staff here any more than I have to. I'll speak to some of the timber hauliers at their work stations, if you don't mind.'

Making his way along the track into the forest, James came across Harry, softly coaxing Samson in his task of hauling a massive oak tree. 'Good day to you, Harry. I'm looking for the Stockwell brothers, any idea where I might find them?'

Harry brought Samson to a halt and fed him an apple as he replied, 'Ben is at the yard, and Peter is further up the track.'

James admired Harry's close affinity with his horse. 'How do you get on with Thomas Ellis?' he asked.

Harry chortled, 'I don't have much to do with him, nor do many others, you'll find.'

James was beginning to gather that Thomas Ellis wasn't a particularly well-liked work mate. James ended their brief encounter with, 'OK, Harry, I'll let you get on. Catch you later.'

The thud of a striking axe reverberated through the forest. Up ahead the babble of voices informed James he was nearing the main workforce. The scene before him was a hive of activity. He spotted Peter Stockwell adjusting a chain around a fallen oak tree. Other felled trees were being stripped of their branches and made ready for transport to the mill. James found that not all the staff were as amiable and pleasant as Harry. He soon found that Peter was surly and anti social, as were his brothers. They all had a mistrust of anyone in authority, and didn't have a good word for any of their colleagues. It soon became obvious James was wasting his time here.

James ended his day by visiting Mrs Atkinson and bringing her up to date with present developments. He told her, 'I had hoped to have a word with Matthew, but he doesn't seem to be around.'

Her face clouded over, 'That young scallywag is a lazy good for nothing and he is heading for real trouble.'

James was surprised at the old lady's vehement reaction, 'Why do you say that, Mrs Atkinson?'

She treated James more like her son than she did Matthew, and so she confided with him, 'Apart from him being so lazy, and useless within the firm, I've just learned he is having an affair with a married woman.' She seethed, 'She's married to one of the workers at the sawmill.'

James pricked his ears up at this staggering revelation, 'Oh, anyone I know?'

Mrs Atkinson vigorously stated, 'Yes, you know him. You've just spoken to him this afternoon. It's Thomas Ellis's wife.'

James was astounded, 'Really?' he said, with incredulous surprise. 'How many people know of this?'

The old lady was clearly disappointed in her son, 'It's common knowledge by now. After all I've taught them, I can't hold my head up high. I feel so let down by him.'

The following morning found James in Adam's site office once more, as there were many questions James needed answers to. The recent revelation of Matthew's affair was foremost on his mind. 'You told me you put Thomas Ellis on light duties – a fit and able man – because of a favour owed to Matthew, what was that favour?'

Adam shuffled uneasily, 'Oh, I don't know, it was a private matter, none of my business.'

James's hard stare conveyed his disbelief, 'Come on, Adam, it's common knowledge. Matthew was having an affair with the fellow's wife.'

Beads of sweat formed on Adam's brow. 'All right, Tommy found out, and in an effort to hush things up, he blackmailed Matthew into a prime job, we were trying to keep it quiet.'

It soon dawned on Adam there was no fooling James, as he waited for the next barrage of questions, but what James had to say next shocked him rigid.

'You should have sacked him on the spot, you can't have staff dictating terms. It's obvious the truth will out, get Ellis in here right now.'

Adam was completely overwhelmed and stammered, 'He's not here, he's on the night shift.'

James almost exploded, 'Send for him, get him here now. Don't you understand this puts him in a precarious position? When he arrives I want the local constable present as well.'

Adam was totally out of his depth, but blindly followed orders to the letter. Affairs were escalating at a phenomenal rate. As well as Thomas Ellis and the constable, Matthew was ordered to be present also. James was determined to flush out the truth.

When everyone was assembled, the small office became so crowded it was almost impossible to breathe. James was aware it was claustrophobic, but didn't care.

The constable started the dialogue, 'You all know why you're here, there are certain facts that are being hidden relating to the sudden demise of young Mark. We believe this was no accident; we are working on the assumption that it is murder.'

James glared at Thomas. 'You know a lot more than anyone and have some explaining to do. I find it hard to believe you just happened to come across the tragedy so soon after it happened. We know this to be a fact because Adam left this office shortly after Jacob, when he confronted you at the scene of the alleged accident.'

Thomas was red-faced and looked bewildered. 'I was doing my job,' he ventured as his eyes swept round the room.

James quickly reminded him, 'I find it hard to believe you would venture out in the dark to do your inspection.'

Thomas backed up his night time alibi, 'It was a full moon, you could see as plainly as if it were day.'

James was adamant, 'You were not to know it would stay like that, a sudden cloud could have obscured your vision at any time.'

The constable looked at Thomas and said, 'Something is not quite right with your story, Tom.'

James then confronted Matthew, 'It's no secret, Matt, everyone knows of your affair with Tom's wife, and you pleaded with your brother for Thomas to have a cushy number here, true or false?'

Matthew's barely audible, 'Yes.' It confirmed the many rumours.

James then turned his attention back to Thomas, 'You were supposed to work with Matthew on these night duties – why were you on your own?'

It was plain for all to see that Thomas appeared to be making up his story as things began to close in on him. He gave Matthew a wild look, 'I'm not taking the blame for you. I had nothing to do with it,' he blurted out. At that moment Matthew lunged at him in an effort to stop him saying anything more.

Adam and the constable waded in to separate the pair, and eventually subdue them. It was now just a formality to apprehend them and take them down to the police station for further questioning.

James went straight to Mrs Atkinson's cottage to update her on the latest developments. She was bitterly disappointed at her son Matthew's behaviour, 'That lad's got to mend his ways if he wants to go on living under my roof. It saddens me; he was never brought up that way. As for Adam, he's just encouraging him by trying to cover up his misdemeanours.'

James was full of pity for the old lady, 'They both need a shake up, Mrs Atkinson. I'll be having words with Adam; he needs to take a stronger approach in his job as manager.'

He didn't have it in him to tell her that Matthew would never again have the opportunity to live under her roof, knowing he was facing serious charges. Mrs Atkinson's face clouded over. 'James, do you think Thomas Ellis killed Mark?' She waited patiently while James hesitated, then said, 'I'm not sure, but I do think something is not quite right with his story, we know someone deliberately removed the retaining pegs. We will have to wait for the outcome of the police investigation. I'm going straight down to the police station now to see how things are.'

***

The dusty road into town was thronged with people ending their working day, and heading for their homes. James was beginning to be recognised among the locals, and was known to many as the gentleman investor up at the sawmill. He acknowledged the few who doffed their hats to him as he rode his horse into town. The police station was a foreboding grey-stone building, which doubled up as a temporary jail, having just had new cells added.

Stepping into reception, he rang the bell on the counter to summon the duty officer. He had to wait a few moments before he was attended to. The wait didn't bother him, as he knew the staff would be busy with their new line of enquiry. As he waited in silence, the clock was most noticeable as it sounded out the passing seconds, and the low murmur of voices could be heard in the cells at the rear.

Eventually an officer attended to his enquiry, he disappeared, then returned to lead him to the office of the chief constable, Henry Oaks. As soon as James Williams's name was mentioned the chief constable wanted to be sure he was the one to deal with him personally. The pair were on first name terms, and shook hands. 'Good of you to see me, Henry,' said James, and his friend replied, 'It's my pleasure, James. Have a seat.'

The chief waited until James was comfortably seated. 'I can understand your concern at the unpleasant situation at the sawmill. The suspects we have in custody will have to be detained overnight, I'm afraid.'

James looked perplexed, 'I'm puzzled by these two. What on earth is going on between them?'

'Ah,' the chief said, 'Slightly conflicting stories. They are in separate cells to prevent them from conferring at the moment. One of them is lying; both are blaming the other. I have decided to let them sleep on it, and continue questioning them in the morning.' James was intrigued, 'You don't really believe Matthew has anything to do with Mark's death, do you?'

Placing his hands on the desk in front of him, Henry returned James's steady gaze, 'Too early to say yet, we will know more in the morning.'

James had had a long day, but called on Mrs Atkinson once more. 'I'm afraid Matthew is being detained overnight; he will be interviewed first thing in the morning.'

The old lady was just as mystified as James, 'But why, surely they don't believe Matthew has anything to do with Mark's death?'

James tried to reassure her, 'It's too early yet to say anything. The police want to make sure of some conflicting facts before making any kind of judgement. I'll go down to the police station mid-morning, then let you know as soon as I can of any possible outcome.'

Mrs Atkinson did not sleep well that night, owing to worry over her family. Her husband Seth was in jail for an indefinite period and she was likely never to see him released, and one of her sons had met his death under suspicious circumstances. She was now undergoing a stressful period of time trying to come to terms with her son Matthew's nefarious conduct. She was a God-fearing woman, and it offended her sense of propriety.

Meanwhile, James was being looked after at the police station, while enquiries were ongoing. Henry Oaks had sent out for sandwiches and they had lunch together. James was privileged with up-to-date proceedings. Apparently when the alleged accident occurred, Matthew was at the scene with Thomas Ellis – a fact he had strenuously denied. James was completely bowled over at this revelation.

Ellis continued his story of being innocent, and in truth, it was Matthew in fact who released the timber stack and not him. This was nauseating news. James said, 'I'll have to speak to his mother; I simply don't know how she is going to take this.'

**

Mrs Atkinson was heartbroken as she travelled with James to the police station. In the cell Matthew sat with his head bowed, he had not admitted to anything at that point. With the arrival of his mother, his stubborn attitude changed, then he broke down and cried. He confessed that it was him who released the stack, but he didn't mean for anyone to be killed, least of all his brother Mark. In fact, he was lying in wait for Adam; he was jealous of his elder brother being manager. He thought that, if his brother was injured, the horse handlers would be blamed. It was all a horrible mistake.

James and Mrs Atkinson were alone together in the chief constable's office, while Matthew was being formally charged. James tried to console her, 'I'm sorry, I don't know what to say.'

The old lady, with tears in her eyes, said, 'He has always been an unruly boy. It reminds me of the story in Genesis chapter four, where Cain murders his brother Abel. I suppose Matthew has the mark of Cain on him – his father is even called Seth.'

6

Jack and Jill

There was a stillness in the meadow and an overall feeling of peace and tranquillity abounded, with just a hint of an occasional welcoming breeze. James surveyed his surroundings as he sat by the pond, which was guarded on three sides by bushes and large trees standing as tall sentinels. He felt as free as a newly released prisoner, having left the sawmill earlier that morning on his way back home. With time on his hands, he had taken this opportunity for a well-earned rest.

He leaned on one elbow and tried to empty his head of the impossible events that recently occurred over the last twenty-four hours. As he chewed on a clover leaf, he was fascinated by small insects busy in the grass and by the water's edge. A flash of colour in his peripheral vision altered his view further afield when a dragonfly pounced upon an aphid. He watched spellbound as this aerial master of the skies speedily altered course, forwards then backwards at an impossible rate which was too fast for the eye to follow. He thought back to his schooldays, recalling that they were sometimes mistaken for damselflies, which are morphologically similar.

As there are literally thousands of species round the world, their size depends on which part of the world they belong to. In

Europe, dragonflies are regarded as sinister, known as the devil's darning needle, and linked to injury and evil. In Japan and China, where the species are large, they are a food source. They are caught on poles that are made sticky with birdlime. Children catch them as a game using a long hair with a small pebble tied on each end. When thrown up into the air the dragonfly mistakes the pebbles for prey, becomes entangled with the hair and is dragged to the ground.

He amazed himself as he permitted his thoughts to wander at will, even back to his school days. He had often envisaged some form of flying machine, having studied and admired his long-time hero Leonardo de Vinci. His ideas were inspired by the great man, and would remain within the realms of his fantasy world. At last he disturbed his horse, she'd had her fill of water from the pond and was now busily feeding on grass. It was time to continue his journey.

Maybe it was because his mind was preoccupied with other things that he was taken completely unaware. A ruffian snatched the horse's reins from James's hands, while he stared at the muzzle of a flintlock pistol, levelled at him by a second rogue. He was aware of the third member of the gang behind him, which meant that he was effectively surrounded. Much to his amazement, he recognised the gunman to be Nathan Stockwell, accompanied by his two brothers Ben and Peter.

Nathan smiled. 'Surprised to see me, James, eh?'

James certainly was, 'What are you doing roaming free?' he asked.

Nathan's smile broadened. 'No jail is going to hold me, I'm a free man and always will be.'

James looked at the brothers in turn, then said, 'I don't know how you escaped, Nathan, but you have certain charges to answer. The authorities won't let you get away that easily.' Then, turning to the other two he informed them, 'You two will also have to answer to helping a known felon. You are all on a slippery slope.'

Nathan continued his loathsome grin, 'On the subject of prisoners, it may have escaped your attention, but you are being held by us. Secondly, we give the orders, not you.'

James could only look on helplessly, then Ben said, 'We want your valuables, which also means your horse. Don't give us any trouble and you won't get hurt.'

He could see, in his peripheral vision, Nathan with the flintlock pistol pointed his way as he was roughly manhandled by Ben and Peter. Then, when his timing was right, he viciously grabbed both of them by their hair and banged their heads together. At this Nathan fired his pistol and the shot grazed James's temple. The searing pain caused him much more anger than concern, as he drew his own flintlock from his waistband beneath his coat. Both Ben and Peter were dazed and withdrew immediately when they saw James was armed.

James concentrated his aim on Nathan as a mad scramble for horses ensued. Nathan had just mounted his steed when the loud explosive shot tore into his arm. Then all three rode madly away to escape their formidable foe. As his attackers made off, James instantly reloaded and primed his pistol. This was a lesson for James; his father always maintained if you carried a weapon it should always be backed up by a second. This he resolved to rectify as soon as he could.

The resulting gunfire had aroused the curiosity of a nearby farmer, who observed the fleeing horsemen. He made his way to the pond to find James covered in blood, attempting to clean his wound by the edge of the water.

'Are you all right, sir?' he enquired. James recognised the farmer, who had recently taken delivery of a load of timber from the sawmill for a barn he was building.

'Mr Green, yes I am. It's just a flesh wound, nothing serious.'

The farmer then recognised James. 'Good heavens, it's you, Mr Williams. Whatever is going on?'

As James answered the farmer's questions, he was already

forming a plan of action. 'I was on my way back to London when I was waylaid by the Stockwell brothers, however, I shall have to return to South Downesmere and report to the local constabulary this latest outrage. Nathan Stockwell is an escaped prisoner, awaiting a date to be fixed for his part in an arson attack. His brothers will now be classed as outlaws for helping him.'

***

The chief constable Henry Oaks was in his office, when James arrived at the jailhouse. He was fully appraised and up to date with the escape of his prisoner the night before. He told James the unconscious body of the night shift constable was found in Stockwell's cell that very morning. The previous evening, just after the change over of the night watch officer, the unfortunate constable was overpowered with the help of persons unknown to them.

He was sympathetic on hearing of James's recent experience with the Stockwell brothers and appreciated him coming straight to the police station with his valuable information. They had not yet been able to question the injured jailer, but now knew the rest of the brothers had a hand in their prisoner's escape. Henry Oaks was able to assume that as James was waylaid at Mr Green's pond, which was en route to London, the outlaws must be making their way to the capital.

It was too late in the day for James to continue his homeward journey, and he was persuaded to have the wound to his head cleaned and dressed. He decided to stay one more night. James rented a room at the Red Fox Tavern when he was working at the sawmill. He was about to make his way there after having his wound dressed, when he was requested to attend the police station once more, as a matter of urgency. In the office of Henry Oaks, James received chilling news; he discovered that the injured jailer had died from his injuries. This was now a murder case.

63

Henry Oaks intended sending an officer the next day with the latest information to Bow Street. He wanted James to travel with the messenger as an extra safety measure, a proposition which James readily accepted.

***

The Tolpuddle Martyrs were stepping up activities in the south, and numerous splinter groups were forming at an alarming rate. This was a major headache for the authorities, and it left them at a loss as to how to deal with the problem. James's foundry and workshop were kept busy with repairs, thus slowing down the manufacture for new orders. Jack Collins was a farm hand, as were his father and grandfather before him. He knew nothing else but working on the land.

Although he lived on the outskirts of London, he had never even ventured there. His small world consisted of an area of small hamlets, never straying far from it. It was in one of these small hamlets that he had met and fallen in love with the love of his life. She was nineteen-year-old Jill Harrison, who was in service to a local landowner.

The couple intended to marry soon, but their biggest problem was the conflict caused by the industrial revolution. At the rate new technology was advancing, their future looked very bleak indeed. Feelings were running high among the working class, and the threat of technology to their livelihood meant they had to take drastic action. Influenced by his peers, Jack was attending an illegal meeting where plans were afoot to go on raids to farms. These farms embraced the use of machines and they had to destroy them to save their jobs.

Jack had long thought that what they were doing was wrong, but tonight he was horrified to learn that among the new recruits were the infamous Stockwell brothers. It was common knowledge that they were wanted by the police on the serious charge of murder. Jack was just one of a few who couldn't accept people like this into their fold, it went against their principles.

Owing to increased action by the Tolpuddle Martyrs, James had the security of his engineering firm and foundry reinforced by a fence. Entry could only be accessed via the front main gate, which was manned twenty-four hours by guards specially chosen for their imposing height and no-nonsense attitude. Tonight was Toby Green's first night on duty; he had been successful in securing this post after leaving the army. He was married with two small children, and intended to make a good impression to keep this job. It had just turned midnight. *Time for a cup of tea*, he thought.

He greeted his partner, Tommy Atkins, another ex-service man, who had just completed a tour of the perimeter fence. 'Everything OK, Tommy?' he enquired. The gate house was well equipped, with toilet facilities and small kitchen. James wanted his staff to be well looked after.

Tommy frowned. 'Aye, I'll just have this cuppa, then take another look behind the foundry. I thought I saw something.'

Toby handed Tommy a mug of tea saying, 'You have your tea, Tommy, I'll have a look behind the foundry. I need to stretch my legs.'

Tommy sipped his tea, 'Ahh, that's good. Thanks, Toby.'

It was a full moon as clouds scudded across the night sky, occasionally blotting out the moonlight. Toby made his way silently, pausing intermittently as the light came and went. Owing to his stealthy approach, the intruder on the other side of the fence was completely unaware of Toby's presence as he concentrated his attention on examining the fence. He made his way back to the gate house, there he spoke to Tommy.

'There is an intruder trying to get in behind the foundry. You stay here, I'll go round and nab him on the outside.'

Tommy clutched his mug, 'Just be careful, Toby.' With a smile,

Toby was gone. He was enjoying himself. *This is a grand job,* he thought to himself.

Using the sporadic light of the moon, Toby moved silently and, like a panther, caught his prey completely unawares. Jack Collins struggled wildly but Toby was a big, fit man and quickly overpowered him. 'Right, me lad, you're coming with me back to the gate house.' It was no good Jack struggling, he knew he stood no chance of escaping, so he went along quietly. He was detained at the gate house till the following morning, when James was informed.

'Take him down to the local police station,' James ordered. But Toby respectfully interrupted, 'Begging your pardon, sir, the intruder insists he meant no harm. He was merely trying to leave a message warning you of an imminent attack to your premises.'

James looked puzzled, 'Warning me of an attack? I'd like to see this fellow. Bring him to my office, I want to hear what he has to say.'

Jack Collins was under no illusion that he could escape; he was roughly manhandled by people who were well used to physical violence. Toby in particular remained by his side the whole time since he was detained.

James was direct and forceful in his approach, 'Now then, what were you up to in the middle of the night trying to gain entry to my foundry?'

Jack was resolved to be compliant and answer all questions truthfully, 'I was trying to leave a message warning you of an act of sabotage, which is being planned by the Tolpuddle Martyrs.'

James looked fiercely unconvinced, 'Why should I believe you?'

Jack returned the stare as he withdrew a piece of paper from his inside pocket. 'I wanted to deliver this to prove how easy it was to gain entry, but I was mistaken.'

James took the paper, which stated an attack was imminent,

and was impressed that Jack could read and write. 'Why have you turned against your colleagues?' he demanded.

'Because I want no part with thieves and murderers.'

James was further intrigued. 'Murderers, you say? Who might they be?'

Jack looked sideways at Toby. 'If they knew I was here, telling you all this, I would surely be killed.'

James focused his attention on his security guard. 'Toby, will you go to the outer office and wait there; I need to talk to you before you go.' Jack was relieved when there was just the two of them. 'I didn't believe the rumours when I first heard them that the Stockwell brothers were joining us, but sure enough, they were at a meeting last night.' James raised his eyebrows; this was startling news indeed. 'I appreciate your honesty, Jack, but my advice to you is stay well away from any Martyr meetings. You can be assured there will be a strong attendance of police officers.'

The landlord of the Red Lion public hostelry had agreed his premises could be used by the farm hands to hold their meetings. It was a decision he would come to regret. The next meeting was planned to be held at 7 pm on a Saturday night.

Hidden from view the Bow Street Runners were keeping a close eye on comings and goings, of the customers. At five minutes past seven a blast from a whistle signalled the go ahead for the police to move in. Everyone at the meeting was completely taken by surprise, many arrests were made, including the landlord. It cost him dearly, and his family were evicted while he waited to hear the result of charges relating to inciting illegal gatherings. By a stroke of luck the Stockwell brothers evaded capture; they arrived late to find the hostelry surrounded by police, and made a hasty retreat.

The following Monday Jill Harrison was on her way to the big house, she had been home for the weekend, having spent most of her time with Jack. She feared for her lover's life, after learning what he had recently been up to. They heeded James's advice and kept well away from the Red Lion, consequently it came as no big surprise when they learned of the police raid.

Her mind was on a million things, which was why she was taken completely by surprise when her attackers struck. She screamed as the sack was thrust over her head, then a crushing blow to her skull silenced her.

James had a surprise visit from Jack, who was in a state of shock and disbelief. He had been assured by James his name would be kept out of any dealings with the Bow Street Runners; however, his girlfriend, Jill, had been snatched by members of the Martyrs in reprisal for his part in breaking up their meeting.

Jack wrung his hands in despair. 'They told me they knew it was me, who alerted the authorities of their illegal meeting, and that I was going to be punished.'

James felt truly sorry for the young lad. 'I made it quite clear that your identity must remain anonymous. I'm very sorry, I will do all in my power to find Jill.'

Jack's face was the picture of misery, 'One of your men must have spilled the beans. I cannot think how else they found out.'

James realised this was true, 'I will find out who was responsible, but in the meantime we must keep you out of harm's way. How do you feel about working for me?'

Jack was stunned; he was at a loss for words. James waited for him to assess what was happening, then Jack, wide-eyed, said, 'That's very kind of you, but I still have to face the ruffians. My life is in extreme danger.'

James wanted to convey trust in the lad, and with a smile said, 'You may have noticed my works are heavily fortified. I will find something for you to do, and somewhere for you to sleep also.'

Toby and Tommy reported for their evening shift, to be informed that they were wanted by James in his office immediately.

They were met by a stern-faced James, 'Jack Collins came to see me this morning in a distressed state. It appears his girlfriend has been abducted as a reprisal for his involvement against the Martyrs. Have you any idea how his name has been linked to this situation?'

Both men shuffled uneasily. 'I'm sorry, sir,' said Tommy, 'but a few of us here at the works knew of his involvement. News of this kind could have come from any quarter.'

James had not realised how close-knit his family of workers was. 'Yes of course, I hadn't allowed for that. I feel responsible for his present position, and want to protect him as much as I can. I have offered him employment here and a safe haven, I would appreciate it if you could keep a close eye on him. To be his bodyguards if you like.'

Toby and Tommy looked at each other, and seemed to pass on their thoughts to one another, Toby replied, 'I would be delighted to help out sir, how about you, Tommy?' In answer Tommy grinned nodding his head.

James was pleased at their reaction. 'Splendid, I want you to start right away, Jack is in the foundry. If you stick to him like glue, I will be eternally grateful. I want one of you to be with him at all times.' Toby and Tommy worked out a rota so that Jack was never alone and always in the presence of one of them.

One evening saw the trio enjoying an evening out at a local hostelry, and many hostile eyes were upon them. Jack wanted news of his sweetheart, but many were reluctant to talk to him. An occasional threat was made against him, but his two minders made it obvious they were not fazed by futile sabre rattling. Jack even visited Jill's parents, but they were unwilling to see him, and blamed him for their daughter's disappearance. However James was able to acquire more useful information, but the unsettling news was that the Stockwell brothers were instrumental in Jill's disappearance. It bothered him that the Martyrs were offering them shelter, the Martyrs were fighting for a cause which they considered a threat to their livelihood, and these three were thieves and murderers.

On James's next visit to the sawmill, he made an appointment to see the chief constable, Henry Oaks. 'It's good to see you, Henry. How are you?'

The chief smiled as he offered his hand. 'Hello, James, what can we do for you?'

James settled in his chair, 'I wondered if you had any more news on the Stockwell brothers.' Their very name was as if a dark veil clouded his very thoughts, leaving him very troubled. His face clouded over, 'It bothers me, James, they should have been apprehended by now. Who in their right mind would give them shelter from the law. Now look what's happened, they've kidnapped a young girl. The people helping them do not realise how dangerous they are.'

James was offered tea, which he gladly accepted. Then, ten minutes into the meeting, there was an urgent knocking on the door and the duty sergeant burst in. 'Begging your pardon, sir, a messenger from London just brought this in,' he gasped, and stepped back, to wait further instruction.

A frown clouded the chief's face as he read the message; he then turned to the sergeant, and quietly dismissed him. James could tell there was shattering news to come as the chief solemnly held James in a fixed stare. 'They've just discovered a body in the woods, although formal identification has yet to take place, and as it's that of a female it's assumed to be that of the missing Jill Harrison.' James was horrified.

Jack Collins made his homeward journey a little unsteadily, flanked by Toby Green and Tommy Atkins. They'd had another social evening drinking; the trio all thought how lucky they were to be under the wing of such a beneficial boss.

Tommy said, 'Hey, Toby, why don't you shoot off home? I'll see that Jack gets back to his billet in one piece.'

Toby was only a couple of blocks from his cottage, and replied, 'That's decent of you – are you sure, mate?'

Tommy chuckled, 'Yeah, go on, off you go.'

Toby also chuckled, 'OK, if you're fine with that then I'll bid you gents good night.' He watched them both walking off unsteadily, and felt uneasy, he felt as if he was deserting them. He was halfway down the street, then paused, he wasn't happy with the situation. He thought, *I shouldn't be doing this.*

Tommy and Jack were nearing the foundry when a gang struck, and each was tackled and thrown to the ground. Jack was pinned down, unable to move, such was the weight and strength of his assailant straddling him. A leering Ben Stockwell was grinning at him, and started singing in a rhyme, '*Jack and Jill went up the hill.*' Each word was followed by a slap across the face. '*It was Jill who fell down and broke her crown.*' Through yellow teeth he almost finished, '*But Jack will come after,*' when Ben was smashed over the head, and Jack saw Toby who then started to give a good account of himself with the other two brothers. Tommy was then on his feet; it was at that point the brothers decided to run for it, and disappeared into the night.

Tommy's relief was plain for all to see. 'Am I glad to see you, Toby.' Jack was helped to his feet and then they entered the works foundry and safety. 'What made you come back?'

Toby smiled. 'I got the feeling something was going to happen, sixth sense, I suppose.'

Then Jack asked, 'What do you think that Stockwell fellow meant by singing that rhyme, do you suppose he would hurt Jill?'

Tommy answered, 'I don't know. They're desperate criminals, that's for sure, but you must hope for the best, Jack.' Unseen by Jack, Toby and Tommy exchanged looks, which had he seen, would have totally demoralised him.

The following morning when James returned from his business trip, he sent for Jack. It was a cold and damp overcast morning. When Jack entered the office, he was confronted by two police officers, with his boss. He was offered a seat, and his heart filled with dread at the silent and sombre faces, something was afoot. The weather seemed to match their mood.

7

The Vanishing Vicar

The morning was dull, grey, and uninviting, the mist beyond Jacob's bedroom window promised the day to be sharp and bracing. The moon sank beneath a bank of grey mist before daylight had a chance to break. Jacob had a busy day ahead of him. After he had sluiced himself with cold water, he left a confused tangle of blankets and gathered up his paperwork. With saddlebags packed the night before, he made his way to the stables.

Losing no time, he quickly saddled his horse, and led her outside where he swiftly mounted. An early start to the day ensured he would be at the foundry in good time to meet James. The journey to London gave him plenty of time to mull over all the problems of the sawmill. He was carrying with him detailed plans of machinery he wanted manufactured, and looked forward to his arranged meeting with James. As the morning got brighter, so did his spirits; it was good for him to get away, it was refreshing.

He and his mother were concerned at Matthew's and Seth's plight, it had been decided they were to be deported to the colonies. Some years earlier, the American War of Independence put a stop to transportation across the Atlantic, and the west coast of Africa had earned itself the reputation as the white man's grave;

however, after the success of the first fleeters, transportation to the colonies meant Australia. Whatever their fate, the outcome certainly meant they would never be able to see their family again, ever.

Jacob tried to rid his mind of morose thoughts but the adverse weather wasn't conducive to changing his mood. A constant grey mist had turned into a steady fall of light rain, but he was relieved to come into sight of the foundry and engineering works. James had had the forethought to establish his business premises on the outskirts of London, thus avoiding the hustle and bustle of city life. Jacob had checked himself through security, before James arrived. He had just made himself comfortable in front of a pleasing fire when James arrived.

'Good to see you, Jacob, you chose a wet day for our meeting.'

In reply, Jacob said, 'I certainly did, didn't I?' as he helped his friend out of his sodden raincoat.

Before getting down to business, their small talk turned to Jacob's family problems.

'I sympathise with you, Jacob. I don't know what to say.'

Then, after a period of embarrassing silence, Jacob enquired, 'Enough of my problems, how are you?'

James didn't quite know how to begin, 'You will no doubt have heard of the exploits of the infamous Stockwell brothers.' Jacob pursed his lips and nodded. 'Well,' continued James, 'after the death of Jack Collins's girl friend, I'm afraid the lad's life is in danger. I've got two reliable ex-soldiers watching over him round the clock, but I can't keep it up indefinitely.'

Then Jacob came up with a solution, 'Why not have him sent to my sawmill? No one knows him there, just till the heat dies down.' James raised his eyebrows, 'That's a splendid idea, an admirable solution. He will have to travel with my two security guards, to make sure of a safe arrival.' Jacob was impressed by the two guards, and asked, 'Can you spare these two men for a couple more weeks? I would like them to advise my team. They would probably prevent a lot of damage occurring.' James readily agreed, 'Yes of course, if they agree to it, I cannot see a problem.' He went on to arrange to have everyone involved meet up to discuss the proposed plan.

Toby and Tommy were OK with the plan. They both agreed their wives wouldn't mind; after all they were used to them being away from home for longer periods. James then suggested that Jacob should travel back with the party, as there was safety in numbers. Even the Stockwell brothers were not so foolish as to attack such a strong party. So it was that Jack was sent to the sawmill, escorted under the watchful eye of his two burly minders.

The new intake to the workforce created a huge amount of interest. The ex-soldiers went to work recruiting and training, but as far as Jack was concerned he remained a mystery to the rest of the staff. They wanted to know who and why he was there at all. Jacob was concerned that Jack's cover would soon be blown, so thought it time he had words with him. He wanted Jack to mingle more with the two ex-soldiers, and pass himself off as a security expert; however several days later, Tommy spotted a suspicious-looking character and began to discreetly follow him. The stranger appeared to be concentrating his attention on Jack. Completely unaware of his stalker, Jack made his way to the engine shed.

Workmen were coming and going and the stranger found it easy to merge in with everyone. At a point where the pathway leading from the engine shed met the track to the forest, the stranger hid himself behind a bush. As Tommy moved in closer, alarm bells started to ring. The stranger produced a pistol and cocked it, ready to be discharged. It was as he levelled the weapon at Jack that Tommy pounced. He brought the gunman down to the ground in a headlock, at the same time disarming him. Only now was Tommy able to get a good look at the would-be assassin, due to the fact that he kept his collar up to conceal his identity. 'Well bless my soul,' said a jubilant Tommy. 'If it isn't Nathan Stockwell.'

With a smirk on his face he continued, 'This isn't the first time we've tussled, only this time you haven't got your brothers to help you.'

Nathan was panic-stricken and yelped with pain as he was yanked to his feet, with his arm forced up behind his back.

Tommy marched his prisoner to the yard office, where a surprised Adam slowly took in the relevant facts. Then, when he realised what was expected of him, he sent for Jacob. James had arrived the previous day and was in a meeting with Jacob when they were informed that Nathan Stockwell was being held. They both hurried over to the site office.. He immediately sent for the local constabulary, and for Toby also.

It was good news that one of the Stockwell brothers had been apprehended, but not so good that Jack's cover had been blown. It meant James had to rethink a solution to address the problem of what to do with Jack. He drew Tommy, Toby, and Jack, to one side. 'Right,' he quietly murmured, 'get your things together, and get ready to move out, we have to leave here as soon as possible. It would be safe to assume the other two brothers are here in the area also.' As they left the office, James said, 'Nice work, Tommy.'

Sir Henry Oaks was hoping to have an easy day when the messenger arrived from the sawmill requesting assistance to bring to the police station one of the Stockwell brothers. He quickly despatched a party of officers, and made ready a cell for their new guest. The police station had just had new cellblocks added to the rear of the premises. This was a dangerous prisoner; he didn't want to take any chances with him. Word rapidly spread throughout the village and shortly after the prisoner was booked in, his elderly parents turned up accompanied by the Reverend Walter Peabody. The old couple were quiet and inoffensive, and certainly didn't deserve to be saddled with the disrespectful lawless sons they had sired. They were being supported by their parish vicar, who was a scrawny diminutive individual. His thin neck was accentuated by his clerical dog collar, which appeared to be several sizes too large for him. As soon as Nathan saw the vicar he contorted his face to show his distaste for him, and there was no mistaking his dislike of the man. 'Nathan, you are a big disappointment to your unfortunate parents,' the vicar said as he held his steady gaze, under Nathan's obvious seething wrath.

Nathan replied, 'You're the last person I want to see, you sanctimonious crank.'

The vicar continued as if Nathan had not spoken, 'And a thorn in my side.' Nathan's parents were clearly upset at their son's behaviour, with his father consoling his tearful mother.

The day continued being grey and overcast, as James rode ahead of Tommy and Jack. Toby had been sent up ahead to scout for any trouble. They were travelling through a wooded area, when James was startled at the fast-approaching Toby.

He held up his hand, to bring the party to a halt. 'We must get off the track,' he said breathlessly, 'I stopped just beyond here where there is a clearing, and noticed crows were disturbed and taking to the air, so I skirted round and found a large body of men, concealing themselves in the bushes and undergrowth, lying in wait. I think they are about to ambush us.'

James immediately agreed, 'Right, let's do that, we'll work our way round them. Good work Toby.' As they diverted they travelled quickly then after half an hour got back onto the main thoroughfare. They kept up a rapid pace, until they gained the safety of the foundry once more.

James had to think of a positive way to deal with Jack's safety. He called a meeting with Jack and his two minders. 'Jack, how do you feel about relocating to a new area, where no one knows you? You would still be working for me, then after perhaps say twelve months from now, when the heat dies down, you could safely come back here.'

Jack shuffled uneasily, 'I don't know, sir, I'm a dead man

hereabouts. I'm not ungrateful, I'm just bewildered at the moment.'

James then addressed Tommy and Toby. 'I have a plan which concerns you two also. Owing to increasing orders, I am contemplating opening an office up north in Leeds to deal with our Northern customers. If you are willing I want you three to go and set things up.'

Tommy looked at Toby with a smile and said, 'I'm willing. How about you, Toby?'

Toby beamed, 'Count me in, sir.'

James turned his attention once more to Jack, 'How about it, Jack?'

Clearly taken aback, Jack looked flustered, 'I'm embarrassed to be causing you so much aggravation, sir; I'm immensely grateful.'

James had a twinkle in his eye, 'On the contrary, Jack, it is I who am grateful and your safety is paramount. Right if you will all make arrangements, I want you to leave as quickly as possible.'

The opening of the new office in the north went according to plan. Within a month Tommy and Toby returned with a favourable report for James, Jack was adapting well to his new post as manager. James would visit the new Northern premises as soon as his commitments allowed.

As the sun was slowly sinking in the west, so the light faded also. Nathan Stockwell was facing another atrocious damp night in his cell. He lay ill at ease, fully stretched out with his hands at the back of his head on the hard wooden boards that served as his bed. Above his bed, facing onto a narrow lane, was an open window heavily barred to prevent escape, He thought he was imagining things at first, as a hushed voice uttered his name, 'Nathan, Nathan.' He stirred, and lifted his head, to be sure when he heard the hushed voice again, louder this time, coming from outside, 'NATHAN.' He leapt to his feet and standing on the boards gripped the bars to pull himself in a position to be able to see out. What he saw was the muzzle of a pistol. His last sense was an explosive charge, which filled his vision; he then fell backwards stone dead.

On James's next visit to the sawmill, he was horrified to learn of the demise of Nathan Stockwell. He asked Jacob, 'I know the fellow was a rogue, but who would carry out such a callous act?'

Jacob sniffed, 'Come on, James, the Stockwells have many enemies. How about that lad you're sheltering, Jack Collins, he has good reason.'

James conceded, 'Yes, that's true, he has, but if you knew him, you would soon realise he would not commit murder. Besides he is many miles away from here, it simply could not be him.'

Jacob remained unrepentant, 'Maybe so, James, but like I said, the Stockwell's have many enemies.'

Henry Oaks was under pressure from his superiors, owing to the fate of his high profile prisoner. The praise he would have received from holding such a prominent figure in custody was marred by the disappointment from Bow Street. A fact he conveyed to James on his next visit. He told James, 'Whoever is responsible for Nathan Stockwell's murder is certainly familiar with the station's layout, what with the new cellblocks, and overlooking that back alley.'

James asked, 'How many people came to see him?'

Henry had a steely glint in his eye, 'Just a handful, but mainly his parents, accompanied by their parish priest. There was something funny going on between Nathan and that priest.'

James was immediately interested, 'Oh, why was that then?'

The chief constable frowned, 'Nathan was agitated, and was most hostile towards him. He didn't hide the fact that he wasn't pleased to see him.'

It was James's turn to frown, 'I don't understand. You're not implying the vicar had anything to do with killing Nathan, are you?'

With despair in his eyes the chief constable took a deep breath, 'I don't know what to believe anymore.'

James was intrigued and he wanted to know more about this mysterious priest, 'What's his name?' he asked.

The chief raised his eyebrows. 'Walter Peabody.' He paused as if in thought. 'The Right Reverend Peabody.' Then looked at James as if seeking inspiration. 'I'm questioning all Nathan's visitors, and have requested the reverend calls in at the station tomorrow, James, I don't mind you being present, if you so wish.'

James was delighted to accept, 'That's very good of you, Henry, I was about to ask if I could anyhow.'

In the police station the following day, James was struck by the odd-looking character before him. The reverend did not have a happy face, which led James to think he would not have many natural friends, he would have to work hard to persuade anyone to be his friend, James assumed. Henry asked him about the Stockwell family. 'I've known the family since I came here ten years ago,' he croaked. 'Poor Mrs Stockwell has had a hard life. Her husband took to drink in the early days so he wasn't much help to her, but he has since reformed. Their three boys were such a handful, always in trouble. Because of the added burden, Mr Stockwell had to radically change his ways or they would all have ended up in the work house.'

Henry Oaks then asked, 'It was plain to see that Nathan did not want to see you reverend, in fact he was most hostile towards you, any special reason why?' Reverend Peabody displayed a simpering smile, as he replied, 'All three boys would have nothing to do with me; it was their parents who invited me into their home. Regarding Nathan himself, he was courting a young girl from a village nearby, whose family I knew well. Her family were God-fearing people, and I took it upon myself to inform them of how unsuitable Nathan was. Consequently they forbade their daughter from having any contact at all with Nathan. Ever since he has done everything in his power to harass me and cause me grief.'

The chief constable, nodded. 'I understand his animosity towards you.' Then, changing the subject, he stated, 'You appear to know your way around our newly refurbished police station well, Reverend.'

Peering over the thick lenses of his glasses the reverend answered, 'I pride myself in keeping up with the modern world.'

The Reverend Peabody took the chief constable's last remark as small talk, had he known he was on the list of suspects for murder he would have been much aggrieved. After the other suspects had been questioned, no one stood out more prominently than him.

Meanwhile gossip in the villages had picked up on the interview with the Reverend Peabody, and all kinds of twists and connotations had blown the situation out of reasonable proportions. Eventually the rumours which escalated and gained unbelievable heights of irrational absurdity reached the reverend's ears. Owing to his unpopular reputation this slur on his integrity was too great a burden for him to bear. Knowing that his bishop would inevitably become involved, the Reverend Peabody decided his only line of action was to quietly fade into obscurity. This did not bode well for him, as speculation had it that he was guilty, otherwise an innocent man would have stayed to face the accusations. Nevertheless the Reverend Peabody simply vanished.

As far as Henry Oaks was concerned, it put the reverend in an extremely unfavourable light. The chief constable had exhausted his enquiries regarding suspects, which left him with the vicar, the one guilty perpetrator whose interrogation had to be put on hold for further investigation. He was determined to find him, to facilitate the process he spent more time and resources in hunting him down. However, the elusive reverend proved to be as wily as an old fox, and appeared to have simply vanished from the face of the earth.

On his next visit to see his father, James found the old man was extremely interested in the story of the vanishing vicar, and said, 'I know Henry Oaks, perhaps I could be of assistance to help in finding where the reverend has gone to ground.' James was kept well informed of the latest news regarding the vanishing vicar. He was astounded that a man of the cloth could just dismiss such serious charges and disappear. He was equally taken aback at his father's offer to help the chief constable.

'Come on, Father, you have been retired for a number of years now, how do you think you could help?'

The old man smiled. 'In my job as a bailiff, I was privileged to meet all sorts of men with special skills, on both sides of the law. I may have contacts that Henry has never even heard of.'

James looked at his father with concern, 'I would rather you didn't get too involved, Father. You should be here at home, tending your garden.'

Whatever his son thought Robert Williams was his own man, it amused him to think that he had been written off in his retirement. 'All I am proposing is that I visit Henry for a little chat, it could be to his advantage.' James could see his father's mind was made up, so didn't pursue the point any further.

Henry Oaks was just settling down to his morning cup of tea, when he was informed that Robert Williams had arrived for his appointment. He sent for more tea for his guest, and welcomed him, 'Robert, how good to see you, how is your retirement going?'

They warmly shook hands. 'Very well thank you, how are you?'

The chief constable made himself comfortable, and got straight down to business, 'I'm fine, but bedevilled with this missing vicar suspect.'

Robert sipped his tea and nodded, 'Yes, I understand. I may be able to put you in touch with men who specialise in finding people who don't want to be found. You will need to seek funding from Bow Street when a difficult job comes up like this; there is a team of men who specialise in handling such cases. I might add, they're worth every penny.'

Hearing this lifted Henry's hopes, 'I'm grateful for your interest, Robert, I'll see them as soon as you can arrange it.'

Robert carefully placed his cup on the desk, 'They are a team of three, I can have them here by tomorrow afternoon. It would help if you could arrange for them to stay at the Red Fox.'

Henry beamed, 'I will make the necessary arrangements.'

James and Jacob had just left the sawmill and were heading towards the Red Fox Tavern, where they planned to have lunch. A group of three men on horseback rode past them and came to a halt at the tavern. On entering they found the men had already selected a table near the window. James remembered the men as friends of his father, and nodded to them in recognition.

One of them stood up and held out his hand, 'James Williams,' he said. 'Well, bless my soul, you were just a little nipper last time I saw you.'

James shook the man's hand, desperately trying to recall their names. The man detected James's vague look, and introduced himself, 'I'm Ray Mitchell, friend of your father's.'

James smiled. 'Yes, I do remember you, Ray. It's been a long time.'

Ray turned to his companions. 'You will know David Brown, and Joe Andrews also?'

James shook their hands, 'Dave, Joe, I assume you're here at my father's request?'

They confirmed they were and turned their attention to Jacob. James introduced them, 'This is a business partner, Jacob Atkinson. He runs the sawmill here.'

Ray said, 'Pleased to meet you. We have heard of your troubles here, we hope we can help. We will be staying here tonight, after we have had some refreshment we have an appointment with the chief constable.'

James then took his leave, 'It's good to see you again, if you need anything, come see us at the sawmill.' Shortly after finding a table a raucous shout alerted James's attention towards the door, where his father had just entered. Robert Williams was being greeted by his back-slapping colleagues. Ray indicated towards James and Jacob's table, and Robert immediately left them to say hello.

James stood up to acknowledge his father, 'Hello, Father, you lost no time in recruiting your former work mates.'

Robert looked at Jacob, 'Hello Jacob, nice to see you.' Then, turning to his son, replied, 'Strike while the iron's hot, James, however I can't stay, I've got to get this lot over to the police station. Catch up with you later.'

Jacob observed the rowdy party with interest, while Robert rounded them up to usher them out of the tavern. He was the last to leave, and gave a farewell wave. Both James and Jacob acknowledged his wave, which prompted Jacob to remark, 'What an odd gathering of men, I've never seen the like.'

James raised an eyebrow, 'I suppose they are, but you know, they have to be unique to do what they do. My father's job was special, he had to be ruthless like his colleagues.'

Jacob needed to know more, 'Tell me about them, James, who do they work for?' James was keen to justify his father's association with what Jacob classed as undesirables.

'They are self employed, Jacob, but work mainly from the office of Bow Street and the Old Bailey, as did my father, who was paid by results. These men are ruthless, no-nonsense individuals who have earned respect from high up in the legal profession.'

Jacob was agog, he didn't think people like these men existed, 'The one called Ray Mitchell, seems to be in charge of the other two.'

James agreed, 'Yes it appears so, David Brown, and Joe Atkins seem to answer to him without question.'

Jacob had a look of awe as he delved further, 'They seem to have great respect for your father?'

James agreed, 'Yes, he didn't get to where he is by pussy-footing his way round. He has my respect as my father, and I certainly would not like to cross him.' Jacob seemed to have exhausted his curiosity and said, 'Let's hope they can locate our missing vicar.'

8

The Windmill

The rhythmic clanging of hammer on anvil reverberated round the blacksmith's shop. Luke Armstrong was a big man who often worked stripped to the waist, even in the depths of winter. He broke from his task at the anvil to position his tongs thrusting the horseshoe into the embers of the fire. There he began working the bellows to bring the furnace to life, his bulging muscles glistened in the dancing firelight. The big Shire horse, Hercules, standing in the comer snorted contentedly, as Stan Heslop spoke quietly to him. Stan was an apprentice at the stables, but was unsure of his future owing to modernisation at the sawmill that meant it was dispensing with the use of horses. Luke himself was highly thought of, but he too was also unsure of his future, as the majority of his work relied on the success of the sawmill. The animal he was about to shoe was being prepared for sale, and this was the last he would see of him.

Hercules used to be handled by Karl Kramm until he was sacked and replaced by Nathan Stockwell. Luke remembered when he last shod Hercules, and the blazing rows he had to put up with. The Stockwell brothers left him with unpleasant memories, and he was relieved when he no longer had to deal with them. When Luke finished putting the last shoe on Hercules, he thanked Stan for his help and asked him, 'Have you got any plans, Stan, when all the horses are gone?'

All Stan had ever known was a life with horses, it was a dream come true when he landed a job at the stables. 'I don't know Luke, I can't imagine a life without them.' Stan gazed up at Hercules as he gently stroked the soft velvety muzzle. 'What about yourself, Luke, what will you do?'

Luke splashed warm water over himself from a bucket by the furnace, 'Like yourself, Stan, I don't know, but the powers that be tell me I can diversify and learn different skills within the sawmill.'

Stan watched as the big man dried himself. 'That's just what I've been told,' he answered. As Luke donned his shirt Stan said, 'It's as if they don't want the working man anymore, and they are trying to think of new ways to get rid of us with their fancy machines.'

Stan admired and looked up to Luke, who was shaking his head in disbelief. 'Don't think like that, Stan, since Seth left I believe we have a good team of men at the top. Men of integrity who want what is best for us. Give modernisation a chance, Stan, and don't go mixing with that lot over at Tolpuddle.' Luke didn't want the lad getting in with the wrong sort. 'You'll only get yourself into trouble.'

Stan led Hercules towards the door, thinking how different Luke's ideas were to the majority of the workforce. He called over his shoulder, 'Thanks, Luke.'

The blacksmith looked on with concern and called out, 'Mind what I say, Stan,' hoping his words of wisdom would be heeded.

The huge thirty-foot sails of the windmill swept round, driving clanking machinery inside. The main drive shaft passed through each floor of the mill, producing a repetitive groan and squeak. Mr

Alsop, the miller, pointed to the rotating drive shaft in its housing at the base of the building.

'That's the problem, see how it judders occasionally, it's in danger of being wrenched from its housing.'

Luke nodded in agreement, 'You will have to bring the machinery to a halt in order to effect a satisfactory repair.'

Mr Alsop's face clouded over, 'Can't you do something as a temporary measure? I have orders to fulfil.'

Luke knew closing down the mill was a drastic measure, and was ready for the miller's argument against it. 'I'm sorry Mr Alsop, it would be far too dangerous otherwise, I'm not prepared to risk my life or anyone else's.'

The miller's demeanour grew more menacing. 'Damn it, man, can't you work round it somehow?'

Luke walked towards the door, and turned saying, 'For a reasonable man I would bend over backwards to help; however, you still owe me for work done last year. I need that payment and also the full amount of this job before I will consider any further work.' With that he was gone.

The miller was not a happy man, he was more used to getting his own way. He was now left with the problem of finding someone with skills to enable his machinery to be repaired. He had gone to the blacksmith, who was employed by the sawmill, hoping to get the job done cheaply.

Mr Alsop began asking farmers if they knew anyone else who could do the job. James Williams, who owned a foundry and engineering works, was mentioned several times. So he eventually made contact with the firm, and an engineer was sent to assess the job. He recommended that a new bearing plus the main driving shaft needed to be strengthened.

After speaking with the miller James called at the blacksmith's shop, and asked Luke to manufacture the necessary clamps. 'I would be very careful in any dealings with that man, sir,' Luke warned.

James was eager to know the full story. 'Oh? And why is that, Luke?'

The blacksmith replied, 'Because he is not an honest man, sir, I have worked many hours for that man and to date he has not paid me one penny.'

James showed genuine concern and prompted Luke to go on, 'Tell me more, Luke.'

Nothing was held back as Luke continued, 'I have my own bills to attend to and I struggled to get over a difficult period.' There was compassion in Luke's voice, 'What that man did to me wasn't right. It's nearly a year on now, and fortunately I have survived, but he still owes me what is rightfully mine. If I were to hit on hard times once more, that money would be a life saver for me.'

James continued showing concern, 'You're quite right, Luke. How much does he owe you?'

Luke pulled out a ledger and flipped through the pages, 'I can tot it up for an accurate figure.'

James was determined to help. 'Yes, do that put it all down on paper and give it to me. I will make sure you get what is owed.'

Luke wrote down each item then announced, 'That's a grand total of four pounds twelve and sixpence'.

James took the paper and said, 'Leave this with me, Luke; you will be paid, trust me.'

So James visited the miller once more, and informed him he was aware of outstanding bills that needed to be dealt with. 'I do hope you will address the situation as a matter of urgency as to how much you owe, Mr Alsop.'

The miller was most embarrassed and replied, 'To whom do you refer, sir?'

James was angry. 'I refer to the blacksmith, sir, if there are others, I expect you to do the honourable thing.'

The miller could sense he was dealing with a smart businessman and stuttered, 'It's only a couple of pounds, sir.'

James was infuriated by his response, 'The sum happens to be four pounds twelve and sixpence.' James was staggered, 'Really, Mr Alsop, such a paltry sum, but a small fortune to a tradesman. I expect the blacksmith to be paid as soon as possible, sir, and any other outstanding debts dealt with. Until the blacksmith has been paid no repairs to your windmill will be undertaken, do I make myself clear?'

The miller was totally embarrassed, and red in the face, humbly apologised, 'I'm sorry, sir, I'll see to it straight away.'

It was a surprised Luke who found he had a visitor to his blacksmith shop the following day. The miller didn't want to antagonise the blacksmith any further; he knew he had to be civil. This was his last chance of getting his machinery repaired, he had to grovel. 'I'm sorry, Luke,' he struggled to get his words out, 'I'm having financial problems, times are hard for me.'

Luke took the money from the miller's outstretched hand; he didn't believe a word of the sorry tale that was being spun. 'Times are hard for everyone, including blacksmiths,' Luke said before adding, 'Thank you.'

Clearly embarrassed the miller muttered, 'Right, I'll be off then,' leaving Luke bemused, and relieved. He made sure the money was tucked safely in his breeches' pocket; it would be saved as a back up should times become hard for him again.

That afternoon he was about to have a second surprise visitor. He heard a shout – 'Are you there, Smithy?' – which drew his attention to the door. There he saw a rough-looking character, of similar height and build to himself.

Luke addressed the stranger, 'Yes, sir, can I help you?'

The stranger had a coarse, gravel-like voice, 'My horse has thrown a shoe – can you sort it?'

Luke lifted the horse's hoof, scraped away some dirt, and then inspected the other three.

He heard the coarse voice of the stranger: 'I realise you can't do it right this minute. I'm staying at the Red Fox overnight; if you could shoe her tomorrow, that would be fine.' The stranger appeared to be pleasant enough, despite his rough exterior, and could tell Luke was curious to know more about him. 'My name is Joe Andrews, I'm working with two of my colleagues on the case of the missing vicar.'

Luke held out his hand, 'Luke Armstrong.' It was a firm handshake. 'I've heard of you, how are you getting on finding him, any luck yet?'

Joe clicked his tongue, and rasped, 'No luck yet, but it's early days. He can run, but we'll find him.'

Luke nodded his head. 'This horse, Joe, has been badly shod; I recommend a new set of shoes. I'm not just saying that to make money out of you. There's a vet nearby who will give you a second opinion, if you want it.'

Joe smiled. 'That's fine, Luke, I can tell an honest man when I see one. I will be paying a certain farrier a little visit when I'm next down his way.'

Luke was also pleased to be dealing with an honest man, 'You can stable your horse here for the night; she will be ready before noon tomorrow.'

Stan Heslop had been called to the site office at the sawmill, where he was surprised to find the recently released Matthew. He had informed him of the sale of Hercules. He had been sold to a local farmer, and Stan was told to deliver the horse to him. 'What will happen to me, Mr Atkinson? What will I be doing without Hercules to look after?'

In his own slow ambling way, Matthew took his time to reply, 'Come straight back here, Mr Jacob needs to speak to you.'

It was with a heavy heart young Stan set off on his last duty with his beloved horse. Not only would he not see Hercules again, but he was now unemployed.

When Hercules was safely delivered, Stan slowly made his way back to the sawmill, he was in no hurry to return. Inevitably he was back at the office, he could no longer put off what the future had in store for him. There he was shown into a small office, and awaited the arrival of Jacob. Alone with his thoughts, he imagined that this was where he collects his wages and is wished well in whatever he does in the future.

When Jacob entered the room, he cheerily wished Stan a pleasant good morning. 'How are you, Stan?'

With a glum face, Stan was thinking, *It's all right for you, but I'm out of work.* He replied, 'I'm all right, sir.'

Jacob sensed the lad's feelings, 'We are all sorry to be losing the animals, Stan, but we cannot stand in the way of progress.' Jacob took a deep breath. 'The question is what are we going to do with you, what would you like to do, Stan?'

Stan looked bewildered. 'I want to carry on working with horses, that's my dream, but you have taken it away from me.'

Jacob's face lit up, 'We have not taken anything away from you, Stan, you can still work with horses. We will always need horses, how would it suit you to work alongside the blacksmith? I happen to know he is under a lot of pressure at the moment, he would appreciate a hand with the animals.'

Stan never thought about blacksmithing, his general mood lifted at this unexpected turn of events. 'I would very much like to work with Mr Armstrong; he's a most kind gentleman.'

Jacob was pleased at how the situation had turned out, 'Right, better get along to report for duty then. Best of luck, Stan.'

On his way to the blacksmith shop Stan was confronted by Joe Andrews, who stopped him. 'Hey, you boy, come here.' His grating voice made Stan uncomfortable. 'What do you know of the Reverend Walter Peabody?'

Stan was servile and compliant. 'Nothing, sir, I don't know him at all,' he respectfully answered.

Joe Andrews scowled. 'Do you live here?'

Stan confirmed and replied, 'Yes sir.'

Joe pursued his questioning, 'Where do you work?'

Stan maintained his polite manner, 'At the blacksmith's shop, sir.'

Joe immediately rasped out, 'My horse is stabled there for the night, be sure you look after her well.' With that he turned his back, and left young Stan staring after him in wonderment.

At the back of the blacksmith shop Luke was tending to the horse, as Stan entered. 'Hi, Luke, meet your new assistant. They've put me with you now that Hercules is gone.'

Luke was pleasantly surprised. 'Well that's grand. Where has Hercules been sent?'

Stan's face clouded over, 'He's been sent over to Green's farm. I expect I won't be seeing much of him again.'

Luke ruffled Stan's hair, 'Never mind, lad, he will be well looked after.' He indicated to the horse, 'This fine specimen belongs to one of the men from Bow Street looking for the missing vicar.'

Stan stroked her flank, 'Yes, I know. I've just met him. He warned me to look after her well. He's not a very pleasant fellow, he appears most threatening.'

Luke was interested, 'What makes you say that?'

Stan screwed up his face, 'He asked if I knew the vicar that went missing, and where I lived, and what my job was. He was very menacing.'

Luke chuckled. 'He has to be like that in his line of work; once you get to know him, he's not bad at all. Now that you're working for me, I have to tell you we have an early start in the morning. This horse, as you can see, is minus a shoe. If you look at the rest of them you will understand why she threw it. I will have to make a completely new set and shod her all round. Ideally, I would like to be done by 10 am. You will be responsible for the fire, and looking after the animal's welfare.' Luke reminded Stan, 'You will have to be here around 4 am to get the fire going, don't let me down.'

Stan was excited, 'That's no problem, leave everything to me.'

Stan was so excited about his new job, that he never went home to bed that night. He made sure he would not sleep in, by staying at the blacksmith shop. He kept the embers of the furnace glowing all night, and spent time keeping the horse company. When Luke arrived he noticed all the buckets had been filled with water, and one already heated by the furnace, for his personal use. Luke just had to compliment Stan, 'You've made a good start, Stan, but I don't expect you to live in the shop, you know.'

Stan beamed, 'I know, Luke, I don't mind. I'm grateful for the opportunity to work for you.'

There was much activity at the stables of the Red Fox, where David Brown was preparing for his long journey up to Bristol. With saddlebags in place, he mounted his horse, when the rasping voice of Joe Andrews interrupted his departure. 'Mind how you go, Dave. I'll join you as soon as I get my horse sorted. I've also told Ray I'll let him know what's happening.'

David Brown looked down from his lofty perch in the saddle and confirmed, 'Aye, you take care. I'll see you,' and was soon disappearing down the narrow back lane.

Joe adjusted the saddlebags across his shoulders, and made his way to the blacksmith shop. There he was surprised to discover his horse almost fully shod, and ready for the road. He croaked, 'I didn't expect her to be ready so soon,' as Luke was dressing the last hoof, who looked up saying, 'You've got my able assistant, Stan, here to thank, he's been here all night, to make this possible.'

Joe smiled. 'Thanks, Stan, I'm grateful, and won't forget it.' He put his hand on Stan's shoulder, 'I wonder if you will do me one more service; go to the Red Fox, and ask for Ray Mitchell, tell him my horse has been shod and that I'm already on my way to join David Brown in Bristol.'

Stan willingly agreed, 'Yes, sir. Right away, sir.' He was seeing the lighter side to this man that Luke had told him about.

Henry Oaks was in his office when Ray Mitchell called to keep his appointment as arranged. The disappearance of the vicar was foremost on the chief constable's mind.

'Good to see you, Ray. What progress on Peabody?'

Ray Mitchell took a deep breath, 'The latest news is of a sighting of the vicar in Bristol. My two colleagues are on their way there this very minute; they will check out every last detail. If there is any truth behind these sightings, I assure you they will get to the bottom of it, it's what they do well.'

The chief constable sighed, 'I hope so, Ray, they're getting impatient at Bow Street.'

Ray tried to reassure him, 'Give it another week, Henry, I'm sure we will have some good news by then. In the meantime we will continue our investigations here, I'll keep you informed.'

The arranged date for the repairs to the windmill arrived and the mighty sails stopped turning much to the concern of the agitated miller. James was on site to oversee the smooth running of the repair. The stonemasons had been instructed to move in fast, to prepare a sound base to take the new bearing. James made sure the miller would not interfere with his workmen.

'Mr Alsop I want you to understand that this foundation must not be worked upon for two days. This will give it time to harden before too much stress is put upon it, we will then install the new bearing, and strengthen the main shaft. Luke Armstrong will be in charge of this part of the procedure, and I don't expect to have any interference from you or your staff, is that understood?'

The miller visibly withered under the stern warning delivered by James.

At the blacksmith shop Luke was loading up the handcart with the steel brackets he had manufactured needed for the repair of the main shaft.

Stan, who was helping, paused, 'I think we will need two journeys for this lot.'

Luke wasn't surprised and answered, 'Three. It will mean a third journey with the tools. I don't expect you to handle the cart on your own; we will do it together.'

Stan was full of enthusiasm, 'I don't mind, Luke, I can manage it while you get on with other things.'

Luke admired Stan's attitude, but wouldn't allow any kind of unfair treatment towards the lad. 'It's not often we have jobs to do out of the shop, but if we have to move with the times, I would consider acquiring a horse and cart.'

Stan's eyes lit up, the thought of looking after a horse was very appealing to him.

On their journey to the windmill, Luke realised that Stan would be struggling if he was on his own, as the handcart was creaking and groaning at the excessive forces being put upon it. After they unloaded the cart, Luke sent Stan back to the blacksmith shop with explicit orders to load up with the rest of the steel work, and wait for him to return. On no account was he to attempt to handle the cart on his own.

In Stan's absence Luke went in search of the miller, who he had seen on the first floor of the windmill. Immediately on climbing the stairs to the right was the miller's office, where Luke knocked and waited. He heard the key turning in the lock, and the door was slowly opened, enough for the miller to peer out. Luke wanted to inform him he had delivered part of the steel work, and the rest was to follow. The miller opened the door further, only just enough to squeeze through, then quickly locked the door and pocketed the key. Luke thought, *What's he got in there, the crown jewels?* He was acting most oddly indeed.

When they had delivered the second load of steel work, Luke sent Stan back to the shop to bring the necessary tools.

'It will not be as heavy a load this time, I think you will be able to manage on your own.' While Luke waited, he wandered about the mill, noting what had been done, and what was still needed. Outside he noted the giant sails at rest and the numerous windows on every floor, particularly the window to the miller's office. The reason he focused there was because he caught a fleeting glance of someone inside. He thought that as long as the miller kept out of his way that was fine. Shortly, he spotted Stan on his way with the handcart, and was thankful he could at last get started. Everything went surprisingly well, soon they were lowering the main shaft onto its new main bearing.

'Right, Stan, go find Mr Alsop and tell him we are ready for a trial for the sails to be engaged. You will find him in his office.' As Stan approached the office, he could hear the drone of conversation beyond the door. After he knocked and waited, he heard the key turning in the lock, then the door opened just enough for him to see an eye.

'What do you want, boy?'

Stan respectfully answered, 'My master sent me to inform you we are ready for a trial run, sir.'

The miller scowled, and with a bad-tempered 'umph' opened the door only just wide enough for him to slide out of the office, and just as quickly he locked the door behind him. He then pushed past Stan and hurried down the stairs to join Luke.

'Now then, Luke,' he snapped, 'you've finally finished, have you?' Luke was not going to be drawn into an argument with the bad-tempered miller, and quietly replied, 'Let's see how she performs first then I'll make a final decision.' After everyone was warned to stay well clear of any moving machinery the sails were set in motion. Luke inspected every floor, then returned to the ground floor, to examine the main bearing, and that it was working in a satisfactory manner. In the meantime Stan had loaded up the handcart with all their tools ready for departure, he was intrigued at the workings of this mighty machine. Luke was satisfied that the work he had carried out could not be faulted and lingered a lot longer before giving his final verdict. This annoyed the miller further, who couldn't get them off his premises fast enough.

A couple of days later, Joe Andrews and David Brown returned from Bristol, having exhausted all their enquiries there. The chief constable had called Ray Mitchell and his team for a meeting. Joe Andrews suggested in his croaking voice, 'It's possible the vicar is still in this neighbourhood, and is lying low somewhere.'

The chief constable asked, 'What makes you think that, have you any ideas where he might be?'

Joe replied, 'Before going to Bristol I had my horse shoed by your local blacksmith. On my return I called in to have the shoes checked over, and got into conversation with Stan the apprentice, who told me he had been working at the windmill. He mentioned some odd behaviour by the miller; he was especially sensitive about his office. I suggest an immediate lightning raid on his premises.'

The Stockwell brothers had gained popular support from the general working classes when they joined forces with the Tolpuddle Martyrs. However owing to their brutal, sadistic and cruel disregard for common decency, their notoriety was steadily gaining momentum. Soon they had more enemies than supporters. One such long-time recruit was the Reverend Walter Peabody, who actively made his feelings known against them, while at the same time comforting their parents. He helped people with a grudge against the brothers, but drew the line at getting his own hands dirty.

Unfortunately for him he had allowed his misguided feelings to get him into his present situation, and was now a fugitive from the law. He had overstayed his welcome at the windmill, and now that the workmen had finished their repairs, the miller wanted rid of him. He wasn't aware of how fortunate he really was, because no sooner had he left the windmill than it was surrounded by law enforcement officers.

Mr Alsop was taken completely by surprise when officers of the law swarmed onto his property. David Brown was the first to burst into his office and shouted, 'Right, Alsop, where is he?'

The miller cowered, fear showed on his face, 'Where is who? I don't know what you mean.'

David Brown knew how to deal with men like the miller. 'Don't come the innocent with me, Alsop,' he almost screamed. Behind a curtain at the back of the office was a bed, and evidence of someone having lived there. David Brown came face to face with the miller; he lowered his voice, which made him even more sinister. 'How do you explain all this then, and don't tell me you live here, when we all know perfectly well you have a nice cottage nearby.'

The miller kept up the pretence of not knowing anything, until he was grabbed by the collar and yanked onto his feet. 'You can tell that to the chief constable, he may be more sympathetic than me.' After the windmill was searched from top to bottom, and every floor thoroughly investigated, everyone left and the place became eerily silent once more. At the police station the miller was questioned over his connection with the Reverend Peabody, but remained steadfast in his story that he did not have any involvement with him whatsoever.

As the sun went down over the clearing around the windmill, the huge sails looked like a motionless giant with upraised arms. An owl hooted heralding in the night from the fast disappearing daylight, as slow moving clouds were lit up by a full moon rising. Among night time predators, bats began to take their place in the air, skilfully flitting here and there. In the intermittent moonlight two mysterious figures furtively merged into the shadow of the windmill.

The owl, cruising the airways, had already completed two

circuits of its territory when she was forced to deviate away from her planned route. A huge fireball erupted from the top floor of the windmill. Soon all four sails were ablaze, with the main wooden building totally engulfed by the all-consuming flames. It was too late by the time the villagers arrived for them to save the building, by morning it would be a smouldering pile of ashes.

News of the devastating demise of the windmill was conveyed to the police station. In his cell the distraught Mr Alsop was informed of the catastrophic event, and that his windmill was no more. 'Who would do such a thing?' he wailed. The officers on duty remarked, 'It was a full moon last night so there would be all kinds of lunatics out prowling on the night of a full moon rising.'

9

The Elusive Shepherd

The chief constable was briefing Christopher Ellis, one of his most trusted and reliable officers.

'I want you to deliver this message to James Williams at his foundry,' he said as he folded the paper and tucked it inside an envelope. 'It briefly informs him of latest developments here, but he will be asking further questions, which you can help him with.'

Chris was a trusted and reliable officer. 'Right away, sir. Leave everything to me, I'll be back here before you know it.'

The chief smiled and nodded his head. 'Thank you, Chris, I know I can rely on you.'

Chris loved his job, but was glad to get out of the office. He concentrated on his journey not pushing his horse too much.

Eventually he was at the foundry, he had made good time and arrived before midday. When James read the brief report he was aghast that the windmill had been destroyed. He had numerous questions that needed to be answered. 'Do we know who the perpetrators are? Who would do such a thing?' he asked.

Chris only knew of the gossip that was rife, and replied, 'It's common belief that the Stockwell brothers did it. I can't think the Tolpuddle Martyrs had anything to do with it as they target modernisation. The Martyrs were formed to stop the advance of mechanisation which results in the loss of jobs. Windmills, however, have been around for hundreds of years, they are a valuable and much needed asset to the community, too valuable an asset to lose.'

James looked perplexed. 'Yes, you're right it does look like the handiwork of the Stockwells. You go get yourself some refreshment, while I get some papers sorted out, then I'll travel back to South Downesmere with you.'

As the miller sat in his cell, he watched and followed the shadows cast by the sun traverse the stone floor. His mind was full of troubled thoughts, the worry of the charge of aiding and abetting a known felon paled into insignificance by the devastating fact his livelihood was nothing more than a pile of ashes. He was suddenly brought back to reality at the sound of the lock being turned then the cell door opening. It swung open and the jailer entered.

'On yer feet, Alsop. You have a visitor.'

The miller jumped to his feet, he was beginning to fully obey harsh instructions, until now something he hadn't been used to. Then James entered, and the guard pushed past him and said, 'I'll just be outside if you need me, sir.'

James took in the spectacle before him, with a certain amount of pity, here was a man who had lost everything, even his self respect.

James had tolerance which showed in his voice. 'I'm truly sorry, Mr Alsop, for your misfortune. I wouldn't wish this on anyone.'

The miller accepted James's sincerity with gratitude, 'Thank you, Mr Williams, you're the first one to acknowledge any sympathy towards me.'

James said after a sharp intake of breath, 'You haven't done yourself any favours though, have you?' The miller stared at the floor in silence, James continued, 'It is true isn't it, that you sheltered the vicar, a man who assisted in the death of another?'

The hushed stillness continued, and the miller remained taciturn at first, then silently nodded. James knocked on the cell door, when the guard opened it he joined the chief constable who was waiting for him. 'Mr Alsop has admitted the Reverend Walter Peabody sought sanctuary at the windmill, and was given shelter with his blessing. What will happen to him now?' James asked.

The chief constable ushered him into his office saying, 'It's as we thought, he will be transferred to Bow Street in the morning to be held until the reverend is apprehended. They will be tried together, by which time we will have the name of the person responsible for the assassination of our prisoner.'

***

David Brown and Joe Andrews rode side by side, following Ray Mitchell who set a brisk pace. They were hot on the trail of the vicar, who was riding a small brown pony. They got their information from various sightings of witnesses along the way. They knew he wasn't all that far ahead of them. Ray swerved his horse off the track and cantered towards a man at the edge of a small copse. The man was a woodsman, who carried a saw and an axe over his shoulder: the tools of his trade. David and Joe brought their mounts to a halt, and waited as Ray spoke to the man. Ray quickly returned to the track, and said, 'He's only just ahead of us; he is obviously skirting round the moor and heading for the coast.'

David replied, 'He's probably hoping to get a boat, that will get him to France.'

Joe nodded, and gruffly rasped, 'Let's get a move on, we could have him before nightfall.'

They urged their horses on to a gallop, all three moved as

one, the woodsman was now alone, all was silent around him once more.

As the three riders came to the top of the rise, they had a good view of the road up ahead. The lone rider could easily be seen. The reverend's thoughts turned to elation, he knew the area, and was planning his next move; however the thunderous drumming of the horses' hooves grew louder, as the three riders closed in on their quarry. Alerted to the fast-approaching posse, the reverend halted his mount. He was filled with fear, and realised in an instant he had been tracked down. His mount was a tired old pony, which had no chance of outrunning these professional hunters. He resigned himself to his fate, and waited until he was surrounded by the rough-looking individuals. David went alongside the reverend and grabbed the pony's reins, while Joe manoeuvred himself to the opposite side, and began tying the reverend's wrists behind his back.

Ray faced his terrified prisoner and said, 'We are working under the authority of the Bow Street Magistrates' Court. We hereby take you into custody to answer charges brought against you.'

The Reverend Walter Peabody had gone through life never ever being stuck for words, this time, however, he remained silent, overcome with dread.

***

The sound of heavy machinery was muted, as Jacob closed the window, to lessen the distraction from the work outside. James, who sat opposite him, gave a silent sigh of relief as he grappled with the seemingly impossible set of figures before him. He thought that it would soon be time for a welcome break; he had been hard at it for well over an hour. A knock at the door was answered by Jacob, who commanded, 'Come in.' James looked up to see Chris Ellis enter, he looked immaculate in his new uniform.

'Begging your pardon, sir. The chief constable wishes to inform you that the Reverend Peabody has been apprehended, and is now being held pending his transfer to the Old Bailey.'

Although Chris was addressing Jacob, James replied, 'When did this happen?'

The officer turned to face him saying, 'About 3.30 am this morning. Sir Henry wants to know if you want to see him before we send him off?'

James looked at his friend. 'Jacob, I'll go now, do you want to accompany me?'

Jacob was keen to join James, and replied, 'Thank you, Chris. Tell Sir Henry we will be along shortly.'

Outside the police station stood a sturdily built wagon, which was basically an iron cage on wheels. So heavy in fact, it needed two strong horses to pull it. No thought had gone into the comfort of its passengers, nor for the driver, it being open to the elements. As James entered the station with his friend Jacob, he thought the reverend was in for a further shock for his journey to London. As the heavy oak door of his cell opened, the reverend stood up and placed his bible on the bed. Jacob noted the bible and remarked, 'Been reading the ten commandments, Reverend?'

With his slight body trembling, the reverend turned to face his tormentor, 'I'll have you know I did not kill anyone, Atkinson.' All pretence of chivalry was gone as he spat out Jacob's surname.

Jacob looked at James who said, 'You are heavily implicated with murder, Reverend, how can you justify any form of defence?'

The reverend was passionate in his reply: 'I let my heart rule my head: the Stockwell brothers had turned rogue, they needed to be stopped. I don't understand how they ended up like this, after being brought up in a God-fearing family.'

James appealed to the reverend's better sense of judgement. 'Who was it that did murder Nathan Stockwell? It's in your best interests to name his killer.'

The reverend scowled with obvious disdain written all over his face, 'I had no trouble in finding someone to carry out his elimination; there were many volunteers. Alas I cannot name him, as I gave my word he would have complete anonymity.'

James slowly exhaled in exasperation. 'Then you must know, Reverend, things will not go well for you; the law will hold you entirely responsible for his murder. There is only one verdict: it means the gallows for you.'

The reverend remained adamant, 'Even for the lesser charge of aiding and abetting, my fate is still to end on the gallows, so I have nothing to gain. Consider this my gift of life to the man who helped me.'

There was nothing more James and Jacob could do; outside, they relayed their meeting with the reverend to Sir Henry. He was disappointed; he had hoped they would have been more fruitful and gained information on the identity of the killer. Sir Henry went ahead with plans for the transportation of the miller and the reverend to the Old Bailey. They were scheduled to start their journey early the next morning. Chris Ellis was put in charge, with the aid of two extra officers, who were stowing their wet weather equipment under the driver's seat. There was no provision for the prisoners in the cage, they could only hope for fine weather on their journey.

It rained continuously throughout the night, fluctuating between light rain and frequent heavy deluges. The swollen river levels had risen quite steadily to a serious and dangerous situation. Part of the road, running parallel to the river, became flooded. While further round the bend, part of the steep banking had collapsed, and a landslide had caused the track to be partially obstructed. The heavy prison wagon ploughed ever onward through the flooded road, with the three officers huddled together on the driver's seat. Sir Henry had insisted that no matter what the state of the weather, his prisoners would be transported as arranged; however an act of compassion by the chief ensured the unfortunate prisoners were equipped with long trench coats.

Chris cowered under his hood, trying to keep his eyes on the road ahead. Not so his two colleagues, with their hoods pulled well over they sunk further into the folds of their raincoats. They were suddenly brought back to reality by Chris hauling on the reins, and shouting 'Whoa' to bring the two huge horses to a halt. They had come to the landslip, which covered up to a half of the roadway.

Mr Alsop and the reverend stood up to view the blockage in front of them. Chris was summing up his chances of manoeuvring the heavy vehicle round the obstruction. His two colleagues were not too sure and looked fearfully at the raging torrent below. 'We have got to try,' commented Chris, 'There is no chance of us turning this wagon around on this narrow track.'

His colleagues realised proceeding onwards was the only option open to them. Mr Alsop shouted above the howling maelstrom, 'Hey, hey, Ellis, you're not thinking of going round that, are you?'

Chris ignored his warning shouts and proceeded to instruct his officers on how best to proceed. When they all knew what they had to do the two horses each had a handler to guide them forward, with the sturdy wheels as near to the edge of the drop as they dared. With shouts of panic, from the prisoners, the weight of the wheels broke away the edge and the wagon slowly keeled over to perch precariously near the fast flowing river.

Mr Alsop screamed, 'Get us out of here, Ellis.'

Chris did not need any prompting. He shouted, 'Keep the horses steady,' as he clambered over the top of the cage to unlock the door. When the door did swing open, Mr Alsop lunged at the opening. Chris shouted at him, 'Steady,' and the wagon slipped further down the bank. The two officers kept their horses straining at the weight of the wagon behind them; it was this action which prevented the wagon from going into the river. Mr Alsop clung to the ironwork with his legs now in the fast flowing river, he was quickly followed by the reverend who clung to Mr Alsop's waist. The extra burden caused Mr Alsop to lose his grip, and both were swept into the angry raging waters.

Chris lost no time in scrambling up and off the cage. With the horses still straining at the weight, Chris knew if he didn't act swiftly the wagon would drag the unfortunate animals to their doom. With a rush of adrenalin Chris unshackled the horses' traces, and the wagon was hungrily sucked into the swirling waters. All three men stared in disbelief and shock at the ferocious raging river. It was inconceivable that the wagon and their prisoners had simply disappeared.

Later in the day, Sir Henry looked out of his office window, down the main street wondering when the rain would ease off. He observed two large horses making their way towards the police station. He stood transfixed, as he focussed his attention on the three riders, two on one horse, and one on the other. Then he found it difficult to believe they were his men, he was confused as to what they were doing back here so soon without the prisoners – and where was the wagon?

When the downcast Chris entered the police station, Sir Henry could barely conceal his confused thoughts. He forcefully said, 'Chris, what the hell happened?'

Chris and one of his colleagues took off their raincoats, slopping water all over the office. His other colleague had disappeared with the horses, to stable them. After Sir Henry had heard of their disastrous encounter, he graciously said, 'Chris don't blame yourself, I am as much at fault. Sending you out in such adverse weather conditions was not a good idea.' Chris was visibly in shock: the two prisoners clinging on to the cage, then being swept to their deaths, was etched permanently in his memory.

News of the tragedy spread quickly through the village, it was the main topic of gossip for days on end. The miller's body was quickly found, surprisingly, he had not drowned but had died from a blow to the head. It was not unusual as their bodies had been swept through a narrow gorge strewn with rocks and monolithic boulders. The fact that the reverend's body had not been found was troubling Sir Henry; until it was, no closure could be drawn. It remained a thorn in his side.

As the search continued, James met with Sir Henry, who gave him a personal account of proceedings so far. With the help of a professional cartographer, a clear and comprehensible map of the river was made available to aid the police in their investigations. The focus was between the landslip, and the point where the body was retrieved. James said, 'I'm looking at the area between the gorge and further upstream. I notice various dwellings – can you explain these markings?'

Sir Henry pulled the map towards him. 'Ha, the dwellings that are marked are where we have been able to speak to the householders. The unmarked dwellings we assume are derelict,' he explained. James drew the map towards him again, and studied it in silence.

Sir Henry asked, 'What are you thinking, James, have you got a theory?'

James pursed his lips, 'After this length of time, with no body showing up, I'm thinking it is possible for the reverend to have made it to the bank before being swept through the fatal gorge.' This was an area he knew well from his travels between the sawmill and his foundry. 'Mmm,' he muttered, making a mental note. He wasn't so sure they were as derelict as Sir Henry imagined.

On his return to London, James came across one of the so-called derelict dwellings, where he knocked loudly on the door. There was no answer, but it didn't appear to be neglected, he wandered around the back. It was desolate: curtains were drawn all round, but he couldn't be sure it was abandoned. There were more than just this one cottage, as there were other dwellings regarded as derelict. He gave a lot of thought to how many he could see on the map in his head. Until all these dwellings were checked out thoroughly, no one could be sure of the reverend's fate.

Upon his return from London, he looked up the slope at the cottage, and there it was: smoke from the chimney was most apparent. It was this that was etched on his memory, and which bothered him. He knocked on the door; there was definitely someone in residence. The door opened almost immediately to reveal a weather-beaten old man. The man quizzically looked at James, and waited for an explanation.

James said, 'Good morning, sir, sorry for the intrusion. I don't know if you are aware that the police have been trying to get in touch with you.'

The old man looked horrified. 'Why, what have I done?'

James smiled. 'No, you haven't done anything. It's about the terrible tragedy, of two of their prisoners being washed down river when it flooded.'

The man frowned, 'I know nothing of that, I'm too busy with my sheep.'

James looked at him in surprise, 'You mean you haven't heard anything at all about it?'

He shook his head, 'No I'm out of the cottage most of the day; in fact, a gentleman fell into the river the other day. He was lucky to find me at home when he did.'

James raised his eyebrows, 'Tell me about him – what did he look like?'

A grin lit up the shepherd's face. 'Funny little man he was, very religious. He was most concerned that his bible was wet. Spent most of his time by the fire trying to dry it out. I gave him some warm milk with bread and cheese. He was a cheeky devil: after he left, I found he had taken what was left of the loaf. He didn't stay long, he wasn't at all dry, but was soon on his way.'

James placed his hand on the man's shoulder, 'I really think you should come with me to South Downesmere police station.'

Sir Henry was both surprised and delighted to see James with a witness who could verify that the Reverend Peabody did not perish in the river, and was, in fact, alive and well. Due to extensive questioning, valuable information was obtained, which resulted in hiring Ray Mitchell and his men once more.

***

In a meadow, all was quiet and peaceful as the sun rose warming the land. All around nature seemed to be saying welcome to the sunshine. The hedgerows were thriving with bird life, and rabbits frolicked in the fields. There was slight movement from the haystack, as the reverend peered out. He had stayed there overnight and was now doing some serious thinking. He knew that it wouldn't be long before they got that persistent, and annoying, posse on his trail once more.

He regretted making such a fuss over his bible in the shepherd's cottage, it was such details as that which had led to his previous downfall before. He recalled he must have left a trail a blind man could follow. He resolved to travel by night, and must avoid people whenever possible. It would be a good idea to change direction from time to time. As much as he hated the thought, he had also considered getting rid of his bible.

His thoughts went back to being imprisoned in that accursed iron cage, and the relief of escaping from it. He shuddered reliving the nightmare of being swept away in the current, and the hope of survival when he grabbed at the overhanging branch. It was then his fight for survival began: with the miller hanging on to his leg, he was getting weaker. If he hadn't kicked him in the head, he would most certainly have perished.

***

David Brown and Joe Andrews were languishing in the Red Fox Tavern, while Ray Mitchell was in talks with Sir Henry at the police station. Ray said, 'I didn't think you would be calling on our services for the same man so soon.'

Sir Henry shrugged his shoulders, 'What happened was an unfortunate tragedy, but I don't blame my men. I made a regrettable error in sending them out in such atrocious conditions.'

Ray was impressed that the chief constable was taking responsibility for the tragedy. 'I think you are being too hard on yourself, but I admire you for protecting your men.'

Sir Henry sighed, 'Well we must try and put all this behind us, the sooner we recapture our prisoner the better. As soon as you are able to start, one of my men will take you to the shepherd's cottage. There he can give you a detailed account of the reverend's last sighting. I will forewarn you, he is a difficult man to contact. He may not always be at home. As a shepherd he spends much of his time outdoors tending his sheep.'

Ray smiled. 'Have no fear. If he is there, we will find him.'

Stan Heslop was on his way from the bakery to the blacksmith's shop. He was carrying a crusty loaf of bread wrapped in a cloth: Luke's favourite meal for lunch. The rasping voice of Joe Andrews came from behind and startled him, 'Ho there, young Stan, what have you got there?'

Stan turned to be confronted by a group of horsemen, accompanied by officers of the law. He quickly stood aside, and answered, 'Bread for my master's lunch, sir.' Joe's normal harsh demeanour softened, he had great respect for the blacksmith and his apprentice.

'Good lad,' Joe replied. 'Give him my respects.'

Stan stood aside as the cavalcade of horsemen rode past, he was all fired up with the latest gossip. *Wait till I tell Luke*, he thought. The clanging of hammer on anvil stopped, as Luke patiently listened to Stan's latest version of events.

'He's a slippery one, that vicar,' Stan stated.

Luke frowned, 'You don't want to believe all you hear, lad, we don't know what's going on in that man's head. He may have valid reasons for his actions, I find it strange for a man of God to be in such a predicament.'

At the shepherd's cottage, there was no response to Ray's urgent knocking on the door. Ray turned to the uniformed officers. 'All right, men, you can return to the station, we will take it from here.'

David returned from the back of the property, 'He's definitely not answering, the door is locked and the curtains drawn; he must be out and about,' he announced.

Ray said, 'Right, we will head uphill, fan out; I'll see you at the top.'

Satisfied they had covered all the ground behind them they descended, into a series of gorges. They carefully checked every nook and cranny; eventually the coarse shout from Joe urged them to look in the direction of his pointed finger.

Joe stared into a gully, and, because of his position, he was the only one to see the distant figure.

10

Sometimes Magic Happens

Stan was excited, after a long extended exchange of words with Luke on the virtues of the blacksmith's shop having its own horse, Luke had finally succumbed. He was on his way to the sawmill's stables to take delivery of their very own horse. The horse in question was regarded as having a stubborn streak and wanted too much of his own way. The head stableman thought it prudent that the horse should go, and was all in favour of the arrangement. A small minority of the workforce had little time for a stubborn horse, consequently, the animal had experienced cruelty on odd occasions. This was part of the problem, and only made the animal more determined to have his own way.

Stan eagerly looked into the stable at the horse, who was known as Forty-nine simply because he occupied that stall in the stables. He spoke softly, 'Hello, boy.' The horse turned his head to look at him; then, just as quickly, turned away with a disinterested snort. Further overtures and friendly gestures went unheeded. Stan had gone prepared: in his pockets he had an array of goodies. He held out a carrot, and clicked his tongue; the effect was instant as the horse made his way towards the tempting juicy carrot. Stan had the full attention of Forty-nine.

The head stableman began to wonder how Stan was coping as it was fifteen minutes when he first went in and hadn't yet emerged. He found Stan quietly talking and stroking the animal's soft muzzle; he was amazed at the transformation of wayward Forty-nine.

The stableman said, 'You seem to be getting along very well with Forty-nine. Very few people can.' Stan looked at him and enquired, 'Have you got a bridle and bit?' The stableman said, 'Yes lad, I'll get you one.' He was interested in seeing how the lad was going to manage. As Stan took the bridle from the man, he said, 'It would help if you stood back, sir, he seems to be spooked somewhat by your presence.' The stableman smiled and complied as he stood well away from them. Stan gently put the bridle over the horse's head then slipped him another carrot. Then he finished the manoeuvre by placing the bit in the horse's mouth. The stableman said, 'The management should never have let you go, lad, I reckon they made a big mistake.'

Back at the blacksmith's Luke noticed the joy on his apprentice's face, 'He looks all right, Stan, what's his name?'

Stan replied, 'Everyone calls him Forty-nine; he hasn't got a real name.' Luke scratched his head, 'That's not a real name, you will have to give him a proper name.'

Stan thought for a second, then it clicked, 'Can I name him Charlie?'

Luke was bemused, 'Course you can, as far as I am concerned he is your horse, but why Charlie – any special reason?'

Stan was a picture of joy, 'Because of my Uncle Charlie: he was stubborn, and I loved him for it.'

Luke was pleased with their latest purchase, and went ahead with plans to have a flatbed wagon made, with removable sideboards. As Stan spent all his spare time with Charlie, Luke found he was working alone most of the time. Over time, Charlie was losing his stubbornness; Stan would frequently produce a carrot or an apple, which tended to change the horse's behaviour.

When Stan had to do his deliveries, he always used Charlie, even when the handcart was more suitable.

One day, after he had delivered some hand crafted tools to a local farmer, he noticed up ahead a group of police officers. Chris Ellis held up his hand and brought the wagon to a halt. Stan jumped down and stroked Charlie's rump and listened to Chris Ellis make a most unusual request.

'Stan, I wonder if you would assist the police? We are in a delicate predicament here.'

Stan then went to stroke Charlie's soft muzzle, as he answered, 'If I can help you, Constable Ellis, I will.'

Chris gripped Stan's elbow, and took him aside, as if to prevent anyone else from hearing. 'We have just discovered a body near the road, and we need to transport it back to the police station. The weather doesn't look too promising,' he said, looking skywards, 'Looks like rain or worse, it's even cold enough for snow. We will be very discreet: the body will be well covered and no one will suspect what is in your wagon.'

Stan was wide-eyed, 'I don't suppose my master would object.'

Chris was pleased that Stan was willing to help and stood to one side. With a nod of his head, two officers manhandled the body onto the wagon.

As the group climbed on board, it started to rain – just as Chris had predicted. Everyone was silent as the wagon trundled on. The sombre journey seemed to match the grey day.

Stan was relieved when they arrived at the police station with the gruesome load, he jumped down and was told, 'Just stand aside, we will handle it from here.' He noticed Henry Oaks talking to James Williams as the door was opened to allow the officers carrying the body to enter. As Stan hurried back to the welcome warmth of the blacksmith's shop, the rain turned to sleet, then to snow.

Stan was attending to Charlie when Luke followed them into the stable, and said, 'You've been busy helping the police?'

Stan looked questioningly at his master. 'I hope you don't mind me allowing the police the use of the wagon?'

The burly blacksmith immediately put Stan at ease, 'Not at all, Stan, I knew all about it.'

Looking puzzled Stan asked, 'How?'

Luke answered, 'Unknown to you one of the police officers jumped off the wagon as you passed on your way to the police station. He explained everything to me – you did the right thing.'

Stan looked up to his master with huge respect, and excitedly continued to tell him, 'I noticed Mr James at the police station, as they carried the body past him, he seemed involved somehow.'

There was a frown on Luke's face, as he asked, 'Was the body that of a man, or was it female?' Wide-eyed Stan answered, 'I couldn't tell, Luke, they had it well covered, and it was obvious they were not giving out any indication what so ever.'

Luke gravely took in what Stan was saying, he didn't want him to be misguided and told him, 'Don't be making assumptions about Mr James; he is a man of integrity, better to wait for developments and get the true facts.'

Stan finished making sure Charlie was well cared for, and looked out of the window. He saw it was snowing heavily; the outside world began to take on its winter mantle.

'It's certainly snowing now, Luke. I wouldn't like to be caught out in that lot.'

Luke joined Stan and together took in the winter vista before them. 'I don't want Charlie pulling the wagon in weather like this, Stan. You can ride him, which will be much better for both of you.'

Stan looked up at his master, with a huge grin, and said, 'Thank you, Luke.'

***

The gas lamps cast a welcoming and iridescent warm glow around the snug room of the Red Fox Tavern. James occupied a prime position in the inglenook fireplace, as he waited on the arrival of his friend Jacob. It was a popular meeting place within the village, and tended to get a little raucous as the night wore on. However owing to the inclement weather, few customers were in the snug, which suited James. At last Jacob entered, on seeing James he smiled as he unwound a thick woollen scarf from around his neck. 'James, sorry I'm late.' James replied, 'This wretched weather is slowing everything, and everybody down,' as he helped his friend remove his heavy coat, which reached down to his ankles.

Two hot toddies were swiftly despatched to their table, as Jacob asked, 'Was it your messenger, James?'

Grave faced, James answered, 'Yes, I'm afraid it was.'

Jacob was obviously affected by his answer. 'What was Oaks able to tell you?'

James took a few moments to reply, 'Nothing really, after I identified the body, all he could tell me was that he was shot through the head, which was patently apparent. The prime suspects are the Tolpuddle Martyrs; it looks like the work of the Stockwell brothers.'

Jacob sat back and expelled air with a silent, 'Phew.'

He then looked at James saying, 'The Tolpuddle Martyrs are playing a dangerous game being involved with the Stockwell brothers.'

James nodded his head in agreement. 'They are so misguided, and fail to grasp the benefits of modernisation; it's a force that cannot be halted. The industrial revolution will prevail. There will be no turning back.'

Jacob sipped at his drink, and agreed, 'No turning back, that's the message we need to get back to them.'

James, mesmerised in thought, stared into the fire, then exclaimed, 'Yes that's the key, we must get it through to everyone, we are on a path of no return.'

James said, 'Jacob, I've been giving some thought to our communication system. This latest tragedy highlights the dangers we are putting the messengers in. I have lost a good man, a family man, whose family I will recompense, but no amount of money will bring him back.'

Jacob listened intently, then asked, 'What do you suggest we do then?'

James turned his head sharply, and looked Jacob straight in the eye. 'Don't send any more of your men out as messengers. I will contact Toby, who can recommend tough ex-army types. I want two specially chosen men to travel together while delivering messages. We will fight fire with fire.'

Toby Green and Tommy Atkins found themselves very busy over the coming weeks. They began recruiting, and forming, what can only be described as a private army. They would only accept men who would meet their strict requirements. This elite band of individuals were given specific jobs at the sawmill and at the foundry as security staff, while others were entrusted with the dangerous job of carrying vital information between Jacob's and James's places of business.

***

The Reverend Peabody's slim figure belied the fact that he was a resourceful individual. He had transformed his old ways into that of a cunning and inventive survival expert. He shunned people whenever possible, and lived off the land. Now that the seasons had turned to winter it became increasingly more difficult. However he had discovered a disused tin mine, linked to many galleries that were interconnected to three main entrances. Having stocked up his newfound safe haven with provisions, he had a new problem to deal with. The new season had brought snow; he had to be extra careful not to leave footprints which would betray his presence there.

He had prepared a comfortable bed made up with straw, and in the three weeks he had been there he had slept well. He had explored the many tunnels, and had familiarised himself with the complex twists and turns of numerous passageways. He began to feel more secure in case he had to make a quick exit. His long-term plan was to wait until the weather improved, and only then move on.

He slept soundly and turned contentedly over, but something wasn't quite right. He lay still, his senses gradually bringing him back to reality; there it was again, it wasn't his imagination. The mumble of voices was coming from within the mine. With his heart pounding, he sat bolt upright; now, he was fully alert, concentrating on the alien sounds. Now he was certain there were intruders. He must act swiftly. He made his way to the exit, keeping well back he was able to see outside the entrance. The two dubious-looking characters filled him with dread.

Whatever happens he must not panic. He withdrew back into the shadows, and lit a candle. He went as far as the fork in the tunnel. He listened intently and discerned that the mumbled voices were coming from the left. He quickly made off down the right hand passage. This took him to the third entrance, where he hoped he could escape danger.

On approaching the entrance, he extinguished the candle, and with extreme caution, hung back to scan the outside world. It was most apparent there had been a concentrated amount of activity here, judging by the amount of scattered footprints around the entrance. He ventured further out, in order to find out more of what was out there, when the grating voice of Joe Andrews startled him; it hit him like a hammer blow.

'Good morning, Reverend Peabody,' he rasped, 'or is it Mr Peabody these days?' as he revealed himself from the shadows behind.

The reverend was dumbstruck, as he stared at his tormentor. 'You have led us a merry dance, Peabody,' the annoying voice continued, and sent shivers down the reverend's back.

At last the hunted man began to pull himself together, and asked incredulously, 'How did you find me?'

Joe replied, 'We are professional bounty hunters, we always get our man. We examine every little piece of evidence, no matter how long it takes; then, sometimes, like today, magic happens.'

The reverend glanced back the way he had just come, which prompted Joe to say, 'Don't even think about it, I can assure you we have been very thorough. When our investigations led us to this mine, we obtained detailed plans of the whole workings. You must believe me we have every nook and cranny covered.'

Joe then spun his prisoner round to face the wall; he then cuffed his hands behind his back. The reverend resigned himself to being well and truly caught.

The following day found the reverend back in South Downesmere police station, awaiting transportation to the capital. He perched on the edge of a wooden raised seating arrangement, which served as a bed. Provisions were spartan; there was no heating. The austere harshness of his surroundings was truly soul destroying. He had just finished jumping up and down in an effort to keep warm, and now sat totally tired and dejected. He thought if only he could sleep, it would allow him to escape this impossible situation for a short while at least. The noise of the key in the lock, and the bolts being drawn, caused him to focus his attention on the door.

The door swung open as the jailer barked, 'On your feet Peabody, you have a visitor.'

James pushed past the officer, and informed him, 'You can leave us now, I'll knock when I'm ready to leave.'

The officer, while freely showing contempt for his prisoner, dutifully replied, 'Yes sir.'

The reverend indicated his bed. 'Would you like to take a seat, Mr Williams?' he offered.

They both sat down with the reverend curious to know why

he had such a prestigious visitor. 'To what do I owe this pleasure?' he enquired.

James told him, 'I was in discussion with the chief constable, when I mentioned I didn't care for the way you were being treated. The chief remarked things would be much better for you if you were to reveal who murdered Nathan Stockwell. He then gave me permission to come and talk to you again.'

The reverend appeared to be amused, 'Are you sure? I think you are here because it's the chief's idea; he sent you to get this information from me, didn't he?'

James tried to reassure him, 'No, no, he didn't send me, I'm here of my own accord. I asked him if I could talk to you again because I don't agree with the treatment you're being given.'

The reverend sat silent for a moment, then replied, 'Well thank you for your concern, Mr Williams, I do appreciate it very much. But I did explain when we last spoke my reasons for not revealing who that person was.'

James's face was creased in a frown. 'What I don't understand is how a man of the cloth has ended up like this.'

The reverend smiled and answered, 'There is only so much even a man of the cloth will stand. The Stockwell brothers were running wild; I let my heart rule my head, and stepped over the line. I am now on the wrong side of the law. Despite what people think of me, I still hold dear my Christian beliefs. I gave my word to the man who pulled the trigger for me, that I would not reveal his name. Having said that, I am responsible for murder, and openly confess to that. When I go to the gallows, justice will be seen to be done.'

James took a deep breath, and exclaimed, 'Phew,' then said, 'Well reverend, I don't know what to say to you, it seems to be so tongue in cheek to wish a condemned man the best of luck.' The reverend smiled back at him, then said, 'I do hope I'm not going to be transported to London in one of those infernal iron cages, it's worse than the thought of the gallows.' James was amazed at how calm he was, and in an effort to show compassion, stood up and placed his hand on the reverend's shoulder, saying, 'I'll try to find out about your travel arrangements.' He knocked three times on the cell door, which was instantly answered by the bolts being withdrawn. As the door swung open, James said, 'I'll bid you farewell reverend.' To which the reverend raised his right hand and answered, 'Not farewell, sir; my fate is already sealed, thank you for your compassion, I bid you good-bye.'

The chief constable welcomed James into his office. It was obvious he was keen to learn the outcome of James's visit. 'Well James did he tell you anything?' he asked before James had a chance to be seated. James shook his head, 'No I'm afraid not, he is determined to take the guilty party's name to the grave. But I appeal to your better nature, don't be too hard on him, he is concerned about his transportation to London, will he be caged like before?' The chief constable lit a cigar, 'I hear what you say James, but it would have been better if he had revealed the guilty party. He has forfeited all rights to special concessions, I promise nothing. There is no telling what they will put him through, before his execution.'

11

The Ballad of Ronald Young

Thomas Ellis had been waiting beside the old oak tree just outside South Downesmere for fifteen minutes. They were late and he began to fear the worst. The Stockwell brothers lived an unpredictable lifestyle, almost anything could have happened to them. It was they who should be waiting for him, he thought, as he decided to wait a further ten minutes. Then from the undergrowth behind, he heard his name being called: 'Thomas, over here.' He dived into the bushes, where they were well hidden. 'Where have you been? I was beginning to think something had happened to you.'

Ben sneered back, 'We have to be careful how and when we travel.'

Peter joined in to help his brother, 'Yeah, stop your belly aching; every time we meet you're moaning at something or other.'

Thomas was fearful of these two desperate outlaws and didn't reply; he waited respectfully for their reply.

Ben took up the conversation, 'What have you got for us, anything at all?'

Thomas replied, 'Since I was sacked, I don't get to hear much news from the sawmill, and the majority of people don't speak to me either, but I do know from talk in the tavern that Peabody has been recaptured.'

Peter's eyes glinted in interest as he grabbed Thomas by his lapels, 'Where is he being held?' he demanded in a gruff voice. 'Don't tell me he is already at the Old Bailey?'

Ben eased himself between the two locked men to prise them apart. 'Easy, easy,' he coaxed his brother, 'I'm sure Thomas will help us without any nastiness, won't you?'

Thomas was completely intimidated, and cowered away from his aggressor. Ben continued to fuss over Thomas by straightening his collar, and hoped his gentle attitude would reassure Thomas to be more co-operative.

Thomas told them all he knew: 'He is being held at South Downesmere police station. I would guess they will want to be rid of him as soon as possible.'

Ben looked at Peter. 'It's possible he could be moved at first light in the morning, Peter,' he hissed.

Peter replied, 'We could waylay them and get Peabody before they get past Farmer Green's pond. It's the ideal spot, like we did to Williams.'

Ben scowled at Peter, 'Don't you remember? Williams out gunned us.'

Peter said, 'Yes, but this time we don't reveal ourselves: we remain hidden.'

Thomas looked fearfully at his interrogators, not daring to speak; he just wanted to get away from them as fast as he could. Peter was becoming more hostile towards him every time they met.

Ben turned to Thomas, and began straightening his lapels once more, 'What do you think, Thomas, do you think we are doing the right thing in dealing with our brother's killer?'

Thomas's throat went dry as he struggled to answer, 'I think he will be heavily guarded, given what happened the last time he was transported.'

Peter drew closer to Thomas as he exclaimed, with a snarl, 'Yes, I think we have covered that little detail.'

After his meeting with the Stockwell brothers, Thomas's emotions were running wild. He always knew he was dealing with extremely dangerous men. He had to be careful, which made him fearful, of what might happen to him if he crossed them. The way Peter treated him made him angry, he was already red in the face and gritted his teeth as the anger welled right up until he thought his head would burst. When he first got involved with them it excited him, but due to their treatment, it made him uneasy, and fearful of his life. Of the two he came to the conclusion that Ben was the deadliest, with his sickening, make-believe, friendly attitude. Thomas wasn't fooled, not one little bit.

***

The chief constable was briefing his men on the operation the next morning – of transporting his prisoner to the Old Bailey. Among the group were officers from London; he had also recruited Ray Mitchell and his team of bounty hunters. In total there were twelve men to guard the one prisoner. It was Ray Mitchell who suggested that the prisoner should travel on horseback, rather than in an open-caged wagon. He wanted the group to move fast when it became necessary. Henry Oaks wasn't taking any chances; he had just outlined the minor points, like having the prisoner's hands bound, when he dropped his bombshell. 'Finally, men, I have just received this note informing me that the Stockwell brothers are active in this area.' He held the paper up high, 'This informs me they plan to ambush you on your way to London. It beats me how they obtain all their information.'

Ray Mitchell spoke up, 'My men and I will be scouting ahead for any trouble, this bit of news will make us extra vigilant.'

Chris Ellis interrupted, 'It seems to me they are very

determined to get at our prisoner, they could shoot him without ever revealing themselves.'

The chief constable raised his eyebrows. 'I think Ray is dealing with that problem, by scouting ahead.'

Chris persisted, 'Yes, I acknowledge that, but what if he should fail?'

Ray glared at Chris, to show his disapproval, and growled, 'Well do you have any bright alternatives?'

Chris was clearly embarrassed. 'I'm sorry, Ray, I meant no criticism. I was thinking we could outwit any ambush attempt by dressing our prisoner in a police uniform, while I dressed in civilian clothing and posed as him. With so many uniformed officers it would easily confuse them.'

The chief constable nodded his approval as Chris outlined his plan, then broke into a smile. 'It's a good suggestion, but surely not you, Chris, as the decoy? Look at you, you're twice his size.'

Chris was amused and said, 'We cannot order someone to be a decoy; whoever does it must be a volunteer.'

It appeared all the officers from London had been selected because of their imposing height. The choice of a volunteer was left to a local man, and the chief constable announced he would double the wages of the volunteer. This appealed to Ronald Young, a new recruit to the station. Although taller than the reverend, his slight build was as near as they would get, and he was a volunteer.

***

After leaving Thomas Ellis, the Stockwell brothers went straight to Farmer Green's pond. There they were able to choose a prime hiding place before it became dark. They chose a place where the rise of land was heavily covered by trees and shrubbery. They could see the farmhouse and the track leading past it, and they made sure that they could not be detected by the farmer. Owing to the cold, neither of them slept; they spent an uncomfortable night trying to keep warm, and welcomed the approaching dawn. Their night was long, miserable, and seemed never ending as they waited for their quarry to turn up.

Peter had made himself a comfortable soft bed of conifer ferns, as he scanned the road before him. Now, when he needed to be alert, he found he was having to fight off the sleep his body craved for. Ben was aware his brother was having trouble keeping awake, and placed his boot firmly on his back. Peter was rudely shaken awake, and heard Ben hissing, 'Keep alert. This is no time for sleep.'

Because of his lack of sleep, Peter was beginning to be irritated by his brother. Just as he was about to drift off again, Ben's hushed voice brought him back to reality: 'Don't move a muscle, there is a rider skirting past behind us.'

Peter was now fully alert, and spotted another rider to the right of them travelling over open ground, 'There's another to our right.'

The brothers remained perfectly still, when they spotted a third lone rider on the track, keeping pace with the riders on both his flanks. As the rider nearest to them was safely clear, Ben murmured, 'They are obviously the forward scouting party; the main group will be along shortly, are you ready?'

Peter's heart was pounding madly as he answered, 'Yeah, ready.'

The main party consisted of nine riders: three rows riding three abreast. As they came into view the prisoner was easy to spot: he was in the middle of the uniformed officers. With his hat pulled down over his eyes, the prisoner was well and truly hemmed in. Peter lined up his target in his sights, took a deep breath, and then pulled the trigger. The explosive shot was deafening; the prisoner slumped forward and the officers on each side of him reached out to steady him. Then the main group broke into a well-rehearsed canter.

The Stockwell brothers were also well rehearsed as they mounted, and immediately headed back to become lost in the woods. The plan to use a decoy worked remarkably well, with devastating results. After the initial shock of the attack, the main group halted and met up with Ray and his outriders; however, Ronald Young was mortally wounded, and was urged to stay on his horse. They wanted to get him to a doctor as quickly as possible. The reverend said, 'I'm deeply sorry, but it was a hair-brained idea in the first place. That shot was meant for me; I would gladly have taken it.'

Joe Andrews voice grated out, 'Keep quiet, you're not helping.'

Then Ray spoke, 'The main task is to get the prisoner to the Old Bailey.' He then ordered two of the officers from South Downesmere to take charge of their wounded colleague and get medical help.

It would be two days before Henry Oaks got the full account of that fateful day. The one redeeming factor was that his prisoner had been successfully handed over to the authorities. However, it was a costly exercise, as the chief constable read through the report. Ronald Young had been hit in the neck, causing severe trauma; he was drenched in blood. It was a particularly harrowing experience for his colleagues who witnessed his demise. Shortly after seeing the doctor, he succumbed, but not before he uttered, 'I have no regrets.' His bravery did not go unnoticed: Henry Oaks made sure his family were suitably recompensed. He became somewhat of a legend, a home-grown hero. He was remembered in local folklore, and had a ballad composed in his honour, which sang his praises.

When the full extent of the horrifying event became common knowledge, any sympathy with the Stockwell brothers was quickly diminished. A concentrated effort was implemented to capture the outlaws, as their crimes now included several murders. Their latest escapade had fuelled intense animosity against them, and they were now regarded as being a danger to every law-abiding citizen. The sooner they were caught the better. Thomas Ellis was keeping a low profile, and resolved to end any further meetings with the Stockwell brothers. He prayed the concerted efforts of the law would eradicate any further threats from them. Until they were apprehended he would not be able to breathe easy. It was important he kept his head down, and stayed out of their way.

Owing to pressure from the public, Henry Oaks was forced to act; he must do something about the hazard the Stockwell brothers posed. He was in consultation with Bow Street and it was agreed that special funds would be released to cover the cost of bringing the outlaws to justice. He lost no time in recruiting Ray Mitchell, Joe Andrews, and David Brown. It became obvious the criminals must be receiving help from somewhere, and the bounty hunters were quick to investigate any loose talk, especially in the taverns. Henry Oaks was staggered at the amount being spent by them, but they just shrugged it off, explaining information was costly. People knew the bounty hunters paid well for any little snippets that might help them. Thomas Ellis on one of his rare nights out at the Red Fox Tavern happened to hear David Brown in conversation with some locals. Throwing caution to the wind, he thought, *I could earn a little pocket money here,* as he sidled up alongside the bounty hunter. He eventually got to speaking to David Brown, nervously looking around every other second.

'I might be able to help you, for a small remuneration.'

David Brown was instantly interested, 'I don't chuck money around willie nillie; tell me something positive, and I might just fill your tankard up.'

Thomas had to be careful not to give too much away, and replied. 'I know a friend who is in contact with the brothers. I might persuade him to tell me where they meet.'

The bounty hunter's first thoughts were euphoric: he knew that this man knew more than he cared to give away. He waved the serving wench over, 'Fill this man's tankard,' he ordered, as he patted Thomas on the back.

The bounty hunter pressed for further information. 'Thomas, who is this friend?'

Fear gripped Thomas, as he realised he may have gone too far with his loose tongue. 'Oh I'm sorry, I can't give you his name,' he blurted.

David Brown secretly thought, *By George, you will give me his name*, as he put his arm round Thomas's shoulder saying, 'You can't just leave it at that. Don't you see, Thomas, I must, and will, find out. Either tell me now, or come down to the police station, this very minute.' There was no turning back, for Thomas, he realised he had got himself into a corner, and pleaded, 'Don't take me to the police station, if I'm seen there, everyone will know I helped you catch the Stockwells.' David Brown smiled benevolently.

'But that's good Thomas, don't you want to be known as the person who helped catch these criminals?'

Thomas was desperately trying to enhance his lame excuses, 'But if the Stockwells find out it was me who shopped them, I'll be next on their list for vengeance.'

David Brown chuckled, 'Ho, ho, Thomas, not at all. They will be apprehended, you will be quite safe.'

Thomas never had his tankard of free ale, as he chose not to reveal his fictitious friend; the alternative was the police station. On locking Thomas up for the night, Henry Oaks was surprised at the latest outcome, and planned an intense interrogation the following day.

As the cell door firmly shut behind him, Thomas momentarily stood still, taking in his spartan surroundings. Below the heavily barred window was the wooden contraption which served as a bed; to one side stood a slop bucket. He shivered and noted the window was open to the elements. The only luxury he could see was a flea-ridden blanket; he was in for an uncomfortable, and miserable, night.

He sat down draping the blanket around his shoulders, and pondered the fate of Nathan Stockwell in this very cell. He imagined the unfortunate Nathan standing on this bed, after hearing his name being called from the alleyway outside. It was a sobering thought. He mulled it over through his mind that if someone should call his name from outside, he resolved to remain silent, and, most importantly, stay where he was. While the sense of survival was foremost in his mind, a shiver ran down his spine. The full horror of his present situation was dawning on him. How could he have been so stupid in front of one of the bounty hunters? These men were not fools. Once they got hold something, they were like Rottweiler: they would not let go.

He thought of the reverend. He didn't think for one moment he shot Nathan Stockwell, but he was implicated in his death, therefore just as guilty as if he had pulled the trigger. He knew if he was found in league with the Stockwell's, he would follow them to the gallows. He would have to convince the police he made up a story of knowing someone who was in contact with the brothers. If he couldn't, they would show no mercy.

As he mulled over his fate in the darkened cell, his attention was drawn to agitated voices coming from the corridor leading to the front desk. The dispute drew nearer, there was some sort of altercation going on, then a loud shout: 'You've no right to arrest me. You're making a big mistake.' The bolts on the door were noisily withdrawn, then the cell was flooded with light as the door was flung open. Thomas Ellis drew his legs up to his chin as a tumbling mass of struggling bodies now intruded upon his tranquillity.

One by one the officers turned, leaving their victim bruised and bloody, on the floor of the cell. The officer with the keys held his lantern high, and with a parting last-minute piece of information he smiled, saying, 'Very sorry, we have no single cells available at the moment, Foxy, but we know you won't mind sharing.'

The heavy wooden door was slammed shut with an earth-shattering bang, like that of a gunshot blast. Thomas stared at the unfortunate figure through the gloom. The only illumination came through the door hatch, from a lantern in the passageway.

Thomas said, 'They certainly escorted you in with dignity, and charm.'

Foxy sat before him as he rubbed his head, and remained silent. Thomas realised this man wasn't going to give out information freely about himself, and he continued, 'You must have ruffled their feathers to receive such treatment?'

Foxy painfully got to his feet, as he struggled to get to the wooden bunk bed. Thomas was rudely pushed to one side as Foxy laid himself full length. With a low groan he murmured, 'They very nearly broke my bloody arm.'

Thomas was alarmed that this newcomer was laying claim to his bed. 'You cannot sleep here,' he stated.

Foxy sneered as he enquired, 'Why not?'

Thomas was incredulous. 'Because it's my bed,' he blurted, stating the obvious.

Foxy continued with his contemptible attitude, 'Not anymore it ain't. Besides which, you've got the blanket.' Thomas couldn't believe his stay here was getting steadily worse.

Here was a hardened criminal; there was no telling what he might resort to if he was to irritate him.

Foxy smiled, as he asked, 'This is the first time you've been locked up, isn't it?' Thomas gloomily nodded. 'It's like this,' Foxy continued, 'on this side of the law it works on supply and demand. At the moment I have a bed while you have a blanket, I'm willing to share my bed with you in exchange for an equal share in your blanket.'

This was a deal Thomas could not ignore; it seemed more than a fair solution. This man, thought Thomas, was fair-minded;

he knew the ins and outs of the police system, and was beginning to warm towards him.

Regaining some of his confidence, Thomas ventured, 'What have you done, to be imprisoned here?'

Foxy had an infectious smile. 'What haven't I done? My mother isn't very proud of me.' Turning to Thomas he said, 'Enough about me, what about you? Why are you in here?'

Thomas was feeling relaxed, and completely at ease. He obliged Foxy saying, 'I met this bounty hunter in the tavern, looking for information on the Stockwell brothers.' Thomas sighed, and asked, 'Have you heard of the Stockwell brothers?'

Foxy's grin widened. 'Who hasn't?'

A dejected Thomas carried on with his tale of woe: 'I told him I knew a guy who might be passing on information, in the hope I would be rewarded with a tankard of ale. Well, he insisted I gave him the name of my friend, and when I declined he had me thrown into jail.'

Foxy chuckled, 'I would have thought a tankard of ale was a good price just for mentioning a name, why on earth didn't you tell him?'

Thomas fell silent, staring into the gloomy surroundings. Foxy sat upright, and with a giggle said, 'You haven't got a friend have you, because it's you, isn't it?'

Thomas wrung his hands in despair. 'I'll have to convince them there is a friend, otherwise I'll be joining the Stockwells when they are caught.'

Foxy got up and walked towards the door. 'They will never believe that; you are not dealing with fools here. I think you are in deep trouble.' Thomas was amazed when Foxy banged on the door, and shouted, 'Guard!' He was further confused to hear Foxy telling the guards to let him out, that 'It was time.'

Thomas sat open-mouthed as the door opened for Foxy, who turned with a smile, and apologised, 'Sorry, Thomas, only doing my job. My name isn't Foxy, it's Constable Harold Easton.'

The full implications of what had just happened slowly dawned on Thomas. As the heavy door slammed shut once again, he contemplated on what a fool he had been. If he hadn't been so avaricious, he could have still been ahead in the cat and mouse game. Instead he had betrayed himself for the price of a tankard of ale.

The next morning, Henry Oaks was at his desk bright and early. His first job was to organise the interview room, and he wanted to start interrogating Thomas Ellis as soon as possible. In his cell, Thomas had just finished his breakfast, which was an unappetising watery porridge. When he finished, his bowl was whisked away and he was immediately instructed to follow the guards to the interview room. There he was ordered to sit facing a desk where Henry Oaks sat, flanked on each side by uniformed officers. There was a fourth officer standing behind in the shadows. When his eyes became adjusted to the gloom, Thomas was aware the fourth officer was none other than Foxy. Thomas stared at Foxy; he was filled with animosity towards him. What made Thomas more incensed was the fellow's annoying smile. He noticed the beaten-up face, with its new cuts and bruises: his colleagues had gone to extreme lengths to present Foxy as a true villain, as his injuries were by no means fake.

After an hour of frustrating interrogation, Thomas was in no doubt of the precarious position he was now in; however his hopes rose when the chief constable threw him a lifeline. Maintaining a steely eye contact, the chief said, 'If you help us in the capture of the Stockwells, I'll see what can be done to ease the serious charges against you.'

Thomas met the steely gaze, 'I would need to know for sure that I would not be following them to the gallows, otherwise it would be pointless me helping you.'

The chief constable gave a sigh of resignation as he leaned back in his chair saying, 'All right, Thomas, we appreciate your concern, but you must realise our job is to uphold the law. We don't make the rules.' He paused awhile to look at the officer writing notes to his left, then nodded and watched the man stop writing, then closed his book. Clearing his throat, he focussed on Thomas once more, saying, 'We are going to leave you in the capable hands of Constable Harold Easton, who you will remember you have already met. We will resume this conversation later.'

The chairs made a scraping noise, as the chief and his staff cleared the table, then left. Constable Easton stepped forward to fill the vacant seat left by the chief. 'Now then, Thomas, I do hope we can come to some kind of arrangement.'

Thomas was very hostile, and vented his rage in his reply: 'I think you look very distinguished in your smart uniform, but I will always remember you in your other guise as Foxy.' He almost spat the words, which resulted in that annoying smile from Foxy who good-humouredly told Thomas, 'That's fine, Thomas, it's a role I have been playing for quite some time now. Refer to me with whatever you feel comfortable with. My superiors have given me the title of 'Special Operative' – with this position I have special privileges. Sometimes these special privileges override a chief constable's authority.'

As Thomas listened intently, to every word, he was formulating a plan, there were certain questions he needed answering. Thomas leaned forward, hostility still showing, 'Listen, Foxy, before I agree to helping you, I need a firm commitment from you that I will not end up on the gallows, is that understood?'

His latest outburst merely caused Foxy to turn on that irritating smile once more. 'I understand perfectly, Thomas; however Henry Oaks is not in a position to promise you that. I am the only one who can grant you that wish.'

Thomas was still battling in his inner mind, as whether he could accept this man as a friend or not.

'How can I trust you, after you trapped me in the first place?' His voice had mellowed.

The smile never left Foxy's face, 'Ah there is the rub: you cannot. All you can do is put your faith in me.'

Thomas was grasping at straws, 'I want a signed, written statement from you guaranteeing my safety.'

Foxy seemed to find it all so amusing as he broke into a laugh and spluttered, 'You don't really believe I would do something so incriminating, do you? There is something you must realise, Thomas: you are in no position to demand conditions, but if it's any consolation to you, I had a similar situation a while ago in Croydon. After everything was cleared away and dusted, the person involved was whisked out of harm's way. I arranged for him to go to one of the colonies.'

Thomas thought it over; it seemed he had no option, as he reluctantly nodded his head.

12

Foxy's Judgement

Mary Williams had just shown the doctor out after his visit to her sick husband, Robert. She returned to the kitchen where she finished making a hot drink for her patient. In an upstairs bedroom, Robert lay back in his bed, extremely weak. He had been a very active man throughout his life, now however age took its toll. Now he found himself in an unfamiliar, bedridden situation. When Mary entered she placed a tray on his bedside table, and he asked, 'Does James know?'

She looked at him with compassion, and answered, 'You mustn't worry so, dear. I expect he will be here shortly.'

She could tell he was agitated, when, in barely an audible voice, he said, 'Mary, my dear, I fear I have not much time left.'

James had got the call, and made haste to be at his father's bedside as soon as he possibly could. He had no idea what to expect as he hurried up the stairs to find his mother with the doctor, who was in attendance once more. The doctor moved to one side, as his mother said, 'Thank the Lord you are here, James, your father has been asking for you.'

Robert's eyes fluttered slightly open as he became aware of

his son's presence, 'I want you to know that I have followed your career with pride.' James had to concentrate hard to catch his father's voice, which had tailed off to a whisper, as he laboured to communicate his feelings.

James was filled with emotion, and he replied in a hushed voice, 'Thank you, Father.'

Robert opened his eyes wider as he continued to tell his son, 'You are doing the right thing in opposing the Martyrs.'

James firmly gripped his father's hand. 'I know, Father. We cannot allow them to stop progress. Our policy is that we are committed to progress, no turning back.'

Robert sighed, 'That's right, son, look to the future. I'm so proud of you.' He continued, his voice still in a whisper, so that James was the only one in the room to make out what he was saying. 'I haven't much time left; I want you to have my two flintlock pistols. The one pistol you carry is useless on its own, it should be backed up with a second.'

James moved closer, so that his head was nearer to his father, and so that he could speak directly into his ear. James knew from his experience of being ambushed that his attacker's got the fright of their lives when he fought back, but once his weapon was discharged, he was vulnerable once more.

'I know, Father, I will take good care of them, thank you.' He didn't have the heart to tell him that weapons such as these were being superseded by a new generation of handguns. James had already acquired a multi-firing handgun, which did not require a second backup weapon. He remembered as a child being told how dangerous those pistols were and on no account was he to play with them. Then when he was twelve years of age, his father gave him lessons. He taught him all there was to know about the weapons and to have respect for them.

James was now whispering back. 'I want you to know, I could not have wished for a better father than you.'

With that Robert smiled, then urgently whispered, 'James, I

want you to know I haven't always done things right. When I was younger, most of my wealth was gained unlawfully.'

James was quick to hush his father, 'We all have our faults, Father; no need to admonish yourself so.'

Robert urged himself on, 'You remember the mystery of how I got myself across a flooded river near South Downesmere?'

James did, but never pressed for a detailed account, until now, 'Yes, Father, what really happened?'

Robert was fighting to remain lucid, 'It was as I told you: Angus appeared as a ghost, and charged me three pieces of silver.' Barely audible Robert's voice tailed off as he whispered, 'It's the only story I've got, I tell people to believe it or not.' Then, he slowly took his last breath, as he peaceably settled into his pillow, and shook off his mortal coil.

It came as a huge shock to James in coming to terms with the loss of his father, as he took on the role of looking after his bereft mother. Fortunately, his engineering business was firmly established, and required no input from him. Eventually he found time was a great healer; his wake up call came in the form of an invitation to meet with Sir Henry Oaks over in South Downesmere. He had got into the habit of spending his days with his mother, and it was she who urged him to get back to work. He had learned a lot about his mother over the last couple of weeks, and realised she wasn't the weak, simpering mother he at first thought she was. He marvelled at her strength of character, and thought what an asset she must have been to his father.

James visited the sawmill before his meeting at South Downesmere police station. It occurred to him how long he had been away. However, he was soon brought up to date with the running of the business.

At the police station he was enthusiastically welcomed by the chief constable, 'James it's so good to see you again. We are all terribly sorry to hear the sad news of your father, how is your mother coping?'

James took the seat that was offered to him, 'She's managing remarkably well, thank you, Henry.'

The police chief quickly explained how Thomas Ellis was detained in one of his cells overnight. Then the sting operation used to trap him into a confession. They were shortly joined by Constable Harold Easton, who was introduced to James as a Special Operations Officer. The chief explained, 'Constable Easton has been on numerous undercover operations, with a high success rate. He is authorised to use certain incentives in his privileged position, and has persuaded Thomas Ellis to co-operate in helping to apprehend the Stockwell brothers.'

James was intrigued by Constable Easton; the wounds to his face were healing nicely, soon to join the rest of his scars, which were to be worn as a badge of honour.

James asked, 'How do you endure such treatment, and inflicted by your own colleagues?'

Constable Easton's face lit up into a radiant smile, 'It's not a problem to me, sir, I'm well used to it. Besides, it makes for a grand and interesting entrance, don't you think?'

James smiled back, warming to this unusual young man. 'I'm amazed at the lengths to which you go.'

The constable winked back at James. 'It's the easiest way to gain respect, from old lags especially. In the case of Thomas Ellis, I spent little more than half an hour in his cell. Only once did I have to spend a night in a cell, it was a well-learned lesson.' The constable's smile faded as he concentrated, 'Enough about me, we are here to discuss the problem of the Stockwell brothers.' Sir Henry chipped in, 'Indeed we are, it's a problem which affects James here more than anyone else. I'm sure he is keen to know what we are doing about it.' James said, 'Well as you know, they are an annoying and disruptive force, proving to be extremely costly. When they included murder to their cause, they stepped over the line.' The chief constable replied, 'Constable Easton will bring us up to date.'

The constable rose and went to the door, saying, 'I want to bring in Thomas Ellis at this point.'

He was gone barely seconds and returned with his prisoner. Thomas Ellis sat in the chair that was indicated for him, and scowled at everyone. James remembered him well from the time he had him fired from the sawmill. He certainly didn't enamour himself to anyone, and it left James with the memory of him being a thoroughly distasteful fellow. Thomas Ellis made his feelings towards Constable Easton very plain indeed, referring to him as Foxy, as that was the way he first remembered him. He used the term in a derogatory fashion, to show his contempt for the law.

Constable Easton smiled back at his prisoner, 'Now then, Thomas, I'm sure you know Mr James Williams. We've kept him informed of developments, and he is impressed that you are helping us with our inquiries.'

Thomas glared back, 'I'm sure he's impressed, and yes I do know who he is, Foxy,' he snarled.

Constable Easton carried on, 'By the time Thomas finally agreed to help us, he had already missed one appointment to meet up with the Stockwells, owing to the length of time we held him in custody.' The constable went on to explain, 'They keep in touch by leaving messages in an old oak tree. I have left a note arranging to meet them this weekend; however, I believe Thomas shouldn't be anywhere near them. I believe there is a strong possibility his safety has been compromised.'

James was amazed that Constable Easton could show such compassion for someone so disrespectful, and said to him, 'I'm surprised at your obvious animosity towards this constable. He is doing you a massive favour, Ellis. Don't you realise your life is on the line here?'

Thomas faced James, 'My animosity towards him is for the underhand way he tricked me, by pretending to be a bona fide prisoner. I will always remember him by the name of Foxy, and will never address him as an officer of the law.'

James saw the hatred in his eyes, and replied, 'The truth is you were breaking the law. This man was only doing his job – a fine job, too – and ensuring your safety.'

Thomas remained churlish, James had failed to change his attitude. The chief constable was not impressed by his prisoner's unpleasantness, and abruptly brought his attendance to an end. 'That's all then, we have no further use of you,' turning to Constable Easton, he instructed, 'Take the prisoner out.'

Alone once more with the chief, James asked, 'What will happen to him now?'

The chief took a deep breath and slowly exhaled, 'He is in between the devil and the deep blue sea: at the moment his life is in danger from the Stockwell brothers; however after they have been caught, and taken out of circulation, he will no doubt follow them to the gallows. If he should be spared that fate, a long-term prison sentence awaits him. His future is most bleak. Many people have a deep-set grudge against him for helping the Stockwells. He has alienated himself to so many, he has not got a friend in the world.'

James couldn't help but feel a little sorry for him, and quietly said, 'Poor fellow.'

The chief was impressed at his compassion. 'He may have a lifeline through our special operative, Constable Easton. He has unique authority to overrule chief constables. His informants have been known to simply disappear; what happens to them is known only to him.'

The road followed the river round its elegant sweep, taking the two horsemen ever onward towards their final destination. It was a quiet early evening, which lent itself to a pleasant journey for the riders. They were in no hurry and time was of no consequence, as they leisurely wound their way to their final destination. Their objective was to reach a rising knoll, which was covered by trees and undergrowth. This position commanded an all-round view of the many roads stretching into the far distance for miles. Ben and Peter Stockwell were on their way to meet up with Thomas Ellis the following day at noon. They intended to spend the night in the wooded knoll.

After unsaddling their horses, it was the perfect place to spend the night; no one would suspect they were even there. Soon it would be dark and they could light a fire with little chance of smoke being spotted to give them away. They were both hungry, and looked forward to cooking the rabbit they had caught earlier.

The following morning saw Ben up early; he had had a restful night. He had slept well after his meal of cooked rabbit. He made sure the embers of their fire were completely dead as his brother slept soundly. They had stayed here before. Nearby stood a tall tree, which when climbed gave them an excellent view of the countryside all around. Ben climbed the tree and made sure he could not be seen up on his lofty perch on high. After a while, he heard his brother calling, 'Ben, how long have you been up there?'

Ben looked down, at his brother. 'About half an hour. I thought I'd let you sleep.'

Peter replied, 'Thanks, have you had any breakfast?'

Ben shielded his eyes from the early morning sun as he answered, 'Not yet. There is bread and cheese in the saddle bags. I'll be down shortly.'

After Peter had his breakfast, he went back to the base of the tree with his brother's breakfast. Ben was on his way down, excitement lit up his face, 'There's lots of activity on all roads leading to South Downesmere. It's as I thought, I don't trust Thomas.'

Peter grimaced, 'Aye, something is afoot, after he failed to turn up for our last meeting.'

Ben replied, 'That last letter we picked up didn't look quite right: he was using words he wouldn't normally use.'

With a snarl, Ben grabbed the bread from Peter. 'He had better find a good place to hide,' he said, as he bit savagely into the bread.

Later that morning, by 10 am all police officers were in position, ready to spring the trap, to apprehend the two fugitives from the law. Constable Easton was concerned at the huge numbers of police personnel, an issue which he pointed out to Sir Henry Oaks. The chief constable was also having misgivings at the massive police turnout. Constable Easton asked, 'Who ordered so many men onto this job, sir?'

The chief constable replied, 'It was all arranged from Bow Street. When I ask for extra men for a job, I was reliably informed that it's not possible. Today I think they have gone over the top; there is no way the Stockwells will come anywhere near this place. They are not fools, and this is the best tip off they could possibly wish for.'

The long wait for midday came and went, and, as predicted, there was neither sight nor sound of their intended quarry. In his report to Bow Street, the chief constable lay the blame for the failure of the operation, fairly and squarely, on their doorstep. Thomas Ellis's life was now plainly at risk and reprisals from the fugitives were a real threat. The chief constable ordered Constable Easton to organise a party of police officers to form an escort to take Thomas Ellis back to Bow Street, while there were still so many officers to hand.

James requested a further meeting with Sir Henry, after the botched attempt to capture the Stockwells. James shook his head in disbelief, 'What a wasted opportunity. A perfect set up to rid ourselves of a massive thorn in our side, all to no avail.'

The chief constable threw up his hands in despair, 'I know, James. No one is more disappointed than I. It's clear the taskmasters in London have very little understanding of operations in the field.'

James nodded, 'Absolutely, it was painfully clear from that turnout. What about Thomas Ellis? It's now blatantly obvious it is he who is the informant. What have you done to protect him?'

The chief sighed, 'Well, he will be detained, and if he should escape the gallows, he will be well taken care of.'

James hoped he would be looked after; he had helped the police, now he stood to lose everything, including his life. Over the following weeks James requested an audience with Thomas Ellis, pleading that, although he appeared an unsavoury type, he deserved to be treated with compassion. His voice went unheeded, but Thomas Ellis was not to be seen again, ever.

At Bow Street prison, Thomas was held in a cell by himself, where he languished for several days. He was, in fact, in solitary confinement, and the solitude was beginning to have its effect on him. Eventually he had an unexpected visitor, in the shape of Constable Easton. Although he would never admit it, he was extremely pleased to see him. 'Well, if it isn't my old cell mate, Foxy,' he sneered.

Constable Easton smiled. 'I'm glad you're pleased to see me, Thomas.'

His pleasant attitude annoyed Thomas, who replied, 'Don't fool yourself, Foxy. You may think I'm grateful to you, but get this into your thick skull: I think you are the scum of the earth.'

The smile on the constable's face broadened. 'Oh, come now, Thomas. I don't think you really mean that.' His jovial demeanour seemed only to inflame Thomas all the more, who silently scowled, as he looked down at his feet. The constable paused for full effect, then explained, 'The powers that be are finding your presence here slightly embarrassing. Normally, you would be held here until the fugitives are apprehended, then you would be tried alongside them. However, owing to the fact you helped the police in their enquiries, they believe some form of leniency is called for.'

Thomas looked up questioningly. 'So what's going to happen to me then?'

Constable Easton's face had changed dramatically, the smile had vanished, as he answered, 'All the time you were being disrespectful, and abusive towards me, how do you think I felt?' Thomas was speechless, Constable Easton broke the silence, in a subdued voice he said, 'They have left it up to me to deal with your case.'

All pretence of friendliness was gone to be replaced by a chilling, dark, evil look, as he answered, 'Remember how I told you I make people disappear?'

Thomas looked puzzled at the sudden change, then felt his throat constrict as he realised the full implication of what the constable meant and he was filled with horror.

13

Rebecca's Encounter

Winter had seemed to drag on for ever for James, now he felt a little more positive in anticipation of the oncoming spring. The attacks from the Luddites had intensified, but it was inevitable that the advancement of modernisation could not be halted. Nevertheless the assaults were a nuisance and costly to anyone involved in the advancement of modernisation. After a consultation with heads of businesses directly affected, it was decided a huge sum of money was to be put up for the capture of the Stockwell brothers. James had been in talks with Ray Mitchell and his bounty hunters, who were most interested. It had proved a costly exercise for the police, when they had last used the bounty hunters. However, funds had risen to unimaginable proportions for the capture of the outlaws. Several hundred pounds were now on the table, which James made up to £1000.

Ray Mitchell and his bounty hunters were seriously interested, and enlisted the aid of Arthur Fletcher, a dog handler. Arthur specialised in bloodhounds, and in the past had worked for the prison authorities. He was instructed to stand by; in the event he was called out he would be handsomely rewarded on results.

Ray Mitchell, David Brown, and Joe Andrews concentrated their search on last known previous sightings of the outlaws. The coming spring was in favour of the outlaws, as the wooded areas took on their extra growth. Consequently, the dogs would be a god-send.

Joshua Kennedy was a woodsman, and had been all his life. He had turned his back on civilisation, and people, choosing to live the lonesome life of a hermit. Only occasionally did he venture into a town or village, when he needed supplies or equipment. He had built his log cabin as a young man many years ago. Today he was replenishing his wood store with logs. After felling a tree, he was cutting it into manageable lengths, ready for hauling back to his cabin. The snorting of a horse alerted him to an approaching rider. The horse had to have a rider, for the animal to be under that amount of stress. There was no need for an unnecessary confrontation, so he dived for cover into the nearest bush, and waited until the way was clear.

Later he skirted round back to his cabin, still keeping undercover, and saw not only one horseman but three. He continued to remain unseen, as one of the men knocked on the cabin door. When no one answered, he tried the handle to find it locked. Joshua watched, as the men entered his stable, where they would find his horse. After spending some time looking around, they finally mounted, and left. When Joshua estimated they would be well clear, he immediately went to the stable. He looked over the place, then checked his horse, and decided he would have to visit the farrier in the morning.

Stan Heslop was on his way back to the blacksmith's shop from the bakery, when he spotted a customer's horse, tied up ready for shoeing. On entering, Luke said, 'Stan take Mr Kennedy's horse round the back, we will be working on her later.' Stan recognised the customer as the hermit who occasionally came into town.

When he was younger Stan and his friends would view the hermit with suspicion. He noticed his master treating him with the utmost respect, and referred to him as Mr Kennedy.

Joshua said, 'I had some rough-looking characters poking their noses round my cabin yesterday. They didn't see me though; I kept myself well hidden.'

Luke assured the old man, 'They would be the bounty hunters, Mr Kennedy, they mean you no harm. There's a big push on to flush out the Stockwell brothers.'

Joshua's eyes lit up, 'Oh, I understand now. If they come round again I will reveal myself.'

Luke was keen to put the old man at ease, 'That would be for the best, Mr Kennedy. Maybe after they have spoken with you they will leave you alone.' Joshua nodded in agreement.

Luke said, 'If you come in at the same time tomorrow, we will have her ready to go, Mr Kennedy.'

The old man asked, 'Are you sure, Luke, that you won't be charging me? I don't want to be in your debt.'

As Luke dried his hands on an old rag, he smiled and replied, 'Of course I'm sure, Mr Kennedy, it is I who am indebted to you.'

Joshua nodded, 'I'll see you tomorrow. Take care of Annabelle for me.'

When Joshua left, Stan asked, 'Luke, how come you are giving your services free to that hermit?'

Luke sat down, 'We go way back. When I was just a young 'un, my elder brother and I were messing about near the river. I fell in; I was not able to swim at the time, and so my brother jumped in after me. The river was in full flow, and we were being swept downstream. I swallowed half the river, and blacked out. When I regained my senses I was on the riverbank and there was Mr Kennedy, soaking wet. He had jumped in after us and saved our lives. I would appreciate it if you didn't refer to him as the hermit: his name is Mr Kennedy.'

The enlightened Stan said, 'Sorry, Luke, I meant no harm.

It's just we lads were always wary of him, what with him being so different. We always steered well clear of him.'

Luke smiled as he said, 'That's just what he wants; he needs to be left alone.'

There was a stomping of hooves, and a general commotion coming from the stables, Stan jumped up, 'That will be Charlie, getting frisky with Annabelle,' he commented.

Luke said, 'Better bring Annabelle into the shop Stan, I wouldn't want Mr Kennedy to receive spoilt goods when he comes to collect her.'

The following day Joshua trekked to the blacksmith's shop, and collected his horse. He took her straight into the forest to start hauling his timber back to the cabin. He had already hauled one heavy tree length, and was on his way back for another, when he first heard the dogs.

Joshua brought Annabelle to a halt, and stood quietly by her head. The dogs could plainly be heard drawing ever nearer. Even when their baying and howling were almost upon him Joshua still reacted with fright as they burst upon him. There were three dogs attached by long leads to a red-faced Arthur Fletcher. He appeared to be glad the dogs had stopped dragging him, as he was out of breath, and glad to bring his breathing back to normal.

Arthur produced a whistle, which delivered long shrill blasts. In between blasts he spoke to Joshua.

'Hello, Joshua, I'm the dog man.'

The dogs began sniffing round Joshua and the horse, but Annabelle was in no way perturbed by their presence.

Arthur said, between blasts, 'They won't hurt you, they're incredibly docile.' One more shrill blast, and the first horseman appeared, in the shape of Joe Andrews.

His gravel-like voice rasped out, 'Hello, Joshua, at last we meet.'

They were quickly joined by David Brown, then Ray Mitchell,

who was in charge of Arthur Fletcher's horse. As he passed on the reins to Arthur, he spoke to Joshua, 'We called to see you two days ago.'

Joshua replied, 'Yes, I know, I was aware you were here, but, living here on my own, I have to be careful. There are some undesirable types about.'

Ray fixed him with a stare. 'Yes, we knew you were not too far away: we observed smoke spiralling out of your cabin chimney. Bringing the dogs was the only way we were going to meet you. It's the undesirables, as you call them, that we have come to question you about. We have been commissioned to track down the Stockwell brothers – have you seen them lately?'

Joshua replied, 'As I've already said, living alone as I do, I don't see many people, and when I do I have to be careful.'

Just before Ray left, he steered his horse round ready to leave, and said, 'All right Joshua, you take care now, if you see anything suspicious, let us know.'

Joshua held onto Annabelle with one hand, and raised the other in a farewell gesture, as he said, 'Oh to be sure I will, thank you.' But what he was really thinking was, *I'm glad you're leaving, I've had enough of the lot of you.*

The bounty hunters, together with their dog handler, met in the Red Fox Tavern. There they discussed their latest venture. David Brown raised the problem of their elusive quarry.

'That's the third time we've been to that area.'

Joe agreed, and said in his rasping voice, 'I think it's more than a coincidence. Maybe the old hermit knows more than he is letting on.'

Ray spoke forcibly, 'I tend to agree; I think we should force our way into his cabin, if we need to. Until we have been inside, who knows what kind of a setup he has in there.'

Arthur Fletcher spoke up, 'Hang on there, fellows, you have never struck me as being heavy-handed, let's just think about this.

The last two times you traced the outlaws' movements to this area, and lost the trail, you didn't have me and my dogs with you. Think about it: they have come up with an ingenious plan to spirit away their horses. What you need is my dogs, with their super enhanced sense of smell. Just because you can't see them doesn't mean they are not there. Wherever they are my dogs will sniff them out.'

Ray reflected on Arthur's words, and said, 'What you say makes a lot of sense. I suppose we are so frustrated, we are becoming impatient. It will not be unreasonable if we were to ease up a little. We will continue to make our usual enquiries, but the next time we trace them to this area we will be more prepared.'

Charlie stomped his hooves, as he became aware Stan was entering his stall. He had become accustomed to little treats, such as an apple or a carrot, and occasionally, like this morning, the odd sugar lump. Stan spoke softly and caressed the horse, while the clanging of metal being forged in the shop next door echoed round the walls. It sounded like music to Stan and made him wonder what Luke was making. His curiosity got the better of him, and he left Charlie to investigate. Luke was just finishing an order, consisting of bolts, hinges, and steel brackets.

Stan asked, 'Who's all this lot for, boss?'

As Luke stacked the components near the door he answered, 'It's for Mr Kennedy. He is repairing and upgrading his stable. If I know Mr Kennedy, he will make a proper good job of it. He's not one to skimp on things. He will be coming in later, so I will need you to help him shift it.'

Stan was elated, he thoroughly enjoyed working Charlie with the wagon, 'OK, Luke. I'll bring the wagon round to the front, but I've never been to Mr Kennedy's cabin in the wood.'

Luke informed him, 'Don't worry, Mr Kennedy will be travelling with you.'

When Joshua arrived at the blacksmith's shop, he was staggered at the size of his order, which was fully loaded on the wagon, and ready to go. He mentioned his concern, and Luke shrugged his shoulders, 'I've put extra bolts and brackets in, Mr Kennedy, but don't worry. I knew you couldn't shift it on your own, so young Stan here will help.'

Joshua was clearly embarrassed, 'But Luke, I can't pay for the extra, it's too much.'

Luke didn't want Joshua to feel awkward, and said, 'There is no extra charge, Mr Kennedy, and it's free delivery, naturally.'

No matter how much Luke dressed it up, there was no mistaking Joshua was most uncomfortable about the whole thing.

On the trip to the cabin in the woods, Stan got to know Joshua, and saw a different hermit to the one of his youth, whom he and his friends used to be so wary about. He began to feel more relaxed.

During the conversation, Joshua asked Stan, 'Can you have a quiet word with Luke and tell him how uncomfortable he makes me feel?'

Stan told him, 'I'll speak to him, Mr Kennedy, but you know he feels terribly indebted to you.'

Joshua wasn't happy with Luke's generosity, and tried to get across to Stan exactly how he felt, 'I'm well aware he is, but he doesn't realise how uncomfortable it makes me feel.'

As Stan helped the old man unload his steel fittings outside his stable, he reflected how wrong he and his friends had been about the hermit. He resolved to speak with his employer, and make known the true facts.

Stan got to wondering what on earth all the fittings were for. When he enquired, all the old man would say was that he needed to upgrade his stable. He wanted to make a proper job of it, one that would last him to the end of his days.

***

Rebecca Ellis had just finished her shift as a chambermaid at the Red Fox Tavern. Her days were one long round of unending toil. When she got home she would have to start work on the laundry she took in to make ends meet. Her husband had been transferred to London's infamous jail to be tried at the Old Bailey for aiding and abetting known enemies of the Crown. Weeks later he had mysteriously disappeared. She had tried several times to find out what had happened to him, and more importantly where he was. Alas, no one could enlighten her.

However times were getting a little easier, now she was on her own. Without Thomas at home, he could no longer constantly rob her purse for beer money. Owing to her unswerving work routine, she found her financial state to be considerably healthier.

Rebecca straightened up; her back was aching due to her constant bending over her work. She noticed the light was fading fast, to continue meant she would have to use the last of her precious candles. It was time she left the laundry shed and headed home. She mused on her illicit affair with Matthew Atkinson, son of the owner of the sawmill. He gave her money and she never wanted for anything. How things had changed; now he was gone, along with his father.

She balanced the clothes basket on her hip as she took out the key from the pocket in her apron. As she opened the door she was pushed violently inside and fell to the floor. It was then she was aware that Ben Stockwell and his brother had so easily entered her home. She slowly got to her feet, gathering the strewn clothes back into the basket.

Ben leered at her, 'Hello, my dear, how nice to see you again.'

Rebecca was paralysed with fear. She stared back in silence at these dangerous men.

Peter said, 'Lost your tongue, have yer?'

She placed the basket of clothes onto the kitchen table, her mind racing in turmoil. Then she found the strength to fearfully speak, 'What do you want here?'

Ben said, 'We are fast losing supporters, and thought you might be willing to help us. A hot drink and perhaps some bread and cheese would be nice.'

Rebecca replied, 'I only have a small amount of bread, take it if you must. Since I am on my own with no support, I find it very difficult to make ends meet.' She found she was gaining more strength, and anger was taking over. 'If I'm caught helping you, the law will deal with me as it did my husband.'

Peter, who was rummaging in the kitchen drawers and cupboards, called over his shoulder, 'Oh him.' Then followed up with, 'She's got less than us, there isn't anything to eat here.'

Ben glared at his brother, 'Nip out and get some bread from my saddle bag, you'll find a leg of lamb there also, bring that.' On Peter's return, all three feasted well, Rebecca hadn't eaten so well in weeks.

At first light the two outlaws were long gone, leaving the confused Rebecca most disturbed by their unpleasant visit. She was very fearful that she would be in serious trouble, if it became known she had given shelter to the Stockwells. She resolved to inform the authorities, come what may. She was fully aware she may be on the Stockwells' hit list as an informer, but didn't want to end up like her husband.

James was at a meeting with the chief constable. They were interrupted by a junior constable, who informed Sir Henry that Mrs Ellis wanted to see him as a matter of urgency. She had something of grave importance to tell him.

Sir Henry told James, 'Stay here, James.' Then, to his constable he commanded, 'Show her in, constable.'

When she entered, James knew who she was having had her pointed out one day in the village. She was like a timid mouse; she was trying to make herself small, as a means of protection.

The chief constable welcomed her. 'Take a seat, Mrs Ellis. Don't be so afraid, no one is going to harm you. You can speak freely in front of Mr Williams here.'

There was a difficult period of non-communication, as she took the offered chair.

The chief constable broke the awkward silence, 'You look terribly distressed, Mrs Ellis. Would you like a glass of water, to compose yourself?'

She nodded, gratefully accepting the glass, and took a gentle sip, before placing it on the table in front of her. The chief constable continued to make her feel more comfortable, 'In your own time, Mrs Ellis.' She was more at ease when she responded, 'Last night, come twilight, I had just finished my laundry, and as I opened the kitchen door, I was pushed inside by the Stockwell brothers.' She paused while she dabbed her eyes with her handkerchief.

James and the chief exchanged glances, at the seriousness of her statement. 'Did they harm you at all, Mrs Ellis?' asked James, showing genuine concern.

She looked at James for the first time, 'When they threw me to the floor, I hurt my shoulder. They demanded food, but when they knew I had nothing to give them, they provided their own.'

The chief constable asked, 'Did they stay long, my dear?'

She was more composed now, 'They stayed all night, sir, but were on their way before the break of dawn.'

James said, 'We will have to inform Ray Mitchell and his team.'

As the chief was busy organising his men and briefing a messenger, Rebecca asked James, 'Can you tell me anything of my husband, sir? I don't even know where they are holding him.'

James sympathised, and answered, 'Well, he is answering serious charges, but the law is protecting him,'

With a gentle sob she uttered, 'Will I ever see him again?'

James was forthright with her, 'Probably not: my guess is that he has been transported to the colonies.'

As soon as Ray Mitchell received news of the Stockwell brothers' last known sighting, he quickly mobilised his team. Arthur

Fletcher was also included this time, bringing three of his hounds. On reaching Rebecca's cottage, the kitchen door was left open, allowing the dogs free to roam wherever they chose. Their excitement grew; then they sniffed their way into the woods.

The hounds were closely followed by the horsemen, deeper into the woodland. They skirted round thick foliage, coming back to where they first started. Arthur Fletcher rode round once then after dismounting, he announced, 'The hounds appear to be interested in this piece of foliage, which seems to be impossible to penetrate.'

All four riders were now dismounted, as Ray said, 'Have a good look, lads. Try to see if there is a way through.'

Eventually Joe's voice croaked out, 'Here it is, boys.'

Everyone dashed towards Joe, who was dragging aside a large sapling to reveal the entrance to an enclosure. Inside there was evidence of horses being kept there.

Ray Mitchell said, 'Well now, isn't this just cosy?'

David Brown added, 'They could have been hidden in here the last time we were hot on their heels.'

Arthur Fletcher responded in an I-told-you-so voice: 'Just shows how good my dogs are, doesn't it?'

Then Ray said, 'They've got too big of a start on us. They will be miles out of the county by now. Let's put things back the way they were; they may be tempted to use this again. They seem to have an inkling to return here on a frequent basis. You never know, this might just be the break we are looking for.'

Meanwhile, James was kept busy, with his thriving foundry, and engineering business. Apart from the day-to-day running of his enterprise, he had invested heavily in the railways, which were reaching out to isolated parts of the country. Many fortunes were being made by the investors as the rail network expanded. James was one of many investors who had made their fortune this way.

Railways were reaching out to all parts of the country: previously isolated regions were linked up to towns and cities, in a way never before imagined. It was heartily embraced by businessmen, such as James, who could travel to previously unheard of distances in a day.

Owing to general unrest within the workforce in Lancashire, James's office in the north was being kept very busy. Mill workers were keeping up a concentrated attack by damaging machinery, they assumed to be a threat to their livelihood. His manager, Jack Collins, had made a request to have an emergency meeting as soon as it was possible.

When it was arranged, James arrived in Leeds with four of his staff. Apart from Toby Green, the other three accompanied him in an advisory capacity. Jack was concerned that replacement parts were taking too long to arrive at his depot. Consequently rival firms were cashing in grabbing the extra trade.

Jack put it to him, 'Is there any way we could speed up the delivery time?'

James was impressed with Jack's mature demeanour, any doubts James may have had, about Jack's suitability as manager, were now completely dispelled. 'Yes, of course, Jack, we will look into it as a matter of urgency.' His advisers were busily taking notes, as he carried on speaking, 'The railways are continuing to expand, and so too, their freight business.'

Jack knew James would get things moving, 'I had to bring this to your attention, sir. The orders seem to be taking longer and longer to get here. Local firms are moving in taking business that should be ours.'

James replied, 'I've also noticed how shabby-looking these premises are, I think we could do with a spot of modernisation. It doesn't inspire customers coming into a rundown building.' He then informed Jack, 'I intend spending a few days here, Jack. Can you arrange to have two horses ready for Toby and myself for tomorrow morning?'

It came as no surprise to Jack, as James normally spent extra time when he visited.

Jack answered, 'Certainly, sir, I'll arrange everything.'

The following day, the horses were made ready, and James and Toby were soon on their way. In the past Tommy Atkins had always accompanied James, however this was Toby's first trip and he was excited at the prospect of exploring Yorkshire. He was further elated when James informed him they would soon be leaving Yorkshire and be heading for Burnley, in Lancashire. Then, if time allowed, he wanted to visit Helmshore, which was in the Rossendale Valley. He was not surprised at the spartan conditions around the mills. *It must be a hard life for the workers*, he thought. But away from industrialisation, some of the countryside he found was breathtakingly beautiful.

14

The Last Sanctuary

'Are you OK boss?' Toby asked, after they had been riding for two hours. James was amused at how the men he employed with a military background all called him boss.

'I'm fine Toby, we're making good time,' he replied.

The term boss they used while referring to him was meant as a term of endearment, and James felt honoured to have their trust and enthusiastic support. The pair travelled in silence, for a while, concentrating on the journey ahead, both lost in their own private world, until James observed, 'It's pleasant countryside up here, Toby, don't you think?'

Toby readily agreed. 'It certainly is, boss.'

James followed up with the remark, 'Once over this rise, we will drop into a valley; then, further on, we will be in Burnley, where you will see a dramatic change in our surroundings.'

When they did eventually reach the town, and were riding past the Market Cross, Toby thought, *It's definitely grey and soul destroying here.* This being due to several coal mines in the area, which provided fuel for the many steam engines along the Calder Valley. He remembered a forest of chimneys, spewing out an inky black cloak, which embraced the whole city. The market town of Burnley was expanding rapidly, due to the link of the Leeds-Liverpool canal. It enabled goods in bulk to be transported easily. Owing to the Irish potato famine, there was also a large influx of immigrants, who established a community in Parker Street. The locals dubbed it Irish Park. To James's delight he learned a plan was put forward to create a rail link from Accrington to Burnley in the near future.

A short way out of the market town, by the side of the canal, was the first of many mills. It was here that James had first visited in the past to solve a problem with one of their steam engines. Once out of the town, the two riders came to a neat stone built cottage which overlooked the cluster of houses surrounding the village square. The cottage was surrounded by a well-kept garden of flowers, mainly of roses, which adorned the front door. Both riders took in the sight of the tower of the grey-stone church, which stood out prominently below them.

Further along the valley, the first of many mills could be seen. With its huge water wheel slowly churning the passing river into a seething mass of foam, before allowing it to resume its peaceful pace once more. A young girl sat on a stool outside the entrance of the cottage busily knitting. She wore a plain gown of dark heavy wool, a square of white linen round her neck and on her head was a stiff linen bonnet – she was dressed in the manner of the Puritans of old.

James touched the brim of his hat, saying, 'Good morning, fair maiden.'

She looked up with a smile and nodded her head. From the side of the cottage, a man suddenly appeared.

He looked at the riders with concern. James addressed him saying, 'Good morning to you, sir.'

The man wore a wide-brimmed hat. He had a neat white linen collar, and wore knee breeches. His coat was tightly buttoned up. As he looked at the two riders, he was assessing them as he replied, 'Good morning to you, also.' The man decided that James was arrogant, and that the other rider, Toby (although he looked dubious), must be his manservant. The man turned his attention to the girl, and nodded towards the cottage. She immediately rose, vacating the stool, and vanished indoors.

The man looked on at the two travellers with an intense stare, and waited on James to continue the discussion. Because he and his family were different they had been the target of local bigotry; he was extra vigilant when it came to strangers. James could sense the man's resentment towards them, and hastened to convince him they were no threat.

'You have a beautiful garden, quite splendid in fact – you must spend a lot of time gardening?'

The man seemed to relax a little, he said, 'It's not a burden; my daughter helps a lot.' Then he asked, 'Are you travelling far? I see your saddle bags are well laden.'

James and the man, it seemed, had broken the ice and accepted that each was of no threat to the other.

The man told them his name was Andreas and he lived alone with his daughter Hannah. He looked quizzically at James, who readily told him he was a businessman from London, and was on a courteous call to some of his northern customers.

Andreas then invited them inside: 'Can I invite you to refresh yourselves before you continue your journey?'

James and Toby were happy to accept his invitation. Andreas told them he lived alone with his daughter, and had lost his wife Esther in tragic circumstances when Hannah was a baby. He told them that, during the riots, people were scattered all over the countryside, fleeing from the militia. Gunshots and screams rent the air as crowds stampeded past their cottage. A dishevelled woman ran up the garden path, and banged desperately on the door, begging to be let in. Esther answered the frantic hammering on the door, as she faced the woman, she saw over the woman's shoulder, a soldier aiming his rifle at them. Esther grabbed at the woman's clothing to drag her aside, as the deafening explosive shot tore through her heart – she died instantly. James was horrified at the savage account portrayed.

Andreas was equally interested in James's story as he offered them carrot juice. 'You will understand we don't have anything stronger: we belong to a temperance society, and don't advocate intoxicating liqueur.' Before Esther's death, Andreas had planned on taking his family to America, to join the Amish sect in Dutch Pennsylvania. Andrea explained, they were not Dutch at all, as the word Dutch is a corruption of Deutsche, or German.

After the family's tragedy Andreas decided his place was to help others start a new life in America. He made his cottage into a staging post, assisting families on their journey to Liverpool. They would arrive from the Continent, to the Port of Hull, then have to travel across country to Liverpool, where they would board a ship bound for America, the Promised Land.

Andreas made a living by opening a temperance bar, serving the local community; then, later, he opened another a few more miles away in the more heavily populated mill town of Rawtenstall. Life became a little more kind to Andreas, after the tragic loss of his beloved wife Esther. His enterprising temperance bars were a financial success; he was able to support both himself and his daughter Hannah. Now in her twenties, Hannah had no wish to move on, and instead she remained by her father's side. She regarded it her duty to stand by him. There were plenty of opportunities – she was a pretty girl – but she remained steadfastly by her father's side. He himself took a protective stance, making his presence known in the face of unwanted overtures, by any young man captivated by his daughter's beauty.

Hannah came out with a tray of refreshments, and waited on her father's guests. It was pleasant relaxing with Andreas and Hannah, but James was mindful of the time.

He stood up to reluctantly inform them, 'Well thank you,

Andreas, for your kind hospitality, but I'm afraid we must be on our way.'

Andreas stood also to shake James's hand, 'You're welcome, James. You and your man, Toby, how long do you plan to stay in Helmshore?'

James was touched by the kindness shown to them. 'Not long, we will be returning tomorrow.'

Hannah collected their glasses; as she took Toby's glass, and stacked up her tray, she said, 'You must stop here on your way back, we will look out for you.'

That was something both James and Toby looked forward to.

The huge water wheel relentlessly turned, urged on by the fast flowing river, as the two riders caught sight of the mill. They had arrived in Helmshore; this was the first of two mills, run by the same family. The clattering noise of the weaving machines could plainly be heard, as the yard staff helped to hitch their horses outside.

Toby told James, 'I'll wait outside with the horses, while you're seeing to business, boss.' James replied, 'I may be some time, Toby, a couple of hours maybe, you OK with that?'

Toby smiled. 'I'll be fine, boss, take your time.'

Knowing he had time on his hands, Toby was fascinated by the huge water wheel, and decided to take a closer look. It amazed him how much energy the river could deliver, as he looked up at the huge mill, every floor had machinery of some sort, each contributing to the cacophony of noise. In the lower levels, a row of what looked like giant hammers crashed down in a steady pounding rhythmic beat. He pitied the workers, who had to endure the racket in such confined areas.

As Toby made his way back along the towpath, he could hear a commotion and shouting, coming from the yard. He was startled as two horses came hurtling towards him, both ridden by young boys. In an instant he recognised the horses as his and James's. As the first horse flashed past him, he lunged at the second, grabbed its reins and hung his arm round its neck. It brought the horse to a halt, by which time Toby hauled the youth to the ground.

They were instantly surrounded by workers from the mill.

Toby shouted, 'Detain this fellow, I'll follow his friend.' He then leapt into the saddle; by chance it happened to be his own horse. He was soon in hot pursuit, and rapidly gained on his quarry. When he drew alongside the other horse, he reached over and grabbed at the reins, bringing the horses to a halt. Toby was angry at the horse thieves, but struggled not to show it. He reached into his saddlebag, and withdrew a length of cord. He said to the youth, 'Sit very still and you won't get hurt,' as he bound the thief's hands together behind his back. He then led his prisoner, at a sedate pace, back to the mill.

The yard was thronged with workers, among them was James with the mill owner. In the midst of the crowd, the other youth was being firmly held by a burly worker. He looked sullenly round as if seeking a way of escape. He was going nowhere. As Toby dismounted, he hauled his prisoner down to join his comrade.

James said, 'What have you got there, Toby?' As he untied the cord from the youth's hands, Toby answered, 'A horse thief, boss; he very nearly got away.'

James asked the mill owner, 'Do you know these miscreants, John?'

The mill owner nodded, 'Yes, they're well known in these parts. If there's any trouble, you can be assured these two won't be too far away.'

Toby glared at them both, and said, 'Where we come from, horse thieving is taken very seriously.'

John the mill owner said, 'What do you want us to do with them, James?'

The youths physically withered under James's dark stare, as he addressed the pair, 'What would you have me do? Shall I get the police involved, or would you rather have me deal with you?'

The eldest boy spoke, 'I would prefer the matter to be dealt with by your good self, sir.'

James smiled. 'If that's what you want, boys, but if you think I'm a soft touch, think again, you may come to regret it. I leave such matters for my aide to deal with.'

Then facing Toby he said, 'This is who will be dealing out your punishment, who, by the way, detests horse thieves.'

Toby asked the mill owner, 'May I take the boys into that shed, sir, when I administer their punishment? It's not for the faint-hearted.'

The mill owner consented. As Toby pointed to the shed with his horsewhip, indicating for them to enter, he said, 'This is going to hurt you probably more than having the police involved.'

Toby worked on the boys for one minute each, by which time, justice had been done. It was a lesson they would not forget for a long time, it would also be a considerable time before they would be able to sit comfortably. The boys were released, and allowed to go home shortly afterwards. James and Toby also left to go to a tavern, where they had booked rooms for the night. On their way they passed the boys, and Toby enquired, 'Can we offer you boys a ride, maybe?'

The elder of the two, replied, 'No thank you, sir, we prefer to walk.'

James grinned, saying, 'You are such a wicked man, Toby.'

The following day saw James and Toby up early, and well on their way, looking forward to refreshments with Andreas, and Hannah. Little did they know what atrocities were about to unfold before them. It was a cold damp morning, after heavy rainfall during the night, and the day remained grey, and uninviting. The fire the previous night had ravaged the cottage: the thatched roof had completely gone, leaving only the stone walls standing. The neat tidy garden, with its well cared for flowers, was trampled underfoot.

James and Toby stared at the chaotic scene before them in abject horror, as faint wisps of smoke struggled to rise from the still smouldering embers. Toby looked on open-mouthed, then faced James to ask him, 'What do you think happened here, boss?'

James was still taking in the scene before him, then replied, 'I cannot imagine, Toby.' He was struggling to make sense of the impossible situation, 'I can only think something incredibly evil has occurred here.'

He noticed people in the distant fields working, and spurred his horse towards them. On reaching them, he confronted an elderly farm hand, and asked, 'Can you tell us what happened over there?' as he pointed to the remains of the cottage.

The farm hand took off his cap as he faced James, 'Andreas has been plagued by a gang of ruffians over the years, who could not accept them into our community. Last night I think they went too far.'

James listened to the macabre tale. The farm hand was clearly affected by the whole affair, and twisted and screwed his cap between his hands.

James asked, 'Do you know where Andreas and his daughter are?'

The old man looked up at James through watery eyes, 'I believe they are at the police station. Andreas looked in a bad way, sir, I do hope he is going to be all right.'

James thanked the man and wheeled his horse round to meet Toby, who asked, 'What's happened, boss?'

James said, 'Come on, we're going to the police station – that's where Andreas and his daughter were taken.'

At the police station, James enquired where Andreas and Hannah were. The duty constable said, 'After the doctor left, he arranged for them to be cared for by a lady in the town. Andreas was in a bad way, the doctor said he had done all he could for the poor chap.' James was becoming more concerned for the welfare of

Andreas, all he was hearing was how critical a state he was in. 'Can you direct me to the house of the lady who is caring for them?'

It appeared the lady concerned was an Irish immigrant, who had been helped by Andreas years ago, when she and her husband had first arrived in the area. She was well known to the locals who all referred to her as Ma O'Donnel. She had become a widow after the death of her husband in a mill accident. Due to her kindly nature and warm personality, she had been well looked after by all who knew her. Her local church had gone out of their way, and made sure she wanted for nothing.

When James and Toby arrived at her home, they were surprised at how small her cottage was, having just one bedroom, which she had willingly given over to the very sick Andreas. However Ma O'Donnel had some devastating news, for them: in her lilting Irish accent she said, 'I'm sorry to have to tell you that your friend passed away just one hour ago. The doctor has just this minute left.'

James was visibly shaken, and asked 'How is Hannah, can we see her?'

Ma O'Donnel wiped her hands on her apron, saying, 'Course you can. The poor dear is devastated, as you can well imagine.'

In the darkened bedroom sat the shadowy figure of Hannah, silently weeping, by her dead father's bedside.

Ma O'Donnel quietly whispered, 'Hannah, some friends to see you.'

James put his arms around her shoulders to comfort her, and told her, 'I'm so sorry, Hannah. I'm appalled at what has just happened. I cannot understand why these people have perpetrated such an evil act.' Hannah was grateful for the support being shown to her. James went on to tell to her, 'I know it's too soon to ask what your plans are for the future, but if there is anything I can do to help, you only have to ask.'

Hannah stifled a sob, 'I haven't the faintest idea of what to do, I have no family, and now no home.'

James listened intently, then asked, 'What happened, Hannah, when these people attacked your home?'

Ma O'Donnel handed Hannah a fresh handkerchief, as she tried to compose herself. 'I was in my bed for the night, when I heard shouting, and loud threats coming from outside. I heard my father trying to reason with them. They had set the thatched roof alight, and soon the whole cottage appeared to be on fire, it was terrifying. My father came into my bedroom to get me out; he left me outside in the rain, and went back inside to retrieve some of his possessions. The roof timbers then collapsed on top of him, trapping him. It was some of the townsfolk who got my father out.'

Ma O'Donnel had made up a temporary cot in the corner of the bedroom, making space at a premium. She led the grieving Hannah towards it and tucked her in as you would a child. Then she ushered James and Toby into the kitchen, where she proceeded to make them tea. James was impressed by the old lady's compassion; she had not had an easy life, after fleeing her native Ireland.

James told her, 'I'm most concerned for Hannah's welfare, and will do all I can to help her. You're most kind, Mother O'Donnel, by taking her in. It must be a strain on you, making life more difficult.'

Ma O'Donnel busied herself making tea, and chuckled, saying, 'When I was a young girl in Ireland, I lived my life as was immortal. Whatever life decided to throw at me, ze me in the least; now, in my twilight years I realise I all I can to help myself, and that it's just as important to ers.'

es and Toby were served tea, round the small kitchen table, oy said, 'Your cheery nature is admirable, Ma O'Donnel.' e old lady smiled, and said, 'I've been on my own for many now, and have lots of happy memories to look back on. I often let my imagination run riot, and think what might have been. I think imagination is my last sanctuary.'

James continued to be overawed by the old lady's tenacity, and positive outlook on life; in particular, her last remark, about her imagination being her last sanctuary, remained etched on his mind.

The following weeks saw Hannah slowly coming to terms with her life, and she accepted James's offer of help. He sent people to help, sustain, and promote Andreas's temperance bars, which became Hannah's main source of income. He saw to the rebuilding of the fire-gutted cottage, which was restored back to its former glory, the only difference being the roof was finished off with tiles, instead of being thatched. This was done on the insistence of Hannah.

Once installed in her newly rebuilt home again, Hannah blossomed into a highly efficient business woman. She insisted Ma O'Donnel leave her tiny home, and come to live with her in her cottage. She looked to the future, and envisaged looking after the old lady when she would most need it.

And so it was, James fulfilled his promises: Ma O'Donnel never again had any financial worries to contend with. She was overwhelmed by the generosity shown by everyone but mostly she was humbled and indebted to James. Ma O'Donnel had arrived with happy thoughts to her last sanctuary.

15

The Fool Who Stands before Me

James arrived at the sawmill just before noon; he was surprised to find there was not much activity in the yard. It was unusual for a Monday morning, which normally would be full of frantic workers, all bustling about their respective tasks. As soon as he entered Jacob's office, he immediately knew by his friend's solemn face, something was amiss.

'What's going on, Jacob?' he asked even before reaching his desk.

Jacob sighed, 'Adam's gone missing; we don't know where he is.'

James reached the window that overlooked the yard. 'When did you last see him?' he enquired, as Jacob looked up from resting his head in his hands.

'Saturday morning, about 9 am. I assumed he had gone home, which is most unusual. We were first aware something was wrong when I got home. My mother asked, "Is Adam working late this evening?" That was the start of our worries.'

James turned from the window to face Jacob, 'You must get the foreman to take charge, Jacob, the whole workforce is standing idle.'

Jacob replied, 'I've already got him on to it. I supposed he is doing his best.'

James frowned, 'Have you reported Adam missing to the police?' James could plainly see his friend was upset, and wasn't thinking clearly.

'Yes I reported him missing earlier this morning, they told me it was too soon to take action just yet, they said if he doesn't turn up by tomorrow, they would look into it.'

James was concerned that the business had virtually ground to a halt, due to the absence of one man, and said, 'Come with me, Jacob, let's get things moving downstairs.'

The pair went into the manager's office, where they found George Johnson, the yard foremen, trying to make sense of Adam's paperwork. James told him to see to a wagonload of timber he had noticed ready for despatch, then come back to the office immediately. James sympathised with the harassed foreman, who had been thrust in at the deep end, and was struggling to make sense of Adam's filing system. While Jacob poured over the order book, James attempted to sort out the chaos.

James told Jacob, 'In future, it would be wise for the foreman to work closer with management. I realise it places a bigger burden of responsibility on the poor chap's shoulders, so he should be amply rewarded by an increase in wages.'

It appeared Adam's filing system left a lot to be desired, but gradually they began to get on top of the muddle. While sifting through the paperwork, Jacob came across an envelope marked urgent. James became aware that Jacob's face had turned ashen, after reading it.

James was shocked as he read the ransom note, which informed they had until 12 noon Tuesday, to hand over £200 or it would be all the worse for Adam. The money was to be placed behind the engine shed by the yard foreman, and on no account were the police to be involved, otherwise Adam would lose a finger every time they did not comply with the ransom demands.

Jacob stood transfixed, and exclaimed, 'What have we done? We have already informed the police.'

James was quick to reply, 'Don't you see, Jacob? We mustn't bow down to these people; we must involve the police. We must keep them updated with the latest information. I'm taking this letter to them right now.'

Jacob stood bewildered, 'Who do you think is behind this?'

James was putting his coat on as he approached the door. 'I could make a pretty good guess,' he retorted, as he closed the door behind him.

At the police station, the chief constable was made aware that this was now an official ransom demand, and that Adam was being held somewhere against his will. He was also aware the Atkinson family had many enemies. He told James, 'There is one thing for sure, we're spoilt for choice as far as suspects are concerned.'

James agreed, 'I'm thinking this whole business smells of the Stockwell brothers.'

The chief constable frowned, saying, 'The constabulary has spent an absolute fortune trying to capture those two outlaws. I'm having to answer questions as to why they are still at large.'

James nodded his head, 'I can imagine the strain you're under, Henry.'

The chief constable raised his eyebrows, saying, 'However, this could be the breakthrough we've been waiting for. I suggest we pretend we are complying with their demands. We get the yard foreman to leave a bag, supposedly containing £200; then, when they come to collect, we pounce.'

James agreed, 'It's a plan which could work. I just hope for Adam's sake it does.'

Jacob wasn't pleased when he learned Henry Oaks had a plan to capture the Stockwell brothers.

'But he is putting Adam's life in jeopardy,' he complained to James. 'What if it should go wrong?'

James tried to placate his distraught friend, 'It won't go wrong. If it's planned carefully, it could rid us of the problem of the Stockwells for good. Besides, Henry is doing something positive. He knows what he is doing; he is nobody's fool.'

But Jacob wasn't going to be swayed so easily, 'You know it could go horribly wrong, James,' he protested. 'I don't know how my mother would react, should anything happen to Adam. She is out of her mind as it is, owing to worry. She has had to come to terms with the loss of one son. Then when another son and husband fell foul of the law, it's like being bereaved three times over.'

James understood the precarious situation the family were in. 'We cannot allow these people to get away with bribery, we must fight them.'

Jacob was thoroughly miserable, but there was nothing he could do about it; everything was in place and it was out of his hands. George Johnson was brought in, and it was revealed to him the part he was to play. The bag had to be in place that evening, ready to meet the kidnapper's demands for collection the next day. It was impressed upon the foreman the importance of secrecy, not even his wife should know.

Constable Christopher Ellis pulled the hood of his waterproof further forward to cover his face from the constant drizzle of rain. He had been given a prime position behind the engine shed, but unfortunately the only shelter was a row of bushes. He had to squat down, and was basically open to the elements. His colleagues were stationed in far more favourable positions, and, although not in close proximity, they were protected from the persistent rain. The monotonous damp grey morning dragged on into the afternoon. It seemed to Christopher he had been in this cramped location for an eternity. He had seen no one go near the bag.

He thought the whole population had taken shelter from this diabolical, damp, cursed day when, in the half-light of the approaching evening, he spotted his boss and the yard foreman go to the bag. It was some time before the chief constable turned to face Christopher and indicate for him to come forward and break cover. With the bag was a dirty soiled rag, which when opened contained a spine-chilling object. Both the chief constable and the foreman were ashen-faced, and observed Christopher's reaction as he looked open-mouthed at the bloody severed finger.

Later that evening James escorted Jacob to the police station, where all the officers involved in the stake-out were assembled. Henry Oaks had interrogated every officer, to find that no one had witnessed a soul go near the bag. The mystery intrigued all and sundry as to how such an impossible feat had been accomplished.

The chief constable asked the foreman, 'Is there any means the bag could have been accessed from inside the engine shed?'

George Johnson was clearly embarrassed being the focus of everyone's attention. 'I don't think so, sir. It's a brick-built building,' he informed them.

Jacob's face was like thunder, 'I knew something like this would happen, we were warned not to involve the police.'

Henry Oaks intervened, 'I'm sorry, Jacob. We certainly didn't see this coming, until we unravel this mystery, we will have to think positively.'

James remained deep in thought, totally baffled as to how the Stockwells had accomplished such an enigmatic and impossible feat. He thought the kidnappers had prior knowledge: someone, somehow, was keeping them well informed. There was only a few who knew of the money exchange, but he hadn't accounted for the many police officers involved.

Later in a private meeting with Henry Oaks, James queried how many officers were taken into his confidence. He was surprised to hear that no one knew of the true kidnapping, all they understood was they were on a routine stake-out. They were to keep a low profile, and watch for anyone acting suspiciously. This narrowed the field down considerably. James turned his attention to the yard foreman, and why was he chosen to be part of the ransom deal.

His suspicions were further aroused, when the foreman drew their attention to a letter, which turned up the following day. It informed them the deal was still on for the transfer of money, from the same location on Thursday. If the police were still involved the deal was off. Disturbingly, it reminded them Adam had only nine digits left. James thought it prudent not to let Jacob see the letter.

At a prearranged meeting, James decided he would accuse the foreman outright, to see how he would react.

'George,' he asked, 'Why do you think you were involved with this ransom business?'

The foreman frowned, 'I have no idea, sir.'

James continued, 'I'm rather puzzled' and paused for a moment, as he held his steady gaze. The foreman was most uncomfortable under the hostile stare, 'Did you see anyone delivering the letter?'

The frown never left his face as he replied, 'No, sir.'

James began to put more pressure on: 'You see, George, we only have your word for it, but no one else has seen the mystery person delivering letters.' George was clearly struggling to maintain his innocence, as James pressed home his interrogation. 'I think you know more than you're telling us, I'd advise you to come clean. This is a serious business you're mixed up in.'

James could tell he was on to something, as George hung his head, not knowing how to handle James's damning insinuations. After a moment's silence, James carried on, 'I believe when you positioned the bag last night, you also placed Adam's severed finger there; that's the only possible explanation as to how it was done. The bag was under constant surveillance the whole time, with not a soul being observed going anywhere near it.'

The foreman placed his elbows on the table, and cradled his head in silence.

James quietly said, 'I think we ought to visit the police station together, and you can come clean.' Without a hint of protestation, he rose to his feet, and followed James to face more questions from the chief constable.

The truth when it came out was, in fact, unbelievably stranger than fiction. James was present in the interview room with the chief constable, and Constable Chris Ellis, who was taking notes.

The chief constable asked the foreman, 'Do you admit to being involved in the extortion of money by abducting Mr Adam Atkinson, from Atkinson's Sawmill?'

In a subdued voice George Johnson answered, 'Yes, sir.'

The chief's next question was, 'Are you working with the Stockwell brothers?'

George said, 'No, sir, they are not involved.'

Everyone exchanged glances, in disbelief, 'Who else is involved in the abduction?' His answer was all the more puzzling, 'There is no one else involved, sir.'

George on the face of it appeared to be a mild-mannered man, not in the least would anyone imagine he could be capable of such a diabolical scam such as this.

'Are you asking us to believe this is all your own doing?'

The mild-mannered George further managed to amaze them when he answered, 'No, sir, I'm only following instructions.'

The interview proved to be throwing up more impossible facts than could be believed.

Henry Oaks asked, 'From whom?'

His reply was more shocking than anyone could imagine. 'From Mr Adam, sir.'

There was stunned silence in the room as Christopher Ellis feverishly recorded the unlikely facts on paper as they unfolded before him. The question everyone wanted to know was where is Adam now.

It was James who finally blurted out the question: 'Where is he hiding?'

George was completely compliant and at ease by now, and told them he was hiding in the loft of the manager's office.

Henry Oaks then took charge again. 'Right this interview is now terminated,' glaring at the foreman he instructed, 'Lock him in a cell. We have business to attend to at the sawmill.'

James asked the chief constable to delay his mission for five minutes, before he descended mob-handed at the sawmill. He needed to explain to Jacob what was going on, he felt he owed him that.

Jacob was in his office, when James arrived.

'Jacob, listen very carefully,' he hurriedly blurted out, 'we haven't much time.'

Jacob was startled at being interrupted by James, who was in a highly belligerent state, 'In five minutes' time, the police will raid Adam's office, where he is hiding in the loft.'

Jacob was struck dumb, by this shock announcement, and sat open-mouthed, as his friend went on to explain the situation as quickly as he could. Jacob managed to say, 'But why would he do such a thing?' James grabbed Jacob's sleeve, 'That's what we need to find out, come on move; the police will arrive shortly.'

On the short walk from the engineering shop to the sawmill manager's office, they were overtaken by a rush of bodies, as police officers hurried to secure the area. They arrived at the office, simultaneously as the chief constable, and Constable Ellis. James and Jacob followed them in, as Henry Oaks pointed at the loft hatch, above their heads. The chief said, in a loud voice, 'Come on down, Adam, we know you're up there.' They all stood in perfect silence, till the chief followed up with, 'Stop playing silly games.

Adam, we don't want to have to smoke you out. You wouldn't want that now, would you?' A few more moments of silence, then the hatchway lid was opened, followed by a ladder. As Adam descended, his heavily blood-soaked left hand was most noticeable, and Jacob and the others were awe struck at the sight of him.

James spoke, and asked him, 'Adam, what the hell are you playing at?'

Adam faced them, and hung his head in shame.

Jacob also said, 'What's going on Adam? This is crazy.'

Adam eventually explained, 'I needed the money: I have been gambling heavily and the people I owe money to threatened me with violence.'

Henry Oaks asked, 'Adam, have you lost a finger?' indicating his bandaged hand.

Adam held up his damaged hand, and affirmed, 'Yes, I have.'

Henry followed up his questioning. 'Did they do that to you?' he said.

'No.'

'Then was it George?'

Adam's answer was all the more shocking.

'I wanted George to do it, but he wouldn't. He helped me in the engineering shop, where I amputated the small finger of my left hand. I did it myself on the guillotine. I had to make it look genuine.'

Jacob was sickened listening to his brother's macabre story: 'Adam, did you not stop for one minute to think of what this will do to our mother? She has already lost a husband, and two sons, and now she has to deal with your stupidity. You are her eldest son, you should be setting an example to me, her youngest son.' Jacob left his brother no place to hide, but Adam remained reticent.

Henry Oaks motioned to Constable Ellis to step forward, who proceeded to charge their prisoner.

'Adam Atkinson, I am arresting you on conspiracy of falsely demanding money from the firm that you manage.'

The constable's voice droned on, then their prisoner was handcuffed, ready to be escorted to prison.

As they were leaving Adam turned, and asked, 'I assume George has ratted on me?'

Henry Oaks was quick to reply, 'Yes, he has. He is being held at this moment in police custody, where you are soon to join him.'

Adam said, 'The man's a fool, if he had held his nerve, I could have made him a rich man.'

Jacob looked at his brother with contempt. 'The only fool I see is the fool who stands before me.'

16

The Woodsman

It was early morning. *Once the sun rises higher, the grey mist will soon disappear*, thought Mrs Atkinson. She was a strong-willed woman, and had dealt with family problems that would have destroyed many women. It was testament to her character that she kept her head after all the heartache she had had to endure. On Adam's insistence, she had just employed a maid, but she preferred to do all household chores herself.

Now Adam was encouraging her to buy a cottage near the river, which was pleasantly located away from the village but nearer the sawmill. It meant she would lose all her friends and neighbours and live a life of solitary confinement, if she went ahead with Adam's plans. She had already made up her mind: it would never happen.

Mrs Atkinson looked out of the kitchen window, at the brightening skies, and called to her maid.

'It looks like it will be a nice day, Alice. I think we will give this carpet a good beating. It's some time since it was last done.'

Alice nodded her head in agreement. 'There's no need for you to do it, Mrs Atkinson, after all, that's what you're paying me for.'

Mrs Atkinson had known Alice since she was born, and chose her to be her maid for her trustworthiness. The truth was Alice was more a companion than a domestic help. She had recently married her childhood sweetheart, Ken Cooper, who worked at the sawmill.

It was because of Ken's down-to-earth attitude that he was well thought of and his devotion to his work soon saw him rise to the ranks of foreman. He was an automatic choice for the vacancy of manager.

Alice began to roll up the carpet, when a knock on the door announced the arrival of Ken.

'Good morning, Mrs Atkinson,' he greeted her, 'Am I in time for a cup of tea?'

Mrs Atkinson smiled at him. 'Of course you are, lad – that is after you have helped us lug this carpet on to the line, ready to be beaten.'

The pair had just recently married and were very much in love, he took every opportunity to see his beloved wife.

He chuckled pleasantly. 'It would be my pleasure,' he chortled. He then took on a more intense stance. 'I can only spare a couple of minutes, as I'm on my morning break,' he announced. 'I cannot be out of the office too long.'

Mrs Atkinson asked, 'Ken, how are you settling in to the manager's job?'

Ken dragged his eyes away from Alice, and replied, 'I'm enjoying it. It's challenging. This morning I have a meeting with James; he is interesting, and has taught me so much.'

Alice looked at Ken adoringly, and told Mrs Atkinson, 'I'm so proud of him, and he looks after me so well.'

The old lady replied, 'Well, that's what husbands are for, dear, and you also must treat him accordingly.'

Ken quickly dealt with the heavy carpet, and was soon settled in the kitchen with a cup of tea. Mrs Atkinson tried to encourage him to try one of her cakes, which he politely refused.

'I cannot stay long; James could turn up any minute. I would hate to keep him waiting.'

The old lady smiled. 'He wouldn't take offence; he is one of life's gentlemen,' she said. 'Ask him to call here afterwards, if he has time.'

Ken gulped down his tea, then stood up. 'I certainly will, Mrs Atkinson.'

Then he was gone, but not before he had given Alice a quick peck on the cheek.

On his way back to the sawmill he passed Blind Billy, who was playing his violin. 'You're up early this morning, Billy,' he greeted him, 'Most people are still in bed at this hour.'

Ken noticed the open violin case at his feet was empty, as he dropped a coin in. Billy stopped playing, as he conveyed his thanks.

'God bless you, Ken. I'm so glad you have been promoted to manager.'

Ken slowed down his walk, as he replied, 'Thanks, Billy. Can't stop – duty calls.'

Billy was still playing his violin two hours later, when he became aware of an approaching horse. He listened intently at the jingle of the bit in the horse's mouth, and its distinctive breathing pattern.

He stopped playing when it got nearer, and called out, 'Good morning, Mr James. How are you?'

James brought his mount to a halt. It amazed him how Billy could recognise individuals owing to his highly developed hearing.

'I'm quite well, Billy, how are you?' he asked.

Billy's attention was drawn to his pet spaniel, Daisy, as he patted her and answered, 'I'm very well thank you, sir.'

The dog wagged her tail in appreciation, as she wandered around behind him and between his legs.

All the time Billy followed her movements as if he could see, which prompted James to ask, 'How do you know where Daisy is all the time?'

Billy grinned. 'I can hear her breathing, sir.'

James was full of admiration for Billy's tenacity, and how he coped with his disability.

'I haven't any change on me at the moment, Billy, will you be in the Red Fox tonight?'

Billy looked up as if he could see, while he stroked Daisy.

'That I will, sir.'

James urged his horse forward as he said, 'I'll see you there then. Leave your purse at home.'

Billy raised his voice to be sure James heard him: 'God bless you.'

Mrs Atkinson was delighted to see James. 'Did you want to see me for some specific reason, Mrs Atkinson?' James asked.

The old lady put on her best theatrical stern face. 'Do I need to have a reason, specifically, for you to come see me?' she demanded.

James replied light heartedly, 'No, of course not, Mrs Atkinson. You know I like seeing you, and the delightful Mrs Cooper also.'

Alice blushed, and tried to make herself look busy. The old lady brought the conversation round to police actions, and the threat to the timber business from the diehard Martyrs. James was able to tell her he was about to meet with the chief constable concerning that particular problem.

James was able to put her mind at rest. 'I have an appointment to meet with the chief constable later today,' he informed her.

Mrs Atkinson sighed. 'I wish you well, James, my heart goes out to the Stockwell family. Such a well-meaning Christian family… to have their sons bring so much disgrace upon them, it doesn't bear thinking of.'

James could only nod his head in silent agreement.

Much later James met up with the chief constable, who outlined plans he had to bring the Stockwell brothers to justice. 'You see, James, they lost popularity when they murdered Police Constable Ronald Young. Now that we have increased the bounty on their heads, their days are surely numbered. It will be a massive burden lifted from my shoulders when we bring them to answer for their crimes.' Henry Oaks shuffled through a pile of paperwork, to produce a folder, with the title, 'Stockwell; Bow Street'. He showed James a questionnaire.

'Look at this. Yet another progress report to fill in on the Stockwell case. I'm inundated with the damned things.'

James sympathised with him. 'Never mind, Henry. With so many turning against them, I'm pretty sure you won't be troubled by them for much longer.'

James rested awhile in his room after the evening meal at the Red Fox Tavern, and he heard a lively jig being played on the violin. Blind Billy was starting his repertoire early in the bar. Just a handful of customers were gathered when James at last joined them. He placed two tankards of ale on one of the tables near the front.

After Billy finished a lively jig, James said, 'Evening, Billy, have a rest. Your ale is waiting here for you.'

Billy was wearing his dark glasses, but if you didn't know any better you wouldn't think he was blind, as he made his way towards the table. 'Good evening, Mr James. God bless you, I've been looking forward to this.'

James was pleased he was turning Billy's evening into a pleasure, as he had the utmost respect for Billy.

It amazed him how Billy coped with adversity, and so he asked, 'Have you been blind from birth Billy?'

There was a pause as Billy sipped his ale, 'No, but my eyesight began to deteriorate from the age of about four years, so I can picture colours in my head and also the general shape of an animal, say a horse for example. Don't feel pity for me, Mr James, my other senses are highly developed, and I don't miss much. I can pick up on things that most people would miss.'

Billy further amazed James, when he continued, 'There are two men sat at a table behind us. What you don't know is, they are most interested in your good self, Mr James.'

It most certainly aroused James's curiosity.

'How do you know that, Billy, and why are you covering your face, like that?'

Billy smiled as he whispered, 'There are folk in here who have worked in mills. Because of the noise of machinery, they have learned the art of lip-reading – much like my highly developed hearing, which has compensated for the loss of my sight. It makes sense not to let them know what I'm saying.'

James was intrigued that the two men were interested in him.

'Perhaps we should invite them to join us, Billy; what do you think?'

Billy was shaken at this remark, and urgently hissed, 'No, no, Mr James. They don't wish you well. They are bad news.'

James began to feel uncomfortable, when Billy asked him to pull up his collar in the pretence of feeling cold.

'This will partly obscure your face, making it difficult for the lip-readers.' James tried to listen above the low mumbling noise in the room, to see if he could hear what Blind Billy could.

He leaned nearer to him, and asked, 'Do you know who these men are?'

Billy replied, 'I don't think so; I cannot think who they might be.'

Billy was in deep concentration, listening; he then whispered, 'This is more serious than I at first thought: one of them has mentioned the names of Peter and Ben. You know to whom they are referring.'

James confirmed, with a nod of his head.

'Whatever is going on, it's happening tomorrow night,' Billy whispered.

James had turned his head slightly, so as to observe the two in his peripheral vision. He was able to tell Billy what his ears couldn't.

'They are on their feet and about to leave, but why did they mention me in their conversation?'

Billy said, 'I suppose everyone in here would be interested in you, what with your involvement at the sawmill, and I'm not surprised they're moving on. David Brown and Joe Andrews have just come in; they will not want to be around next to bounty hunters.'

James looked towards the door as the two left and observed the two bounty hunters in conversation together. Then David Brown also left, leaving Joe Andrews to make his own way to the bar.

James nodded his head as Joe passed and asked him, 'Come and join us when you have your ale, Joe, I need a word.'

It wasn't long before Joe's gravel-like voice filled the room.

'Ahh,' he rasped as he lowered his frame into the chair next to Billy, 'Evening James what can I help you with?'

James replied, 'Those two ruffians who just left, Billy was able to pick up on some of their conversation. They appeared to be most interested in me. They're up to no good the pair of them. Tell Joe what you heard, Billy.'

As Billy relayed what he had heard, Joe didn't seem to be too interested, until Billy mentioned that they spoke of their involvement with the Stockwell brothers. Joe's rasping voice was urgent as he informed them, 'We have already got them under surveillance; David is keeping a close eye on them.'

If Joe first appeared disinterested, he was now most attentive at the news something big was planned for tomorrow night.

He wasted no time in emptying his tankard, and asked, 'You didn't hear more detail of what was happening tomorrow night, did you?'

Billy said, 'No, sorry.'

Joe sighed. 'Thanks very much for your input. I must get along and inform Ray, he will be most interested.'

***

Ken Cooper was in his office, bright and early; he wanted to be well prepared before the day shift reported for duty. He was acting on advice from Henry Oaks, to be prepared for some unusual activity. What that unusual activity would be was a mystery; the chief constable wouldn't or couldn't tell him.

Right now his main interest was overseeing a new building, to further enhance the modernisation of the plant. Duncan was general foreman of building works, and was glad Ken was also in the office early.

'We have a problem, Ken, there's some kind of hold-up at the quarry. I cannot find out what is going on down there.'

Ken reassured Duncan, 'I'm going to the quarry this morning, Duncan, to see Mr Smales. Why don't you accompany me?'

Duncan, who admired his boss, exclaimed, 'Wow, straight to the top, eh, Ken? I'm impressed.'

Ken liked Duncan, they got on well together, and said, 'We will get the day shift sorted then go just before midday.'

In the office at the quarry, they were asked to wait, as Mr Swales was in a meeting. They couldn't help but notice the absence of the quarrymen, and had to wait a full fifteen minutes, until the meeting was concluded, and when they entered were surprised to find James sitting there. Mr Smales welcomed them and apologised.

'Sorry to have kept you waiting, I'm sure you have the same questions, as Mr Williams wants answers too.'

James took the lead, saying, 'While all the relevant people are here, I'd like to assure you that the problem here at the quarry is being quickly being dealt with.'

Ken had a frown on his face as he enquired, 'What I want to know is, what's the hold-up with materials from this quarry, and where are all your staff?'

James looked at Mr Smales, as he replied, 'Well, Ken, it's no fault of Mr Smales here, or his workforce. The truth is he has been asked to suspend all business for a short while until further notice.'

The incredulous Duncan looked at Mr Smales, and asked in a puzzled voice, 'Why would anyone want to suspend business?'

Mr Smales answered, 'The request came from the chief constable.'

They all sat in stunned silence, as the facts came to light. 'We had a break in at the quarry where a substantial amount of explosives were stolen. The police believe the Stockwell brothers are involved: they have information that the brothers are planning a major incident, and in an effort to prevent a general panic, they are keeping the knowledge of the theft quiet. That's why the workforce has been stood down. However it's just a matter of time until it becomes general knowledge. The police have further details that an atrocious barbaric act is planned for tonight. They believe the target is the sawmill.'

Christopher Ellis, like his colleagues, had been briefed of an impending attack at the sawmill, and was on standby on high alert. He remembered his last stake-out at the sawmill and the miserable hours he spent through that rainy night, drenched to the skin. It was thought to be more likely an attack would be carried out after darkness. He was positioned in a workmen's hut near the partly constructed walls that were to become the new engine shed. The race was on to complete the project in readiness to receive new machinery, but it appeared that delays kept cropping up.

Meanwhile Henry Oaks sat in a chair in Ken Cooper's office, opposite Ray Mitchell. Outside daylight was fast diminishing; soon the yard would be in total darkness.

Ray said, 'I'm not happy with the amount of men you have deployed on this job, Henry. Remember what happened the last time when so many officers were tramping around?'

The chief constable was quick to defend his handling of the exercise.

'I certainly do, Ray, that's why I declined the offer of extra men from Bow Street.'

Ray was not convinced, 'I still think we are sending them a clear signal for them to steer clear.'

Henry Oaks was still on the defensive, 'I don't think I can do anything more, under the circumstances.'

Ray followed up with, 'I'm certain nothing will happen here tonight: they are much too wily to be caught and there are far too many officers out there.'

Henry Oaks asked, 'Why? What would you do differently?'

Ray replied, 'I anticipated this very scenario: I have got my team out on different locations altogether.' With that he arose from his chair, 'I'll catch up with you later, Henry.'

Arthur Fletcher was being dragged along behind his three excited dogs as they headed for the wooded enclosure that had been previously discovered. Joe Andrews and David Brown lagged a few paces behind on foot, leading their horses. On reaching the enclosed compound, the dogs remained in an agitated state, while Joe and David caught up. Joe immediately removed the sapling to reveal the entrance, and was almost knocked over as the dogs barged through, dragging Arthur behind them.

With the rapidly diminishing daylight, they were able to ascertain the brothers had been there. The most important evidence was the discovery of two boxes of dynamite.

Joe rasped out in his gravel-like voice, 'Arthur, see if the dogs can pick up their trail quickly.' In the meantime, David loaded the boxes onto his horse, ready to be put into the custody of the police. They had arranged to meet up later at Joshua the woodsman's cottage, while Joe followed Arthur and his dogs. When Joe caught up to Arthur he found him and his dogs wandering around in circles, going nowhere in particular. It was obvious they had lost the trail, there was nothing more they could do, but to meet up as previously arranged. It was dark anyhow.

At the woodsman's cottage, there was no sign of life; the place was in darkness. 'He's got a knack of not being able to be found, that hermit guy,' said Arthur, as he tried the back door, which to his surprise he found to be open.

He stepped inside, and shouted, 'Hello, is anyone at home?'

David and Joe followed Arthur inside, David had found a candle and hastily lit it, bathing the kitchen in an orange glow. It was then they discovered the place was in a state of disarray; the small kitchen table was turned on its side, as was the kitchen chair. It was as they crunched their way through broken crockery they came upon Joshua's legs protruding from beneath the sink.

He had been brutally beaten; his face was heavily bruised and swollen. He was breathing, fortunately, and as they bathed his wounds with water he began to moan.

David reassured Joshua, 'Easy there now, Josh, we will take care of you. Joe, you take his legs; let's get him on to his bed. He'll be more comfortable there.'

Meanwhile Arthur began sorting through the mess in the kitchen, and soon had the kettle on.

As the evening wore on, it was decided David and Arthur would report to the police station, leaving Joe to look after Joshua until help could be given to the old man. Joshua was slowly coming round, trying to make sense of what had happened to him.

Ray Mitchell soon joined Joe and was keen to know what had happened.

'What do you remember, Josh?'

The old man struggled to sit up, but was advised to lie still. 'I remember it all,' he said shakily.

Ray pressed on with his questioning. 'Josh, who did this to you?'

Josh replied weakly, 'It was those Stockwell boys. After all I did for them. I used to help them but when they turned their hand to murder I refused any further help.'

News of the assault soon spread like wildfire through the village and Luke Armstrong, the blacksmith, was quick to respond. He was the first to visit Joshua, showing concern for the old man's welfare. It was Luke who resolved the predicament of Joshua's wellbeing. He contacted Rebecca Ellis, who was always looking for ways to support herself, and paid her to nurse Josh back to health.

For Joshua, the road to recovery was as alien to him as anything he had experienced in his life. He always found the world was full of evil, hence his preferred way of living – alienating himself away from society to live a life in the woods, and to live a lonesome existence as a hermit. He found it rather odd, because in his time of need, he had seen a different warm side of humanity.

David had delivered the dynamite into the hands of the police for safe keeping, and help was being sent to look after Joshua. Ray was getting more frustrated that the Stockwells had once again eluded them.

Once an officer arrived at the cottage, he said to Joe, 'Can you find the place where Arthur lost the trail?'

Joe rasped out, 'Yes, I believe I can.'

17

The Haven Hotel

Ben Stockwell looked behind him, to make sure his brother Peter was keeping pace with his horse's mad, headlong dash through the forest. It was twilight, and visibility was beginning to be a problem. They came to a halt, and sat listening for a few seconds.

Ben said, 'I think we may have shaken them off.'

Peter had his head at a slight angle, listening intently. 'I hope so, they're using dogs more frequently now,' he replied.

Ben grunted, 'Uh, if we continue for another half hour we should be clear of the county.'

Peter remarked, 'Why did you have to beat up the old fellow like that?'

Ben scowled, 'He annoyed me, with whining on about murder. Silly old fool.'

Peter shook his head, 'We haven't any friends left now to aid us; their support was a great help. I suppose they will have found the dynamite too.'

Ben urged his horse on at a walking pace. 'I reckon they will have found that, but don't worry, we can manage without any help.'

They continued their journey for a further two hours, until they decided to settle for the night. The pair were well used to roughing it, having spent many nights in the open. Peter saw to the horses, while Ben busied himself making a fire for hot drinks.

'We were that close to using the dynamite,' Ben said venomously.

Peter agreed, 'Yeah, just think: with that fancy new engine shed blown up before it was finished, it would have set them back weeks.'

Ben's face lit up in a grin, revealing yellowed teeth, 'Then we would have hit them again, even harder.'

Peter laughed, 'Yeah, then they would be set back for years.'

Ben was carried away with euphoria. 'We could have finished them for good, even,' he beamed.

Then Peter gravely said, 'But we haven't got support anymore, Ben. You gave that old hermit a right good going over. I thought you were going to kill him. It was out of order.'

Ben glared at his brother. 'Don't you start.'

Peter cowered under the admonishing stare; he knew when to keep silent. He was well aware it didn't take much to tip Ben over the edge, and he knew the signs.

What Peter had to do now was to allow Ben time to simmer down; he would come round in his own good time. This was a good time for Peter to turn in for the night. Ben was still in a state of seething anger, as the rhythmic steady breathing coming from Peter tended to further inflame him. Owing to Peter's sleeping pattern, Ben knew he could break into a spasm of loud snoring at anytime. It was because of this that Ben often slept some distance away. Not because he couldn't sleep, but it was as an extra precaution against their position being detected.

As the night wore on, the stillness of the forest was interrupted by nocturnal predators: an owl hooted, while the full moon seemed to be dodging fast-moving clouds as they scudded across the sky. In the intermittent light of the moon, Ben had located a suitable tree, which offered the perfect sleeping accommodation. Being off the ground, Ben dozed fitfully in his elevated position.

He could hear the low, laboured snoring of Peter some way off in the distance, but what alerted him was something quite different – something that caused him to be fully awake. Something was moving stealthily and with purpose. He strained his ears as well as his eyes, searching for the cause of disturbance below. Then he caught sight of a jumbled mix of shadows merging back into the darkness. If it was an animal it hadn't sensed his lofty presence. A gentle snort assured him that it came unmistakably from a horse.

Ben waited while the tell-tale rustling of the stalkers had passed below, then he descended from the tree. Two hunters were on foot, leading their horses, and homing in on the sound of snoring, while Ben circled in a wide arc to reach his brother before they did. He moved swiftly, making as little sound as he possibly could. Peter lay under a bush, and his snoring was abruptly brought to a halt by Ben's gnarled and callused hand over his mouth. Peter stared wide-eyed into his brother's face, as he realised they were in danger. They lay silently together, completely camouflaged in the shadow of the bush.

Ray and Joe stood silently together, the noise of snoring had mysteriously stopped.

In the office of Henry Oaks, the following day, the general mood was solemn. The chief constable was once again filling in yet another report for Bow Street. He seemed to be forever trying to justify his failure to capture the Stockwell brothers. He had just finished interrogating David Brown and Arthur Fletcher. What he wanted to know was where were Ray Mitchell and Joe Andrews. The officer who was sent to the cottage in the woods to look after Joshua could only assume the pair had continued the hunt for the fugitives on their own.

It would be evening before Henry Oaks had his question answered, with the arrival of Ray and Joe. They told him of going to the place where the trail of the recalcitrant brothers was lost, and how, despite it being dark, they headed in the general direction they believed their quarry might be going in. They told of trying to track a sleeping outlaw by his snoring, but when they got close to their quarry, the snoring stopped; they decided it must have been some kind of animal, but little did they know how close they came to success. Also the brothers were incredibly lucky that their horses, which were tethered nearby, were not discovered. After that episode Ray abandoned their search, which was useless in the dark, and decided to return.

James was brought up to date, after meeting with the chief constable. It concerned James that Joshua had been left in such a vulnerable position, but he was assured that Luke was seeing to his wellbeing. Luke informed James how he and his brother were saved from drowning by the old man, and would for ever be in his debt. He was prepared to finance Mrs Ellis to nurse Josh in his hour of need. James decided to intervene, and resolved to lift the burden from Luke's shoulders, insisting he would finance Mrs Ellis to nurse Josh.

It unsettled James, that so many people were leading troubled lives, and made him more determined than ever to help where ever he could. He visited Mrs Ellis, who told him her life was made more complicated than ever. She had to visit the cottage in the wood every day to see to Joshua's needs, and was also burdened with the extra responsibility of being in charge of her niece.

James asked, 'How old is your niece?'

Mrs Ellis sighed, with the weight of her troubles. 'She is eighteen, sir.'

James was surprised, 'Eighteen? She should be fending for herself, surely.'

Mrs Ellis replied, 'She has a disability, and was until recently

197

cared for by her mother. However since her mother passed away last month, I am her only remaining relative. She has no one left to care for her.'

James was intrigued by what he was hearing. 'Where is she now?'

Mrs Ellis mopped her brow, her face a picture of trouble and strife. 'I have set her to work seeing to the laundry, but I must leave shortly to attend to Joshua.'

James could see she was under a lot of strain, 'Can I see her, I'd like a word with her, if I may?'

Mrs Ellis called into the kitchen: 'Leave that for a minute, Ruth. Can you come in here, please?'

James was taken aback when the girl entered the room, she appeared to be fit and able, but on closer inspection displayed signs of a slight limp.

Mrs Ellis introduced her, 'This is my niece, Ruth Harper.'

James smiled as he said, 'Hello, Ruth. I'm James Williams.'

Ruth was timid and withdrawn; she knew who he was, but didn't respond.

She remained silent, and wide-eyed as James asked, 'When did you lose your mother?'

Ruth looked at her aunt, then replied, 'A fortnight ago, sir.'

James noted she replied in a perfectly normal way.

'I understand you have a disability, Ruth, which your mother helped you with, can you tell me about that?'

She was looking at her aunt again, but replied instantly, 'I am affected with a form of bone disease which when I was at school was picked upon. I remember being bullied a lot, but since then have become better at dealing with people. My mother was very protective, and wouldn't allow me to do things on my own. My aunt here also thinks I cannot look after myself,' she returned her stare to her aunt yet again, 'but I assure you I am more capable than you think.'

James turned to Mrs Ellis. 'How do you feel about Ruth

staying at the cottage full time with Joshua, and you could call in occasionally when it was convenient for you?'

Mrs Ellis looked confused, 'Oh, I don't know about that, sir. It's a big responsibility for Ruth, she has never been exposed to anything so demanding.'

James could see Ruth was struggling to accept her aunt's opinion of her and pressed forward his thoughts, 'But, Mrs Ellis, she would be earning money in her own right, which would relieve you of the responsibility of looking after her.'

Ruth was straining to be heard, and in her frustration blurted out, 'When will I ever be allowed to govern my own destiny?'

James was in no doubt, of Ruth's capability as he witnessed her outburst.

James confronted Mrs Ellis. 'It's time to let go,' he said. 'You are not as alone as you think, I will be paying attention to the situation, and will be keeping a close eye on developments.'

Mrs Ellis dried her moist eyes with the corner of her apron as she nodded her consent, and James noticed how beautiful Ruth was as she smiled up at him.

James was pleased at the outcome. Financially he could well afford this act of charity, as his business dealings were going extremely well. Every investor in the railways had made huge profits, and demands for further expansion were going through the roof. In the past a journey up to Scotland could take anything up to five days, travel on horseback, now with the introduction of modern technology, rail travel made it possible to get there in twelve hours. James's affairs were still being handled by Richard Hutchinson's firm of solicitors; Richard was a late friend of his father.

Richard Hutchinson, like his father, had long since died. However, the firm were delighted to have James as a client, and were proud of his achievements. James still had one big headache to deal with and that was the threat from the Stockwell brothers, who were still waging war against the sawmill. It was in his interests to sponsor the police in their pursuit to bring these outlaws to justice.

While things were going relatively smoothly in his life, James turned his thoughts towards his mother. It was some time since he last saw her, and now was as good a time as ever to see her. After a quick visit to his foundry and engineering works, he made his way to Ludgate Hill, which was within sight of St Paul's Cathedral. His mother was always pleased to see him.

'James!' she exclaimed, on seeing him. 'How nice to see you.'

James returned her smile. 'How are you, Mother?'

She hugged him in sheer delight. 'I'm fine, James, but I do miss your father.'

Her smile left her as she contemplated her lonely existence.

James replied, 'I know, Mother, I miss him too.'

She continued with, 'And your dear uncle Richard has also departed; they grew up together and were very close friends.'

As she carried on talking, James saw she was getting melancholy.

She mentioned, 'James have you never thought of marrying?'

James replied, 'I've been so busy with my business dealings that there is no time for socialising.'

She rebuffed him, 'You're not getting any younger, you know. I thought I might have had grandchildren by now.'

James himself just recently had thoughts on that very subject, but remained tacitly uncommunicative, thinking that it was best to remain silent.

***

Stan Heslop covered the contents of the basket with a clean cloth, as he hurried from the bakery back to the blacksmith's shop, where Luke was patiently waiting.'

'Stan, did you get the bread?' he asked.

'Yes, I got a large loaf like you said.'

Luke was washing his hands as he urgently enquired, 'And did you get a fruit pie, also?'

Stan took a deep breath and sighed, 'Yes, yes. I didn't forget. It's all here, look for yourself.'

Luke buttoned up his shirt. 'Mr Kennedy likes a bit of fruit pie. Now, will you be all right while I'm gone?' he said as he picked up the basket.

Stan raised his eyes heavenwards, 'Luke, will you just go! You sound just like an old washerwoman.'

As Luke hurried on his way to the woods, James, who was riding his horse, came alongside him.

'Good morning, Luke,' he pleasantly greeted him. 'I assume you are on your way to see Joshua?'

Luke walked steadily on and said, 'Good morning. Yes, sir, I am.'

James dismounted, and walked with Luke, saying, 'I called at your shop. I just missed you.'

Luke was puzzled. 'Did you want me for anything in particular?'

James told him, 'Yes, I wanted you to know what a fine gesture on your part it was paying for the help Joshua needs. I have employed a carer to live in till he gets back on his feet.'

Luke began to protest, but James informed him, 'You may find it too costly, Luke. A maid-come-nurse doesn't come cheap.'

Luke frowned, 'I don't mind, sir.'

James said, 'I know how he saved you and your brother from drowning, and how grateful you are to him. Everyone knows how highly you regard him.'

At the cottage James knocked on the door, and respectfully waited for it to be opened. It took a moment, as the door was locked and heavily bolted. Then, Luke and James were greeted by Ruth with a smile.

As they entered, James asked, 'How is he?'

Ruth closed the door behind them, saying, 'He is a lot better this morning.'

James told Luke, 'You go in and see him. I want a word with Ruth,' then enquired, 'How are you coping, Ruth? Any problems?'

Ruth smiled. 'None at all, sir. I'm managing quite well.'

James looked at the sturdy lock and draw bolts attached to the door. 'I'm concerned for your safety: you are very isolated in this part of the woods. I'm pleased to see you keep the door locked.'

Ruth followed James's gaze to the door. 'Yes, sir. Mr Kennedy is most insistent I keep it fully locked, at all times.'

Luke came out of the bedroom and joined them, he said, 'I've left him, he seems extremely tired.' James told Luke, 'We are just admiring your locks and bolts.'

Luke raised his eyebrows. 'I'm pleased he has made full use of them; he has made a good job there.' He then squeezed past them in the small kitchen. 'I'll leave you now. I must get back.'

James entered the darkened bedroom, and was appalled at the old man's injuries. In the gloom he was able to make out Joshua's bruised and swollen face. His eyes were completely closed, and James was filled with mixed emotions, ranging from compassion for the old man, to rage at the Stockwells' inhuman treatment towards him.

The old man said, 'I'm sorry for all the trouble I've caused you, but so grateful for all the help you are giving me. People are so kind.'

Mrs Ellis had just taken the washing off the line, and brought the laundry basket into her kitchen, ready for ironing, when James called.

This prompted her to ask, 'Why, Mr James, how nice to see you. I was just about to have a cup of tea, would you care to join me?'

James replied, 'That's very civil of you, Mrs Ellis, I don't mind if I do. I have just visited Mr Kennedy in the woods to see how Ruth is getting on.'

Mrs Ellis busied herself preparing the tea. Amid the clattering of the crockery, she informed James, 'I am trying to make time to visit myself; I don't want to leave it too late. It gets spooky in those woods after dark.

James assured her. 'There is no need for concern, Mrs Ellis. Ruth is more capable than you think, and she is doing a fine job.'

Mrs Ellis poured James a cup of tea. 'When Ruth's mother died, I just did not know how I was going to manage with the added burden of looking after her. She was never allowed to do anything for herself. To be truthful I'm most surprised: she has turned out to be a most strong-willed girl, and has her sights set too high in my opinion.'

James took his tea. 'There isn't anything wrong with having ambitions. If they don't work out then at least she has tried.'

Mrs Ellis went on 'She is all right at the moment, but what will happen to her when Joshua recovers his health?'

James replied, 'I have already thought about that scenario, I have plans for her and I believe it can also involve you.'

Mrs Ellis was most interested. 'Why, what plans do you have that would involve Ruth and myself?'

There was a moment of silence as James sipped his tea, he then said, 'As you know I rent a room at the Red Fox whenever I have business at the sawmill. While it is adequate, and suits my needs, I think what South Downesmere needs is a more elaborate hotel. What I propose is a purpose-built hotel. I would like to employ Ruth and yourself to run it. What do you say?'

Mrs Ellis was dumbstruck for a moment. When she finally found her voice, she stuttered, 'I don't know what to say, Mr James.'

James went on, 'Obviously it's early days at the moment, so if you could keep it under your bonnet for the time being I would appreciate it.'

Mrs Ellis asked, 'Have you approached Ruth yet?'

James told her, 'No, as I say, it's early days yet. I thought you ought to know, so as to put your mind at ease concerning your future. I am due back in London in a couple of days, I intend to start the legal side of the venture – solicitors, architects, builders etc.' James looked at her, and asked. 'What do you say, Mrs Ellis, do we have a deal?'

James had caused Mrs Ellis to get emotional once more, with tears in her eyes, she flung her arms round his neck. 'Oh, Mr James, who in their right mind would refuse such an offer? It's definitely a deal, and I promise not to tell a soul until you sanction it.'

James was kept very busy over the next few weeks not only with the project of a new hotel, but plans were being made for a branch line linking South Downesmere with London. As James was involved as an investor, he made sure his hotel would be conveniently accessible to railway passengers.

In the meantime, Joshua was beginning to recover, and very nearly back to his normal self. However his ordeal at the hands of the Stockwell brothers was indelibly imprinted on his mind, he would forever carry the memory, as would his scarred face.

During the weeks of his rehabilitation, he had grown most fond of Ruth, and she of him. As he reflected on his life, he realised that in his approaching old age, far from shutting himself away from civilisation, he needed the company of his fellow man. He began to look upon Ruth as his daughter, and persuaded her to stay with him, sharing his roof over their heads. Ruth informed him of the offer she had had from James, and the thought of losing her made him sad.

As work started on the preparation for the railroad, so did the foundations of the hotel. To all intents, the general public assumed the building was part and parcel of the railway. This was a rumour James was happy to endorse, and encouraged Mrs Ellis and Ruth to do likewise. Work went ahead at an amazing pace, when the railway was completed, the hotel was promised to be finished before winter.

Ruth sat Joshua down and said, 'Mr Kennedy, the time has almost come when I will have to leave you.'

Joshua looked startled and, wide-eyed, replied, 'Ruth, stop calling me Mr Kennedy, my name is Josh. I've grown most fond of you, my dear, and will be sad to see you go.'

Ruth took his hand, and gently informed him, 'All right, Josh it is then. I have known for some time that the hotel offers my aunt and myself a way out of our predicament. Not only does it offer employment, but accommodation also.'

Joshua sat in silence, as he took in the news, still holding her hand.

Ruth soothingly rubbed the top of his hand, saying, 'Living out in the woods isn't for me, Josh, and it isn't healthy for you either.'

Josh was transfixed as he took it all in and Ruth talked, 'I think you should give up this place, Josh. I can look after you at the hotel.'

Joshua couldn't believe what she was saying, 'I'm happy for you, my dear, but you cannot go making promises you have no right to make. What about the owners of the hotel, won't they have something to say about this?'

Joshua was enchanted at her enchanting smile as she said, 'The owner has agreed and arrangements have already been finalised. All you have to do now is accept the offer already on the table.'

It dawned on Joshua that a lot had gone on without his knowledge.

Ruth further informed him, 'I have arranged for Mr Williams to speak to you; he will answer any further questions you may have.'

Later in the afternoon, James arrived at the cottage in the woods, for his prearranged chat with Joshua. Ruth busied herself in the kitchen, while Joshua entertained James in the dining room.

Joshua wondered what information James could give him as he asked, 'What can you tell me about this railway hotel they're building, Mr Williams?'

James resolved to tell Joshua all the facts. 'Well, Joshua, first and foremost the hotel has nothing to do with the railway.'

Joshua uttered, 'Really?'

James confirmed, 'No, the hotel is one of my projects.'

Joshua was astounded, 'I knew you had dealings with the railway people, but I had no idea the hotel was yours.'

James replied, 'That was a rumour I preferred everyone to go along with, however, it doesn't matter now. It would become general knowledge eventually. I have been keeping a close eye on Ruth, and her aunt. Ruth impressed me; I consider her to have the qualities to manage a hotel of this size. It is one way of helping them, by them helping me.'

Joshua was astonished at this revelation. 'I cannot but admire your cunning sense of business attitude.'

James smiled. 'If you admire me for that, you cannot disagree to my offer of housing you in the new hotel. Living out here in the woods makes you absolutely vulnerable, and, due to your advancing years, it's imperative you accept my offer.'

Joshua knew all too well that James was right.

They sat in silence for a while, then Joshua said, 'I know what you say is right, but it's going to be a wrench for me to leave here.'

James was quick to point out, 'Look at how easy it was for the Stockwell brothers to attack you in such a cowardly way.'

For a moment Joshua sat in silence again, then said, 'You know I'm amazed at how fond I've become of Ruth, and I regard her as the daughter I never had.'

James nodded his head in agreement. 'I know how you feel. I too am most fond of her. Because of her physical impairment, she has had a rough time, particularly in her early years, what with bullying and the like. I have connections with various surgeons, who I believe can help Ruth live a better lifestyle.'

Joshua was most intrigued and wanted to know more. 'What do you think they can do to help her?'

James looked round to see if Ruth was anywhere within

earshot. 'I have not discussed this with her, until I do it remains to be seen what they can achieve.'

Once again there was a moment of silence, as they digested their previous discussion; then, Ruth's voice cut through the silence.

'And what exactly do you think your surgeons can do to help a lame girl?'

They turned to find Ruth glaring at them.

James was embarrassed, 'I'm so sorry, Ruth. I did not mean any harm; I shouldn't be talking this way behind your back.'

Ruth seemed to be on the defensive. 'I have never let my disability get in the way of anything I wanted to do.'

James was clearly shamed. 'I do understand, Ruth. Perhaps we can discuss the matter more fully at a later date?'

Ruth appeared to accept what was clearly an apology from James.

With the opening of the new branch line, James found that travelling to London and back from South Downesmere was very convenient. What used to be hours of riding in the saddle was now condensed into just two hours. He could even deal with some paperwork en route; it was most definitely the way forward.

In ongoing talks between Jacob and James, they decided to connect the sawmill with a rail link to a goods yard; this would further enhance sales wider afield. Horsepower was slowly being phased out, but on the plus side more jobs were being created. Many men from the town, who hadn't worked for years, found employment with the rail company. James could not fathom why some people wanted to keep the old ways and shunned any form of modern change.

Mrs Ellis was excited. Today she would begin work at the newly opened hotel, which was overseen by her niece, who was acting as manager and shadowed by James. Their first day was taken up with the recruitment of local people to staff the hotel. Mrs Ellis was put in charge of head of housekeeping, while the other vacant posts were quickly filled. It would take several days for everyone to settle in to their newfound roles. Two passengers from the rail station came in amidst the recruitment and were dealt with efficiently by Ruth, who allocated them rooms and then quickly rejoined the enrolment scheme.

James had secured a private apartment within the hotel, as had Joshua. At the end of the day's work, James arranged a meeting to sort out any problems. Joshua had been invited in his capacity as a resident.

James asked him, at the end of the meeting, 'What do you think of your new home, Joshua? Have you any ideas as to how we can improve things?'

Joshua was taken unawares; he didn't think he would be asked to involve himself in the meeting at all.

'Well, I must say, I didn't think for one minute I would be asked for my opinion, but I'm so grateful to you, Mr Williams. I don't know what to say, except I think this is my safe haven.'

James was quick to reassure Joshua. 'Your opinion is as valid as anyone else here. It may have gone unnoticed by you all, but we haven't got a name for the hotel yet. In fact you have given me an idea, Joshua, I like what you have just said, about this being your safe haven. How about we call this the Haven Hotel?'

And so the hotel now had a name and it soon proved to be a hit, with its modern up-to-date facilities. It featured conference rooms, a billiards room, a large dance hall, and bar. One of its first customers was the company that owned the railroad, fuelling the myth amongst the locals that the hotel belonged to the railway – a rumour that James was happy to go along with.

18

Ruth's Story

As Ruth Harper descended to the ground floor of the hotel, she struggled to negotiate the stairs. Her legs, which were deformed, meant that her feet pointed inward, making walking difficult. But she was enjoying her new role in management; running the Haven Hotel. As always she put her difficulties behind her choosing to ignore her disability. Her progress didn't go unnoticed as she went about her daily duties; James had a tremendous feeling of compassion and was most protective towards her. However, he had found her to be very strong-willed and that she liked to have her own way. Consequently, any suggestions which affected her personally had to be carefully phrased so as not to cause offence. James had long thought corrective surgery would be beneficial in making her life easier. It was a delicate subject which had to be handled with the utmost care.

All her life, Ruth had been overprotected by her mother. She was never allowed to do things on her own and, in her mature teens, she began to stand up for herself. It was this defensive attitude which sent out a clear message, and a posed a barrier few people could overcome. She fully accepted James was her employer, and that very position allowed him to draw even closer than anyone else had. Over the passing weeks, the two of them got to know each other more intimately. Eventually James found it easier to approach her, until one day she found they were discussing her disability. She had to admit to herself, her feelings towards him were beginning to become more than platonic.

James said to her, 'If you would only consent to have this corrective surgery, Ruth, I'm sure it would be beneficial to you. Your life could be turned around.'

Ruth's opposition had always been negative, mainly because of the huge cost involved. She asked, 'James, how much would it cost?'

He replied, 'You're not to worry over that detail.'

She hastily added, 'But I do worry. I could never raise enough money to cover a surgeon's costs. It will for ever be out of my reach.'

James rolled his eyes upwards in exasperation. 'Ruth, I am not proposing you pay for the operation.'

Ruth tilted her head to one side, questioningly, and looked at him in an admonishing way. 'Why would you pay for me?' she demanded.

James returned her critical stare, and said, 'Because you could manage the hotel more efficiently if we get your legs fixed.'

She answered with a smile saying, 'Oh, so you're thinking of your business interests, are you?'

James smiled back also at the absurdity of the way the conversation had turned, 'Of course, if one of my steam engines developed a fault, I would have it fixed, so that it was working at its best performance.'

They both laughed together, and James knew he had at last succeeded in getting her to think about it.

Ruth said, 'If I consent to have this surgery, you do realise I would be unable to work for a while. I would need time afterwards to recuperate.'

James was still formulating a plan in his head, and said, 'Of course, that's not going to pose a problem.'

Ruth was still catching up, and asked, 'What about the hotel, who will manage it?'

James quickly answered, 'Have you no faith in your aunt? Don't you think she is capable?'

Ruth sat in silence, thinking of the enormity of what lay ahead of her.

The hotel was proving to be a big attraction, because of the many activities they could cater for within the local community. Henry Oaks was one who took advantage of the large ballroom, in which he organised a public meeting. He answered questions from the public concerned in catching law breakers, particularly from those concerned by the threat from the Stockwell brothers. Many disgruntled residents aired their views at the lack of progress in bringing the pair to justice.

In the meantime, James had gone ahead and organised a meeting between Ruth and his surgeon friend, Raymond Hartley, in London. Ruth had never been out of the county before; in fact she had hardly ever left the town where she was born. James wanted to make it a trip she would never forget by showing her the sights of London. For Ruth the train journey itself was an unbelievable experience. James was particularly proud to introduce his hotel manager to his mother. His mother made a big fuss over them, and insisted they stay at her home until they had concluded their business with Raymond Hartley.

On the day James introduced Ruth to Raymond Hartley, he stayed out of the consultation room and then left them alone together. The procedure had already been explained to him during his earlier meetings with the surgeon. Basically, it involved Ruth having the bones in both her legs broken, and then having them reset. It seemed such a barbaric and horrific procedure to James that he resolved to leave Ruth on her own so that she fully understood what was in store for her. He didn't feel he had the right to insist she go ahead with the procedure, as the final decision would have to be hers. After her meeting with the surgeon, Ruth was unusually quiet, causing James to be curious as to what was going on in her head.

On their journey home, James asked her, 'Ruth, are you all right?'

She looked out at the rolling countryside, as the train sped homeward. She paused for a brief instant as she formulated an appropriate answer.

'I have a lot to think about,' she eventually informed him.

She would have left it at that, had James not continued with his prying questions, 'Well, do you think it's a good idea, or not?'

Ruth began to get mildly irritated. 'It's a big decision,' she snapped back at him. 'The surgeon gave me details of all the benefits of the operation, but was quite blunt in telling me the negative side of things. He told me that, should he fail in his attempt to improve the quality of my life, there is the possibility I may never walk again.'

Since Joshua took up residence at the Haven Hotel, he spent most of his days at the hotel's stables. Ruth had insisted he should not give up his horse Annabelle and she had allotted his horse one of the top-of-the-range stalls reserved for special clients. Joshua had a vast knowledge of horses; whenever the stable hands needed advice, he would readily give his opinion. Most of his time was spent pottering around, and he enjoyed the respect shown by the staff. Annabelle too was getting used to star treatment, since taking up residence at the Haven.

Joshua was still wary of strangers, and preferred to keep a low profile, but didn't want to revert back to his old hermit ways. He was in the habit of spending time with Annabelle before having afternoon tea. On one such visit, as he spoke soothingly to her, he noticed across the courtyard two newly arrived clients, who were standing by their hoses. He was about to shout for the stable hands to attend to them, but held back as these clients were acting strangely. One of them lifted the lid of the horse's feed bin, and crouched over it. The other was apparently keeping lookout for him. For this to happen was strange indeed; it was Albert's job to be in charge of the bins. It was a job he took very seriously, and he was never too far away from the bins.

The man crouching over the bin began to hand bags of feed to his companion who loaded them onto their horses. Joshua thought, *Where on earth is Albert?* He was then gripped by heart-stopping fear as he recognised them as the Stockwell brothers. He automatically shrunk further back into the shadows in an effort to make himself invisible. The pair calmly mounted and rode out of the courtyard. When Joshua estimated they were well clear, he came out of hiding. It was then he saw a pair of boots, which belonged to someone lying behind the bin. It was Albert; he had a nasty gash to the back of his head. By the time Joshua raised the alarm, the Stockwells were well gone.

James was unsettled over the whole episode; something must be done about the Stockwells. While the invasive action on his property was too serious an act to ignore, the injury to one of his staff was an even greater threat, which angered him intensely. In talks with Henry Oaks, James promised unlimited funding, and stressed the urgency of bringing to an end the reign of terror posed by the Stockwell brothers.

Ray Mitchell was summoned to an extraordinary meeting with the chief constable and James at his hotel.

James was most disturbed at the experience Albert underwent, and asked Ray, 'Would you be willing to set up your headquarte with your men, Ray, right here in this hotel?'

Ray was thinking of the extra cost, when he replied. 'I woul have to think that one over, James, I can't afford to have my me on permanent standby: we get paid on results.'

James was quick to explain: 'What I want, Ray, is for your team to work as a security force. It was too easy for the Stockwells to leisurely saunter in here and take what they wanted. If your team had been here I don't think they would have got very far.' James paused for a second and then said, 'I believe they may try this again.'

The chief constable cut in, 'We believe they have alienated themselves from the general public and don't have the support they once had. With winter approaching, they need food and shelter. They are not getting information like they used to, and James has the wellbeing of his staff to consider.'

Ray nodded his head, 'Oh that's a different slant on the situation, James. In other words, your hiring my team to work for you.'

James agreed, 'Yes, of course, you will not be charged for rooms or any meals.'

Ray showed a glint in his eyes, as he was already planning ahead. 'Might I suggest, my men and I lodge out in the stables, if they try that again, we can give them a nice little surprise.'

James replied, 'I wasn't thinking along those lines, Ray, are you sure?'

Ray chuckled. 'My lads are used to roughing it. Besides, what more could they wish for, than nice dry warm straw.'

Ruth Harper was on the top floor of the hotel; she liked to check that all the rooms were properly cleaned and ready to be occupied. Now she had to negotiate the flight of stairs to the reception area. It seemed to her that every day her mobility was getting worse. The ascent was a mammoth obstacle, but one she had to face. James watched as she clumsily clung on to the handrail with two hands, he then stepped forward to assist her. She graciously accepted his help – something she would not have done previously. James had resolved to stop badgering her to have the surgical procedure, but he found it very hard.

On this occasion Ruth acknowledged her mobility was steadily getting worse, and brought up the subject.

'James, I've thought long and hard, and realise I'm not going to get any better. Perhaps I should take your advice and trust the surgeons know what they are talking about.'

James was delighted. 'Oh, Ruth. I'm glad you have finally come round to my way of thinking. I'm sure it's the right thing to do. I'm due to travel to London tomorrow; it will be an ideal opportunity to get in touch with Raymond.'

***

It was three weeks since the bounty hunters set up their headquarters at the Haven, the stable staff had become accustomed to them being around. No one was more pleased than Albert, who felt much more secure with their presence. Although the staff had been requested not to discuss their presence there, it was impossible to keep such information from doing the rounds. It was hoped such news wouldn't reach the ears of the Stockwell brothers.

The rain continued to fall steadily, varying between an intense deluge to moderate, then light drizzle. It was after midnight; the Red Fox had almost emptied its customers, except for a few remaining stragglers, who had no choice in their reluctance to brave the adverse weather conditions. Two shadowy figures huddled in a shop doorway, observing the late night revellers.

'Ben, this is madness,' hissed Peter Stockwell to his brother, 'we shouldn't have hidden the horses in the forest.'

Ben growled back at him, 'Quiet, we have more chance at the stables without them.'

Peter mumbled, 'I don't like it.'

Ben replied, 'The stable hands are so relaxed, we can creep in there without anyone knowing. Just think of that nice dry straw, and a good night's sleep.'

Whenever the street cleared, the pair moved nearer to the hotel, but soon disappeared back into the shadows, when two more drunkards appeared. Peter gripped his brother's arm, and stared wide-eyed at these latest two.

'Those two are bounty hunters,' he quietly hissed.

Ben whispered back, 'Are you sure?'

Peter was most agitated. 'Of course I am,' he could not help but to raise his voice, 'I recognise that one with the rasping voice.'

This caused Ben to urge caution, 'Shh, keep your voice down, they will hear you.'

Much to their amazement, they followed the progress of the pair to the hotel, where they vanished into the stables.

Peter asked anxiously, 'Ben, what do you suppose they are doing here?'

Ben narrowed his eyes. 'I reckon they are intent on giving us a surprise, little brother. They know of our previous visit, and rightly guessed that sometime we would come back.'

Peter's jaw dropped and, open-mouthed, he stared at his brother. Then Peter summed up his thoughts with, 'We can't stay the night here, then?'

Ben agreed, 'Oh no, we won't be staying the night here, but we can give them something to think about.'

***

Mrs Ellis had been left in charge of the hotel in the absence of James and Ruth, who had been gone for the past two days now. Her niece would have undergone her operation by now she thought, as a gnawing feeling of unease crept through her entire body. The hotel only had a couple of guests at the moment, and Mrs Ellis took her temporary post as manager very seriously. She slept in a small ante-room, behind the reception desk, so as to be on call immediately should she be wanted. She had kept herself busy all day, trying to occupy her mind with anything to stop her thinking of her niece. Now, in the early hours of the morning, she wrestled between trying to sleep to ease her troubled mind over her tired body.

Someone was shouting outside, she wondered what on earth was going on, and heard the front door noisily open, then a shout – 'Mrs Ellis!'. *That's Albert shouting*, she thought, and she was out of the ante-room as Albert reached the reception desk and garbled, 'The stable's on fire.'

She had to calm young Albert down, 'Don't panic, Albert,' she ordered. Her mind was racing.

In his agitated state Albert told her, 'It's them Stockwells again.'

Mrs Ellis said, 'Right, go straight down to the police station; tell them what happened.'

Before he reached the door, Mrs Ellis shouted, 'And tell them we need as many hands as possible to fight this fire!'

There was frenzied activity as a human chain was formed, to pass buckets of water to the fire. However it was plain to see this was a deliberate act of arson, as there were several different locations of fire. The fire-fighters toiled relentlessly; as more helpers joined their ranks, the flames were eventually extinguished.

Ray Mitchell was keen to question Albert, who claimed to have seen the Stockwell brothers.

'Are you sure it was definitely them, Albert, you're quite sure?'

Albert nodded his head as he confirmed, 'There's no doubt about it. As soon as they finished throwing the lamps into the stables, they ran off. I stayed well hidden till they were gone, I didn't want to be attacked again.'

After the fires were extinguished and the stables declared safe, the fire-fighters automatically turned their attention to a clean-up operation. Horses that had been led out to safety were being comforted as they were brought back to their stalls. Among them

Arthur Fletcher was tussling with his three hounds to get them under his control.

Ray Mitchell told him, 'You can get the dogs onto their trail at first light, Arthur.'

Joe Andrews asked the question, 'They obviously knew of our presence here; how the devil are they getting their information?' Little did he know, it was his distinctive, gravel-like voice that gave them away.

At the break of dawn a posse was up and ready to go. The hounds had no trouble in picking up the scent, which led them to a spot in the forest where the outlaws' horses had been hidden. However it quickly dawned on them that it was once more a hopeless cause, as the hounds soon lost the scent. It was apparent the Stockwell brothers would be well clear of the county yet again.

***

Surgeon Raymond Hartley had finished straightening Ruth's legs. With a nod of his head, he indicated his satisfaction as the last stitches were in place. He then left his team of nurses to complete the procedure and have the patient delivered to the recovery room. James waited outside; his long vigil was now over. He was relieved to see a smile on Raymond's face, which told him the operation went according to plan. But he was warned, 'As far as we know, all is well; however, only time will tell if we have succeeded in a remedy for Ruth.'

Raymond Hartley was fast making a name for himself, he was at the forefront of his profession carrying out unheard of procedures. James was happy with the arrangements his mother had made in caring for Ruth. She had insisted Ruth stay with her during the recovery process. The surgeon called twice a week to check on the alignment of her feet.

He told her, 'Everything seems to be going along nicely, Ruth, now it's just a matter of time for you learn how to walk again. What are your feelings now it's all over?'

As Ruth eased a pillow behind her back for comfort, she winced a little as she replied, 'I'm pleased it's all over and done with. The pain has been horrendous, but I have no regrets.'

***

James had been away from the hotel for a considerable length of time when he was given the full details of the arson attack; he was horrified. He called the bounty hunters together, for an informal chat.

He queried past events with Ray saying, 'I thought in the event of the Stockwells returning, your presence would be a complete surprise. What happened?'

Ray found it most embarrassing, 'We assumed that everyone had turned against the Stockwells; we are at a loss as to how they are getting their information.'

James turned his attention to Arthur Fletcher. 'I don't understand how, on two previous occasions, your dogs lost the scent, Arthur. What's going on there?'

Arthur was fiercely protective of his dogs, often boasting of their tracking abilities. 'Well sir, all I can say is that these two criminals have been incredibly lucky. Twice nature has been on their side, if it wasn't rain, then time would eliminate any trace they left, a scent trail doesn't last forever, you know.'

It seemed to James that something wasn't quite right, but he could not positively put his finger on it, leaving him mystified. There was an ominous silence, which left everyone nonplussed.

He then announced, 'All right, that's all for now. Can you all leave? I need to speak to Ray in private.'

They all obediently filed out of the room as James said, 'Thank you.' Ray took a deep breath as he wondered what James was thinking. The silence continued moments after they had all left, leaving Ray more confused than ever.

Ray broke the silence, he could not wait any longer for James to get whatever it was off his chest.

'I understand how frustrated you must be, sir, having invested so heavily to eradicate the menace of the Stockwells.'

James was quick to respond, 'No you don't, Ray. Something doesn't add up here.'

Ray cowered inwardly as the piercing eyes bore deep into his very soul. 'I have hired the best of the best, but all to no avail. How long have you known your crew?'

Ray now knew where James was coming from. 'Wait a moment, sir. I've known David and Joe for years now, they are the best of the best, as you put it.'

James followed up instantly with, 'And Arthur? How long have you known him?'

Ray felt his throat constrict as he answered, 'Not as long as the others.'

James frowned, then enquired, 'Where is he from?'

It was becoming apparent James mistrusted the dog handler. 'Right here in South Downesmere. What are you suggesting, Mr Williams?'

James answered, 'There are too many near misses where he is concerned to make it coincidental. Leave it with me, Ray, I need to find out more about Arthur Fletcher.'

James's next move was to contact his close friend, the chief constable.

Having explained his concern about the dog handler, he asked, 'One of your officers is the perfect man to assist me. Can I use him, Henry?'

The chief constable was only too glad to be of help, 'Of course you can, James. Who is he?'

James replied, 'It's Constable Christopher Ellis; he is related to Mrs Ellis, my assistant manager at the hotel. If anyone knows about Arthur Fletcher, Christopher is our man.'

The chief told James that Constable Ellis was due on duty that very evening, 'If you want to pop in to the station later, I'm sure he will accommodate you.'

Before James left the hotel that evening, he asked Ray to keep quiet about the suspicions he had regarding Arthur Fletcher. At the police station, James was not prepared to hear what Constable Ellis had to tell him. The constable was amazed at the insinuations that James was making.

'I'm most shocked, that you think the dog handler is in some way helping the Stockwell brothers. He happens to be related to the Harrison family; he is well known for his views on the Stockwell brothers, after they murdered Jill Harrison. Why would he help them? It doesn't make sense.'

James listened, dumbfounded, to what Christopher Ellis had to tell him, then he replied, 'I had no idea of his connections in the town, and that he was related to Jill Harrison. You're right, of course, my assumptions are rather absurd.'

***

Ruth Harper sat in her wheelchair, looking out over Ludgate Hill. She was bored at being confined indoors as she became stronger using her legs.

James's mother, Mary, who was caring for her, sensed her unease as she enquired, 'How are we this morning Ruth, how do you feel?'

Ruth twisted round in her chair, 'I'm fine, Mary, thank you.'

Mary wasn't fooled by Ruth hiding her true feelings. 'You must be getting frustrated, being stuck inside all day long in that chair?'

Ruth accepted she was fooling no one. 'Oh, you know, I think it's time I went home now and began looking after the hotel once more. It's time I started earning my keep.'

Mary fully understood Ruth's feelings. 'I don't think James is bothered about how long your convalescence is taking. I'm expecting him to call tomorrow; no doubt he will be making travel arrangements for you. Something to look forward to, dear.'

Ruth smiled. 'Yes it is, but I don't want you to feel I'm ungrateful, Mary. I don't think I will ever be able to repay either you or James.'

It was a happy day for Mrs Ellis. She was delighted to see her niece back safely, but truthfully she was glad to hand back the responsibility of the hotel into Ruth's hands once more. Ruth still needed assistance, but was becoming more independent as time went by. Then James received an urgent message from Constable Christopher Ellis, who needed to see him immediately. James was curious at the urgency, so lost no time in getting to the police station.

James was ushered into an interview room to be joined by Constable Ellis, who told him, 'After our meeting discussing Arthur Fletcher's integrity, I became aware of some peculiar activity concerning his strange behaviour. I thought it might interest you. It was because of your original concerns that got me involved in probing into Arthur Fletcher's life, and I found some interesting facts emerging. It has been a long known fact that he mixes with undesirable types, however it was not thought unusual, as it was assumed it was to do with his police work. Even when he invested heavily to acquire his bloodhounds, no one thought to question where the finance came from. This is something I would like to follow up.'

What James was hearing rekindled the original doubts he reluctantly had to suppress. He listened intently as Constable Ellis declared his suspicions, and ended his preamble with a question.

'What made you doubt Arthur Fletcher?'

James's original thoughts came flooding back as he recalled his earlier doubts. 'I began to try to fathom the reason why it was becoming increasingly difficult to bring to an end the Stockwells' reign of terror. At first they had the help of the Tolpuddle Martyrs behind them. Then public opinion turned against them when they crossed the line of human decency and resorted to murder. After that it was only a matter of time for them to be captured. When this didn't happen I examined the last two encounters to find on both occasions that Arthur Fletcher was involved. I'm sure he deliberately ended both these hunts. I am well aware he has denounced these two outlaws as cold-blooded, evil murderers, but I am unclear as to what his true motives are.'

Constable Ellis slowly shook his head, then asked, 'Do you think we ought to bring him in for questioning?'

James took a deep breath and slowly exhaled, he then replied, 'Whatever you charge him with, he will only deny it. I think we will be better off keeping all this under our hats for the time being, while also keeping a close eye on him.'

Constable Ellis was clearly as exasperated as James by it all. 'All right, we will remain tight-lipped for the time being, but I'm duty bound to report to the chief constable.'

James stood up and shook the constable's hand, 'Yes, of course. I understand; we will keep in touch.'

At the hotel, James crossed the lobby towards the reception desk and noticed Ruth gingerly descending the stairway. Just lately she had dispensed with her wheelchair, and today was her first visit to the upper floors. James stepped forward to assist her on the last two steps.

'Ruth, you don't have to be going up and down stairs. You're pushing too hard.'

It was the wrong thing for him to have said, as it provoked an angry glare from Ruth, as she replied, 'As manager it is my job to inspect the premises, making sure it is fit for our clients.'

James attempted to justify his comments by saying, 'I'm fully aware of that, but why can't your aunt do all that on your behalf?'

Quick as a flash, Ruth retorted, 'Because I'm the manager, that's why.'

Then James thought, *If my comments are spurring Ruth on to the road to recovery, then, as long as she is careful, it's no bad thing.*

Ruth gratefully sat down, as Ray walked into reception.

'Ah James, the very man. Can you spare a moment, in private?'

James opened the office door and indicated for Ray to enter.

Once they were seated, he enquired, 'Good morning, Ray. What can I do for you?' James detected a slight frown, and surmised it wasn't going to be good news.

'That little problem we discussed concerning Arthur Fletcher, I'm afraid someone has let the cat out of the bag. The lads are freely discussing it; I don't know how it's become general knowledge, but it's no longer a secret.'

James raised his eyebrows in mock surprise. 'Not to worry, Ray, it may work to our advantage.'

Ray was taken aback at James's cavalier attitude. 'How so?' he questioned.

James narrowed his eyes. 'Let's just wait and see what happens. I'm curious to know how Arthur will react when the rumours get round to him.'

Ray was at a loss over the whole affair. 'Well, it's obvious he will only deny everything.'

James displayed a slight smile. 'If we keep silent, he will wonder what we are thinking, and, owing to the uncertainty, it may force him to make a fatal error.'

Ray wanted advice. 'How should I react, if he mentions anything to me?'

James kept his smile, 'That would be perfect: make him believe you have heard the rumours and that you don't believe a word of them, and then advise him to come and see me.'

Ray accepted James's advice, with a nod of his head. 'Right, let's see what happens.'

James rose indicating their discussion was at an end. 'It's important we wait for a reaction from him. Don't lose your nerve, Ray; this is one big conundrum I'd like answers to.'

19

Morgan's Demise

Over the next few days, James's strategy of waiting for a reaction from Arthur Fletcher took a dramatic turn for the worse. While he was happy to wait it out, Henry Oaks wasn't. After his reading Constable Ellis's report, Arthur Fletcher was hauled in for questioning. Needless to say he denied all the charges put to him. James believed it was a mistake making the first move, and told the chief constable so.

Henry Oaks defended his actions when he told James: 'We cannot have this fellow going round as if nothing was wrong, he must answer to these allegations made against him.'

James could not accept the chief constable's decision. 'Don't you see? It was a foregone conclusion. He's done exactly what we knew he would do. What do you intend to do with him now?'

The chief constable stood his ground. 'He will be detained for further questioning, till we get some reasonable answers.'

It was a stalemate situation between the two, on which they both agreed to disagree. James asked if he could be present when Arthur Fletcher was next interviewed that evening, to which consent was granted.

At the hotel, Ray and his team waited anxiously for James to return. They had many issues to put to him. On his return, James was overwhelmed by a torrent of questions, he could not answer. Tensions were high between the trio.

David Brown forced his voice above that of Joe Andrews, 'What can you tell us of Fletcher?'

James speedily retorted, 'It's too early to say as yet. I'll let you know after this interview, when we will hopefully know more of his motives.'

Ray indicated he should accompany James at the interview, to which James replied, 'I don't think that's going to happen, Ray; we have already decided Constable Ellis and I will be the only two present in the room during the interrogation. The chief constable decided a host of people facing Fletcher would be too intimidating, and might cause him to clam up.'

As the sun set that evening, James made his way to the police station, where he was shown into the interview room. He had not long to wait before Arthur was shown in under escort.

He immediately started to profess his innocence. 'It's all lie's, Mr Williams.'

James raised his hands in an effort to silence him. This only caused Arthur to raise his voice, 'I have more reason to want the capture of the Stockwell brothers than anyone else. I have pledged to my aunt and uncle that I would bring them in to answer for their crimes.'

Arthur could see James wanted to hear all this in the presence of Constable Ellis, but still he carried on, 'It was my cousin they murdered.'

James intervened once more, 'Please wait, Arthur, until Constable Ellis arrives; he has certain allegations to put to you.'

Arthur kept on talking, 'Allegations!' he exploded. 'All trumped up lies by people trying to besmirch my good name, where's the proof?'

His rant was brought to a halt when Constable Ellis entered the room. Arthur just stared at the constable as he drew his chair nearer to the table and withdrew a sheet of paper from a folder. Arthur remained silent as the constable acknowledged James. At the sight of the uniformed constable, Arthur seemed subdued and kept silent, as he waited for the questioning to begin.

James studied Arthur's reactions, and thought he must be wondering what evidence have they got, if any.

Constable Ellis started his questions with, 'You are no doubt aware of the allegations being made against you?'

Arthur hotly replied, 'And that's all they are: allegations.'

James stepped in at this stage, 'After months of harassment from the Stockwell brothers, I brought in Ray Mitchell and his team – a bounty hunter with an impeccable past record – to deal with my problem, once and for all. Now, several months later, I agreed that he hire you, with your dogs. According to statistics, with the scheme we had in place, they should have been apprehended by now. On looking at the last two encounters, when they ought to have been caught, I find the weak link is you.'

Arthur was most uncomfortable and visibly shaken, with his voice raised he replied, 'The dogs lost the scent; it's as simple as that.'

James was quick to point out, 'Once I could accept, but twice is too much of a coincidence.' There was a moment of silence.

Constable Ellis wanted to know where Arthur got the money to purchase his dogs – that was the one question that nagged at him the most.

'Arthur, after your cousin was murdered, you pledged to your aunt and uncle to do all in your power to catch the culprits.'

Arthur returned the constable's hostile stare, and answered, 'Of course.'

He maintained his stare of disbelief, as the next question was put to him, 'You then purchased your specialised bloodhounds to aid you in your mission.'

The interview became like a game of tennis, as Arthur returned the volley with, 'Absolutely.'

Arthur didn't see the next one coming, 'Where did the money come from, Arthur? Animals of this pedigree don't come cheaply.'

Arthur struggled to answer. 'It was money I'd saved,' he reluctantly got out.

Constable Ellis exchanged glances with James before he asked, 'As I understand, you were a farm labourer, working for Farmer Green, before becoming a bounty hunter?'

Arthur remained silent, and just stared back. Constable Ellis followed up with, 'Where did the money come from?'

Arthur's silence was his answer. James leaned forward placing his elbows on the table, and forcefully asked, 'Did you steal the money?'

Arthur was incensed, and quick to defend himself, as he barked back, 'No! I did not.'

James kept his calm posture, 'You must realise this is a sizeable amount of money; money you could not have earned as a worker in the fields. Someone helped you – who?'

Arthur maintained his dumb demeanour, which prompted the constable to warn him, 'By your dumb insolence, you are incriminating yourself, which means we will hold you till we get satisfactory answers.'

James tried once more, 'Come on, Arthur, you must know you are in big trouble here. You could be charged with aiding and abetting.'

Arthur looked across the table at both men with a pained expression, then averted his gaze to the floor. Exasperated Constable Ellis rammed his paperwork back into the folder, and shouted for the guard, 'That's all for now.' He instructed the jailer, 'Take him back to the cell.'

Arthur looked back at James as he was escorted out of the

room, as if appealing for mercy. James could only shake his head in disbelief.

At the hotel James relayed the events that had been played out at the police station, much to the astonishment of Ray and his team. In the room Mrs Ellis was busy clearing away the teacups and enquired, 'Will Mr Fletcher be with us for breakfast in the morning?'

James was beginning to get bored, explaining to everyone and answered, 'No he will not, Mrs Ellis.' Then he noticed the puzzled look on her face, and added, 'Mr Mitchell will answer any questions you may have. By the way, Mrs Ellis, are you related to Constable Ellis who's heading this case against Arthur Fletcher?'

She replied, 'That's right, sir. He's my cousin.'

Mrs Ellis, although curious about what was going on, knew she would get more information from Ray Mitchell than her cousin Christopher. He would never talk about what he was doing or anything to do with police work.

In the darkened cell that night, Arthur Fletcher tried to rest, but, owing to the cold, he could not sleep. He drew his knees up to his chin and wrapped his arms around his legs. His mind was in a turmoil and sleep was impossible. He rocked backwards and forwards, contemplating his present dilemma. He had to stick to his story, make them believe the dogs had lost the scent, if they knew the real reason, it would ruin everything. That infernal Constable Ellis was so persistent in finding out who it was that financed him, it was paramount to keep him anonymous. *James Williams seemed a reasonable sort, if I could talk to him, maybe it would buy me some time.*

At the break of dawn, a constable brought Arthur a welcome mug of tea, and a thick wedge of bread. The officer informed him, 'You will be in the interview room in half an hour.' Arthur turned his thoughts over in his mind, reminding himself to stick by his story, that the dogs had lost the scent. It was most important not to reveal his benefactor, when that crops up, that's the time to ask to speak to James Williams – it could save some embarrassment.

At the hotel after breakfast, James received an urgent plea to go at once to the police station; once there he was brought up to date with the latest developments.

Constable Ellis asked, 'Would you speak to Fletcher alone? He seems to think you will be able to help him in some way.'

The constable led James along the corridor, James followed, confused. 'How can I help him?' he enquired.

Constable Ellis replied, 'Search me. He told me he would speak to you and no one else.'

James took a seat at a table facing an empty chair, and waited until the prisoner was escorted in. Arthur was handcuffed and ordered to sit; then they were left alone. Arthur averted his gaze and remained silent, so it was left to James to commence the dialogue.

'Well, Arthur, how is it I can help?'

After a brief pause, Arthur cleared his throat, 'When you asked me if I had stolen the money to buy my dogs, I was horrified. I want you to understand, I am not a thief.'

James was impressed, and asked, 'Where did the money come from, then?'

Arthur felt a little more at ease, and confided, 'What I am about to tell you is between you and me.'

James stiffened, and was quick to inform Arthur, 'I'll have to stop you there. I have to report to the chief constable the outcome of this discussion. If I withhold anything, I will be regarded as flouting the law, and I will be as guilty of the same charges as yourself.'

Arthur's pained expression conveyed the stress he was undergoing. 'I was prepared to reveal all, but it is imperative my benefactor remains anonymous.'

James probed further, 'So you admit there is someone out there who funded you, but you are not about to reveal his identity?'

Arthur anxiously wrung his hands in despair as he said, 'Owing to the nature of your involvement, all I'm prepared to tell you is the person in question wants to settle a score with the Stockwells and recruited me to try and arrange a confrontation with them. With the dogs I was able to join the hunt at close quarters. You of course were quite right, on the last two encounters I held back the dogs, as the person in question wasn't available at that time.'

James was enlightened and relieved that Arthur wasn't in league with the outlaws; he was obviously concerned about his dogs.

'Are my dogs all right?' he asked.

James convinced him they were being well cared for. 'I have plans for them, be assured they will be well looked after.'

The chief constable was pleased that James had secured a little more information from their prisoner. They were now able to hold Arthur on lesser charges. But he would not be going free for some time: he would have to answer to the charge of obstructing the police and withholding information. The chief constable was curious to know what plan James had for the hounds.

James told him, 'I would like my security guards, Toby Green, and Tommy Atkins, in charge of two of them. One for my foundry in London, one for the sawmill here in South Downesmere, and the third to be based at the hotel, on standby with the bounty hunters.'

The chief constable was impressed, 'You certainly seem to have an excellent plan, James, well done. I'm sure your security men will adapt to being dog handlers. Who will take on that role at the hotel?'

James smiled as he replied, 'I have the very person in mind; I will have to approach him first to find out if he will agree.'

James made his way to the blacksmith's shop. The clang of the hammer on anvil rang out, telling him Luke Armstrong was toiling at his trade. As James stepped inside, he shouted, 'Hello' timing his shout to coincide between the ringing tones of the hammer. The melodic rhythm abruptly ceased and Luke grinned as he downed tools to wipe his hands on a rag, before offering his hand of friendship.

'Hello, Mr Williams, what can I do for you, sir?'

James felt the strength of his grip as he answered, 'I have a favour to ask, Luke. How's that apprentice of yours doing?'

Luke rested his arm against the wall. 'He's doing all right. He's a good lad. When we're not busy, I leave him to amuse himself any way he pleases. That means he will be out back with Charlie; he's horse mad, that lad.'

James got straight to the point, 'You will no doubt have heard the gossip about Arthur Fletcher being held at the police station?'

Luke immediately took on an air of intense seriousness. 'Yes, sir, I hear he is in league with those Stockwell boys.'

James hastily corrected him, 'Well, no,. he is not. For them it's a complicated matter, which will take some time to be resolved. The point is I'm taking charge of his three hounds, and I'm looking for a handler for one of them at the hotel, to work with the bounty hunters. I thought young Stan, with his love of animals, would be ideal – that is, with your consent, of course.'

Luke wiped the rag across his forehead, in surprise. 'Well I must admit, this has come out of the blue. Will he be now working in law enforcement?'

James explained, 'No, not really. He will carry on his normal duties here, but be ready on standby when the time comes.'

Luke seemed to breathe a sigh of relief, 'If the boy agrees, I would be happy with that arrangement. To be honest with you, I wouldn't like to lose him, I've come to regard him as a son.'

James replied, 'Splendid. Have a word with him and, if he agrees, tell him to meet me at the hotel this evening where he can see the hounds.'

After tea at the hotel that evening, James was informed that Stan Heslop was there to see him.

'Oh good,' he exclaimed, as he hurried to the reception area. Stan had never been in a hotel before and stood overawed at the grand opulence around him. James's voice behind him made him focus away from this fantasy world.

'Stan, good to see you. Come into my office.'

Stan followed James and sat in the offered chair.

James asked Stan, 'I assume Luke has explained the situation to you?'

Stan nervously faltered a little. 'Yes, sir, I used to have a dog, but I know nothing of bloodhounds. I don't know if I will be suitable to take on such a task.'

James could see Stan was extremely nervous, and tried to put him at ease. 'Oh I'm sure you're capable, Stan. You will soon pick up the finer points of this breed. I've seen that horse of yours, who is very cantankerous, yet you've got his measure.'

Stan shuffled uneasily in his chair, 'Yes sir, but a bloodhound is entirely different.'

James wanted Stan to relax and make a sensible decision. 'Let me show you the hounds, Stan. Come and meet them.'

Out in the stables, the hounds were being kept in a stall. Stan was astonished at their massive size. James suggested he spend a little time with them, to get to know them better. Stan was told one of them was destined to be established at the sawmill, another was to go to Mr William's foundry in London, and if he accepted the offer he could have the pick of the bunch.

James told Stan, 'How about I leave you for a while, for you to get acquainted, I'll see you in about half an hour?' Stan merely stared at the beasts, and just nodded in silence. When he went in among the dogs, they were inquisitive sniffing at his legs, and circling him. He reached out and stroked the animals as they came within touching distance. Feeling more at ease, he then started talking to them, like he did when he first met Charlie. They continued their interest, he then commanded them to sit, which stopped them in their tracks, as if they were ready to obey, but remained uncertain.

He reasoned they must have heard that command before, and reached in his pocket to feel the lumps of sugar he used to bribe Charlie. With a lump of sugar in his hand, in plain view, he then commanded in a more forceful voice for them to sit. One of them did and was given the treat. Several more commands saw the same dog obeying, while the other two surveyed the scene with doleful looks. From then on he gave his full attention to that one dog; then, holding his collar, led him out of the stall.

With another sugar lump in his hand, he commanded the dog to sit in the stable yard and walked away. After a number of yards were between them, he turned around; the dog was still obediently sitting with his eyes intently on the sugar lump until Stan gave the command, 'Come'. The dog rapidly came at him to claim his prize.

Stan was still engrossed in his interaction with the hound when James turned up to ask, 'Well, Stan, what do you think?'

Stan had lost his inhibitions, and was obviously enjoying himself. He exclaimed, 'Of the three, I would choose this one,' as he stroked the animal's head. 'He appears to be the most intelligent of the group.'

Stan then asked, 'Will he have to stay here at the stables?'

James replied, 'Oh, no. It would make more sense for the two of you to be together fulltime.'

Stan's face lit up in a radiant smile. 'When do I start?' he asked.

James was happy to inform him, 'You can take him home right now. I'll be in touch to see how you're getting on.'

The following day, James called a meeting with the bounty hunters, where he brought everyone up to date with the latest news. There was some surprise when they learned the apprentice blacksmith had taken up the dog handler's role.

James told them, 'If Stan should be with you when you apprehend the Stockwells, he will qualify for an equal share of the bounty money.'

Ray questioned this, 'But he's only a boy, Mr Williams, are you sure he's up to this?'

James defended his judgement, 'He's only a boy, Ray, but he has an exceptional way with animals. I guarantee you will be amazed when you see what he can do.'

After Stan had had the dog for a couple of nights and a full day, James paid a visit to the blacksmith's shop. Luke had dismantled the bellows, from the forge, and was doing a spot of maintenance. He welcomed James with a cheery smile.

'Hello Mr Williams, come to check on your dog handler?'

James apologised for holding him up, 'I don't want to be a nuisance, Luke. How is Stan doing?'

Luke didn't mind the intrusion one little bit, 'You're always welcome here, sir, we're not busy at the moment.' With a nod of his head, Luke indicated the stable, 'You know Stan, he's out back with his beloved animals. He's a capable lad; I swear Charlie and that hound understand every word he says. He's named the dog Morgan, after his favourite school teacher.'

It amused James, who reflected, 'Really? I remember old Morgan Wilson. He spent a lifetime at that school allegedly. I believe he's retired now.'

Luke confirmed he had, then invited James to go out back to see Stan.

As James went into the stable, his first sight was of the hound, who turned his head to see who was entering, then instantly turned back to observe Stan putting Charlie's bridle on.

'Oh, hello, Mr Williams. I was wondering when you would call.'

James was impressed by Stan's prowess over these animals. 'How are you managing, Stan? You certainly appear to have the hound's undivided attention.'

Stan walked over to the dog, and fondled the large floppy ears, as he said, 'Yeah, he's an intelligent animal. Yesterday I took him out with Charlie; he stuck with us like glue. I have renamed him Morgan.'

James established he knew the story. 'So I hear, named after your old school master.'

Stan said, 'He's so wise, it was an obvious choice. You don't mind do you, sir?'

James exclaimed, 'Phaw, not at all, Stan. I suppose he already had a name, but to be quite truthful I never knew it. He's your dog now.'

James wanted to know how far Stan had got tracking with the dog.

'Have you tried tracking with him yet?'

Stan smiled. 'He doesn't need to be shown anything about tracking, I started by hiding a lump of sugar; he located it in double quick time. Then I hid Luke's waistcoat in the woods, and after letting him sniff one of Luke's sweat rags he was immediately on the trail, and found the hidden coat. He's a natural and doesn't need training.'

James was pleased with their progress. 'I think it's time you joined up with the bounty hunters and show them what you can do.'

On his first day with the bounty hunters, Stan was overawed amongst the rough and ready, self-appointed officers of the law. It soon became apparent to the bounty hunters that Stan was indeed a competent dog handler. They persuaded Luke to allow Stan to ride with them on Charlie. James watched as they headed out on their first mission. Stan was the odd one out as he rode bareback, with Morgan trotting by his side. James resolved to make the lad feel more like his colleagues by providing him with his very own saddle. Over time Stan got to know Ray and his men, and eventually they were ready as a bonded team.

James kept a close watch on everyone over the following days and detected a change in Luke's attitude towards him. Luke had a problem, which he proposed to remedy immediately.

After Stan had joined with the bounty hunters for the day, James called on Luke, and asked, 'Is something bothering you, Luke?'

The blacksmith made eye contact, and answered, 'Aye, there is. I'm not at all happy with young Stan riding with those bounty hunters.'

James was surprised. 'I thought you were OK with that arrangement, when you consented for him to use your horse.'

Luke was struggling to make his feelings known. 'I was initially, but the time will come when they hunt the outlaws for real. I don't like the idea of the lad putting himself in danger.'

James wanted to convince Luke. 'I wouldn't worry too much, Luke. Ray and his men think highly of Stan; they won't allow any harm to come to him.'

Luke continued to convey his feelings, and said, without rancour, 'Shortly after I took Stan on, he lived alone with his mother. He was so keen he would often sleep here in the forge. His mother was happy with that, as I promised to look after the lad. He lost his mother last year, so this is his home now, right here. I've come to regard him as the son I never had.'

James nodded wistfully. 'I don't know what to say, Luke, but I understand.'

That day when the bounty hunters returned home, James was waiting for them. 'I want to discuss an issue with you all,' James told them, 'you too, Stan – it concerns you.'

The group were mystified as to what the issue might be, and

listened intently to what James had to say. Ray and his team were shocked and disappointed at the thought they might lose their dog handler, and Stan was horrified at the prospect that he may have to end his days with the group.

Stan pleaded with James: 'Please Mr Williams let me talk to Luke. I'm sure I can make him change his mind.'

James could see how keen Stan was to remain within the group. 'It's not me who wants to stop you, Stan, but if Luke isn't happy, we cannot go against his wishes.'

Stan's eyes were moist with emotion as he jumped back onto Charlie. As he rode away, he shouted, 'Leave it to me!'

Charlie galloped down the high street, urged on by Stan, until they arrived at the blacksmith's shop. Luke was startled as Stan rushed into the forge, followed by Morgan.

'Mr Williams has just told me you object to me working with the bounty hunters.' Stan's voice cracked, as he asked, 'Why?'

Luke had never witnessed Stan behaving in such a manner before, and he certainly had never been spoken to like that before.

Luke kept his voice low, and in his quiet way said, 'Stan, lad, I think it's too dangerous. You're putting your life at risk.'

Stan's emotions were running high. 'That's for me to decide, Luke. Don't treat me like a child – you're not my father.'

It was like a knife going through Luke's heart; it pained him to see Stan going through such turmoil.

'The truth of the matter, Stan, is I made a solemn promise to your mother to take care of you. How do you think she would react if she were here now?'

Stan maintained his defiant attitude. 'Luke, I'm not a child. I'm old enough to look after myself. I know you have the power to stop me: it's your horse and your premises, I own nothing. Mr Williams makes out Morgan belongs to me, but realistically he is a valuable dog of a very special breed. I'm not a fool, even the saddle I use was given to me – I never earned it.'

Luke noticed the determination on Stan's face and tried to show him he objected out of love for him.

'Mr Williams saw something was bothering me, and I told him I wasn't happy that you were putting yourself in danger. I'm still not happy, but the last thing I want is to alienate myself against you.'

Stan was aware Luke was genuinely concerned for him, and flung his arms around him. 'Oh, Luke, this is something that means so much to me. I'm sorry for speaking so disrespectfully to you.'

The big man's heart melted as he returned the boy's hug and silently thought, *You're such a child, in this wicked world*. He then said, 'I'm not stopping you from doing anything, Stan; you are your own man, but please, for my sake be careful.'

The bounty hunters continued to receive reports of the Stockwells' activities, and followed every one of them up.

Ray told his men, 'It's only a matter of time when we will catch them.'

Today they were preparing to head out to investigate the latest report. It involved a farmer in the next county, alleging the theft of chickens, but he reported a spate of incidents over several days. This report led them to believe that they had become complacent and comfortable; they were becoming careless.

Joe Andrews had just finished loading his saddle bags, when Stan rode into the hotel stable yard. He rasped out, 'Morning, Stan. It's good to see you're still with us. Has Luke repented, then?'

Stan dismounted to give Morgan some attention and said, 'He hasn't changed his mind; it's just that he worries about me.'

David Brown spoke up, 'I'm glad he hasn't stopped you coming, you would have been missed.'

Stan grinned; he was beginning to feel part of the team.

***

240

Farmer Joseph Clarke, had just come out of his barn, when his attention was drawn to the road leading towards his farm, where a group of horsemen was approaching fast. He withdrew back into the shadows of the barn once more, uncertain as to their intentions. It was not until he heard their leader telling his men to stay mounted until he found the landowener that he felt safe enough to show himself.

Ray asked if he was Farmer Clarke, and he confirmed that he was.

'You reported your hens being stolen?'

The farmer scathingly replied, 'Not only my hens: they cleaned out all the eggs as well; they helped themselves to milk and whatever else took their fancy. This has been going on over a number of days, but I never caught sight of them.'

Ray demanded, 'Show us where you kept your hens.'

Stan, along with Morgan, was the first to follow the farmer. The hound was intensely excited as he sniffed around the buildings.

Stan told Ray, 'It looks like he may have been on this scent before. Look at him go.'

Ray also was beginning to feel excited, with adrenaline coursing through his veins, he told Stan, 'Just let him do his own thing; get mounted and ready to follow.'

And so the hunt began.

Soon the team were following the hound – who picked up a fast pace – over open ground. Stan urged Charlie onward and into the cover of a wooded area. The rest of the bounty hunters were struggling to keep up. Onward through the trees and undergrowth they hurtled until Stan came upon Morgan sniffing around a campfire, in which the embers were still smouldering. The evidence was all around of a hasty retreat: cooking utensils and bedding rolls were scattered, all hurriedly left behind.

As the rest of the team caught up, Morgan was in hot pursuit once again, closely followed by Stan.

Ray shouted to David Brown, the last rider, to join them: 'David, keep up with the boy. Don't let him out of your sight.'

The team quickly regrouped, and resumed the chase. During his headlong dash to follow Stan, David Brown had great difficulty in keeping up.

Ben and Peter Stockwell were taken completely by surprise: they didn't even have time to saddle their horses. Now the bounty hunters were almost upon them; they had just crossed an open clearing and, at the other side, dismounted.

Ben snarled at his brother, 'We've got to take out that hound and the handler.'

As they lay in wait to form an ambush, Ben hissed at his brother Peter, 'You take the hound, I'll go for the handler.'

Ray was most anxious for his team, who were strung out behind in a long line; it was not the most favourable of scenarios. The crack of two gunshots rent the air and Ray's heartbeat almost stopped as he was filled with dread. He spurred his horse on to arrive at the clearing, and saw what he most dreaded.

David was kneeling by the inert Stan, and Morgan was lying in a motionless heap. One by one the rest of the team came into the clearing. Moments later, Stan groaned with the pain of the shot he had taken to the left side of his stomach. All thought of the chase was forgotten; their main concern was for Stan, as they crowded round him. They had to get him to a doctor quickly and stop the bleeding.

Ray watched as Joe Andrews bent over Morgan, their eyes met as Joe slowly shook his head. The magnificent beast had received a shot to the head; there was no hope for Morgan. As the pain in Stan's side intensified, his thoughts were for Morgan.

He looked at Ray, and asked, 'Where's Morgan, is he all right?'

Ray had never experienced such mixed emotions before; he

felt a lump in his throat and was unable to answer. It was as they got Stan back onto his horse that Stan saw the pathetic heap that was once Morgan. It pained Stan more as he took in the tragic scene; tears streamed down his face and he was inconsolable.

20

The Grey Horseman

Angela Dewhirst had recently completed a course as a nurse, and at seventeen she was determined to make a career in the profession to better herself. Having been brought up in the slums of the East End of London, she was no stranger to deprivation and poverty. She considered herself fortunate to have obtained a position with an engineering firm north of London. It meant she had to leave family and friends, but she knew it was the price she had to pay to better herself. Her new employers were forward-thinking and had installed a modern up-to-date clinic, with the wellbeing and welfare of their staff being paramount. She worked alongside a dedicated team of health workers under the leadership of a qualified doctor. She had settled in nicely, and enjoyed her work, and was able to send a little money to her mother.

Her main duties were assisting the staff who had sustained injuries related to heavy industry. The doctor in charge was most capable in dealing with injuries ranging from a cut finger to, in extreme cases, amputations. She got on well with everyone and today the doctor informed her that she had to present herself to the main office, where management wanted a word with her. She was curious why they wanted to see her and wondered if she had done something wrong. She was told to wait and was eventually shown into the boardroom; she had never seen such a long table with an elegant matching shine to it.

Sitting at the far end was none other than the owner, Mr Williams; she was at a total loss as to why he would want to see her.

'Ah, Nurse Dewhirst, come forward and take a seat.' He then added, 'No need to be nervous. How long have you been with us?'

She could see he had in front of him an open file and immediately thought, *He's asking questions he knows the answers to.*

She obediently replied, 'Six months, sir.'

James shuffled the papers, and rearranged them. 'Your superiors speak highly of you.' She remained silent, and didn't comment. 'I'm looking for someone with certain attributes, such as yourself. It says here that you passed a basic nursing qualification, which secured your position here.'

She wondered what this was leading up to. 'Yes, sir. That's right.'

James looked at the confident nurse and posed the question, 'We have a special patient, who requires special treatment. I'm looking for that special someone – could you be that someone?'

Angela perked up and excitedly said, 'I don't see why not.' James then told her, 'If you accept it means you will have to relocate elsewhere. How do you feel about that?'

As far as Angela was concerned, this altered everything, 'Where to?' she asked.

James suspected this might put her off. 'To one of my business locations, in a place called South Downesmere.'

She frowned, 'That will take me further away from my family and friends.'

James didn't want this to put her off. 'If it's the extra cost of travelling back home that's the problem, then I can assure you you will be well paid for your services.'

That's exactly what was on her mind, but she could tell the way the interview was going that the job was already hers for the taking. 'Well, yes sir, that did cross my mind,' she volunteered. *No need for her to appear too keen*, she thought. She may as well be there, as in North London.

James pressed her further, 'Should you accept, you will automatically qualify for a substantial wage increase, together with lucrative concessions.'

Deep inside she was jubilant, but said, 'Can I have a little time to think it over, sir?'

James told her, 'I must have your answer by morning, to be ready to travel with me tomorrow.'

Angela was excited as she packed her few meagre belongings that evening. She had already made up her mind to accept the position before leaving the boardroom. She would let James know of her decision when she reported for duty the following morning. James also had made his mind up about Angela: he was impressed by her positive attitude and was sure she would accept the offer he had made. After studying the notes in her portfolio and taking into account the short notice, he was certain it would be a foregone conclusion she would accept.

At the railway station Angela was helped into the carriage, and joined by James, along with two other men from the administration team.

James asked, 'Have you travelled by train before, Angela?'

She had never met the other two men, and was slightly flustered. 'No sir, I've never been out of London before now.'

The two men ignored them, and appeared to pore over some paperwork together. Here she was embarking on a new phase of her career, travelling to an unknown destination, to look after a special patient that she knew nothing about.

She felt more at ease as the other two men seemingly showed no interest in their fellow passengers whatsoever, and asked, 'Who is this special patient, sir? I know nothing of him.'

James, was apologetic, 'Oh, I'm terribly sorry, Nurse,' he mumbled, 'things happened in such a rush I seem to have overlooked that important item. The patient is a young boy suffering from a gunshot wound. He was part of a team of bounty hunters who were tracking a pair of outlaws when things got out of hand.' James swallowed hard. 'Truth of the matter is, I feel responsible in a way: I talked him into being part of the team, against his guardian's wishes.'

Angela was curious, 'How old is this boy?' she asked.

James thought for a moment, then replied, 'I should think he is about the same age as yourself.'

Angela raised her eyebrows in surprise. 'He seems terribly young to be mixed up in such a dangerous profession.'

James corrected her, 'Well, actually he is an apprentice blacksmith, with an unusual skill of handling animals. It's a long story, as you will find out.'

At the sawmill, Stan was being cared for at a medical centre, similar to the one at the foundry in London. Angela's room was right next to his, and she was ready to be called for at an instant's notice. Stan's condition was serious: he was going into and out of consciousness and was heavily drugged to relieve him of some of the pain. Angela could see the need for round the clock intensive care. During the day, a doctor was on hand and was on call during the night. In Stan's world of drifting in and out of reality, he was aware of someone new caring for him and through the haze got the imprint of a beautiful girl on his mind.

The bounty hunters took it in turns to visit Stan to see how he was getting on. It was from these men that Angela learned what had happened on that dreadful day of the shooting. When Joe Andrews visited, Angela was piecing the last bits of information together.

'How did you get Stan out of the woods and back here, considering the nature of his injuries?'

Joe croaked, 'We got him onto his horse, but his pain was so severe we had to get him down off his horse pretty quickly. David went back to the farm, and borrowed a cart, which we used to bring him home.'

Angela thought of a smelly farm cart, and grimaced.

The bounty hunters resumed their main task of hunting down the Stockwell brothers, and recruited Toby Green, who was now the dog handler located at the sawmill. The team missed Stan, but quickly got to know the new dog handler. As the outlaws had lost all their equipment in the last skirmish, reports were coming in of various thefts around the counties, suggesting that they had made good their loss and were back in business as before.

Going on the information received, the team followed up all leads and Ray began to notice a suspicious-looking character hanging about wherever they went. He didn't pay too much attention to him at first, thinking he was imagining it; however, on one of their missions, lasting two days, he noticed a horseman high up on the ridge, observing them. The mysterious figure caught his eye again further along the ridge: he wore a cloak and appeared to be stalking them. However, he reasoned it was too much of a coincidence and shared his suspicions of the grey figure with the rest of the team.

David Brown had a look of disbelief on his face.

'I'm telling you, David, at first I thought I was imagining it, but when I try to catch a glimpse of his face, he always manages to hide his identity.'

David said, 'OK, Ray, if you see him again, let us know we can round him up and ask him what he is up to.'

Ray, nodded his head, indicating the grey figure on the ridge, 'How about now then? There he is, up there.'

They all turned to look to the grey figure, who immediately turned his horse and vanished from view.

David said, 'Sorry boss, that did look suspicious. We will all have to keep our heads up and take a wider view of what's happening further afield.'

The grey figure was not seen any more that day.

***

Stan could hear his name being called; he was fighting his way through a thick fog.

'Stan, can you hear me?' Someone was shaking his shoulder, he could not understand where he was, this must be a dream he was thinking. It was a dream he didn't want to wake up from, he was more comfortable here. Then there was a violent shake.

'Stan, wake up.'

He forced his eyes open; it was that girl again. *Why is she doing this to me?* He felt his upper body being lifted and pillows being stacked up behind his head. He saw her a little more clearly. *She is beautiful*, he thought.

She is pushy, though.

He looked at her more clearly as she said, 'Come on, Stan. I've made you some porridge for breakfast. Eat this then you can go back to sleep again.'

It all came back to him as he felt the pain in his side, then the pain in his heart, for his dear friend Morgan.

She wiped away his tears as she asked, 'What is it, Stan? Why are you crying?'

Stan was thinking more clearly now. 'Who are you?'

Angela was pleased. This was a breakthrough: he was communicating. 'My name is Angela, I'm here to nurse you back to health.'

He continued to look at this angel at his bedside.

***

Since the team had been made aware of a grey horseman, shadowing their every move, Toby Green was even more diligent at observing his surroundings. It was as he was taking his bloodhound to the hotel that he spotted the shadowy figure and, like Ray, he never got the chance to see his face. It was near the hotel when the stalker took flight after realising his presence was compromised and he disappeared behind the buildings opposite. Toby hurried after him only to find the back lane deserted. It was plain to see the intruder was making sure his identity remained undiscovered. On his way back to the hotel something about the shadowy figure bothered him.

He informed the rest of the team of his encounter.

Ray said, 'Good for you for being alert, Toby. If he keeps this up, we are sure to eventually apprehend him.'

Toby agreed, 'Yes I think we will, but there is something about him which makes me believe I should know him.'

Joe commented, 'Did you see his face?'

Toby shook his head, 'No, but there is something which seems to be familiar. I just can't put my finger on it.'

His train of thought was interrupted by a young police constable rushing in to inform Ray that he was wanted at the station as soon as possible. That could only mean one thing: more information on the Stockwell brothers.

Ray left with the constable, saying, 'Get ready to move out. I'll be back shortly.'

The chief constable was waiting for Ray. 'News just in,' he told Ray, 'there's been an incident with the Stockwells over in the next county. They were chased through Anderson's gorge. Get moving now, you may be able to move in for the kill.'

Ray's heart started pounding at the news; without a word he hurried back to the hotel where his horse was ready saddled up for him.

**

Angela was preparing a meal for Stan when she heard that Toby had been called out with his dog. Gossip had it that the bounty hunters had a solid lead as to the whereabouts of the Stockwell brothers. Angela thought this is just the kind of stimulus Stan needs, whose health was rapidly improving day by day.

Stan said, 'I wish it was me going,' Angela rebuked him with an angry shake of her head. 'You're far too young to be getting mixed up with those murderers. Look what happened to you the last time.'

James called to see how Stan was, and the main topic of conversation was the hunt.

Angela said, 'What do you think of this silly boy, Mr Williams, wishing he was risking his life to be with the bounty hunters again?'

James smiled. 'I agree it's a terrible risk, but I totally understand how he feels, Nurse.'

Stan ignored the care Angela was showing. 'What do you make of reports of a grey horseman shadowing the team, sir?'

James frowned, 'It would appear this phantom is gaining inside information somehow. Perhaps he is Arthur Fletcher's mystery benefactor? There is so much we are not aware of, who knows?'

***

The team travelled through the night, and at the break of dawn, David Brown informed the team that he had spotted the grey horseman. Ray advised them to concentrate on the job in hand; they would deal with the infiltrator as and when the opportunity arose. On reaching the gorge, they occasionally passed other hunters, who were blindly searching for the fugitives, when the bloodhound showed favourable signs, similar to that of Morgan. It appeared likely he had come across this scent on previous hunts.

The hound picked up the pace, and Toby urged his horse on to keep up.

Ray shouted, 'Keep closely together. Don't lose sight of the man in front. Remember what happened to young Stan.'

The steep sides of the gorge eventually opened up, the scent led the hound up the left-hand side of the slope. The team kept together in a tight-knit formation and halted as the hound bolted into a cave.

Toby quickly dismounted with Ray at his side. 'Hold steady,' Ray ordered, 'don't go in there, we don't know where the network system of passages lead to.' Toby called the hound to heel, when the thunderous roar of a gunshot echoed from the cave, followed by a pitiful yelp from the hound.

Joe croaked, 'They're gunning for your dog, Toby.'

Toby called the dog to heel once more, and was relieved when the hound came crawling back to him with his tail between his legs. It was apparent the dog had received one almighty shock as the blast was directed at him. On closer inspection a nasty gash was revealed to his hind quarters, where the lead shot had grazed him.

Toby petted him, and in a soothing voice assured him, 'Only a flesh wound, fella. You'll be fine.'

Ray was aware of strangers joining them, attracted by the explosive sound of the gunshot from the cave. He had mixed feelings: partly jubilant, because here were the Stockwells trapped in a cave, and partly concerned that these men might try to claim the reward by capturing them. That last thought was not going to happen, he mused. He and his team would assert their authority most aggressively.

The number of men gathered around the cave entrance increased, much to the annoyance of Ray, who shouted, 'Keep down, if you don't want your heads blown off.'

This sent out a clear message about who was in charge.

Ray questioned a man nearby, 'Are you familiar with these caves?'

The man replied, 'Sort of, sir, they're a complex system.'

This worried Ray. 'Does that mean there are other exits and they might well escape?'

The man nodded, 'I'm not all that familiar with this system, but I imagine they could.' Just then a further explosive sound of a gunshot startled them, coming from their right.

Ray stood up and ordered the men around him. 'Everybody stay here and guard this entrance. David, you're in charge.'

To the rest of his team he said, 'Right, lads, follow me,' as he set off at a trot along the slope of the ravine.

***

Luke finished his task of making a set of horseshoes ready for a customer. He thought that he must hurry to the bakery to purchase Stan's favourite oatmeal cakes, as he was about to visit. Ironically it would have been Stan going to the bakery, allowing his master to see to the everyday running of the shop. As Luke left the bakery, he met James on his way to the sawmill.

James asked, 'Are you on your way to see, Stan?'

Luke replied, 'Yes, sir, I am. Have you any news of the bounty hunters? Stan's bound to ask.'

James informed him, 'No, it's too early yet; they only left last night for Anderson's gorge.'

At the clinic, Stan had just finished his breakfast, and Angela had got him on his feet for a short walk. It was not long before Stan weakened, and he was ready to lie on his bed when Luke entered. Just as Luke had predicted, Stan was asking if there was news of the hunt, and he noticed the look of disdain on Angela's face.

'Why do you have such a morbid interest, Stan?' she enquired.

Stan looked at his master, as if seeking support. 'Angela doesn't understand the threat these murderers pose, Luke.' Pain showed on Stan's face, as he continued, 'They killed Morgan. I have every reason to resent them.'

With a lump in his throat, Stan's eyes filled with tears, as he recalled the demise of his beloved Morgan. Angela was quick to console him in his grief. Luke noticed there was something special between them.

***

With his hound firmly on a leash, Toby led the team in a headlong dash towards the sound of the gunshot. He came to a sudden halt, rapidly joined by the others, to take in the scene before them. Lying to one side lay the body of Peter Stockwell; it was plain to see he was dead by the serious damage to his bloodied head. Before them, straddling Ben Stockwell, was the grey horseman, who had a firm grip of his hair and was rhythmically banging his head off the ground.

After each thump he repeated, 'Jack and Jill,' thump, 'Jack and Jill.'

Ray dashed across and forced the grey horseman off his victim, saying, 'That's enough. We're taking him alive – and who might you be?'

There was no answer, until Toby enlightened everyone. 'This is Jack Collins, whose bride to be was brutally murdered by these scum.'

Toby helped Jack to his feet, and noticed a dramatic change in Jack from being a scrawny teenager to his now mature adulthood. 'What are you doing down here?' Toby asked. 'You were sent up north to keep you out of harm's way.'

Jack stood back as he observed Ben being shackled by Ray, ready to be transported. Jack had pure hatred in his eyes, as he stared Ben Stockwell down.

He never took his eyes off him as he answered Toby, 'I kept in touch with certain people who alerted me as to where these scum were and what they were doing.'

Jack squared up to Ben who averted his gaze to concentrate

on the ground. Jack spoke directly into his ear: 'When I found out Nathan was imprisoned, I found time to slip away from my duties and then I shot him in his cell.' Jack turned to look at the inert body of Peter, then quietly spoke into Ben's ear once more, 'Just like I did to Peter, your brother.' Jack's controlled voiced turned into a hissing sound, as he informed Ben, 'Given more time, I would have done for you also.'

At this Ben struggled with his captors, as Jack was firmly restrained by Toby. Ray then began to handcuff Jack's hands behind his back, as he told him he was also being taken into custody on his admission of murdering the two Stockwell brothers.

James was in his London office, when news of the Stockwell brothers' demise came through; however, Jack Collins never arrived at the Old Bailey with his arch-enemy Ben Stockwell. He was never heard of again, having disappeared completely into obscurity. It would appear he had more friends than the Stockwells had enemies.